FORGET

Living in Blackrock all her life, Ruth Gilligan attended St Andrew's College from the age of five. Having said an emotional goodbye and finally finished the Leaving Cert, she awaits her results, and looks forward to a quality sixth year holiday and a stunning Debs. She has always been passionate about writing, but her other hobbies include anything to do with music, drama, hockey and partying with her friends. Ruth played Laura Halpin in *Fair City* for a number of years. *Forget* is her fist novel and, even now, she can't believe it has all come true!

FORGET

Ruth Gilligan

HODDER
HEADLINE
IRELAND

First published in 2006 by Hodder Headline Ireland.

A CIP catalogue record for this title is available from the British Library.

ISBN 0 340 92088 2

4

Typeset in Sabon MT by Hodder Headline Ireland
Printed and bound in Great Britain by Clays Ltd, St Ives plc

Hodder Headline Ireland's policy is to use papers that are natural, renewable and recyclable products and made from wood grown in sustainable forests. The logging and manufacturing processes are expected to conform to the environmental regulations of the country of origin.

Hodder Headline Ireland
8 Castlecourt Centre
Castleknock
Dublin 15
Ireland

A division of Hodder Headline
338 Euston Road,
London NW1 3BH

www.hhireland.ie

For Nana, my angel

and

Class 2006, forever young

~ And I know all of this, and yet I still long to be somewhere else. Life is discontent and the future doesn't seem to be bright enough to hold out her hand and pull me through this horrible cloud. Love is so heartbreaking and at the same time the most wonderful feeling life has to offer. I haven't even felt it to its fullest but even the shred of it that has touched me has been amazing. And even though from time to time we go out of tune, the melody is clear and even, and the trickle of happiness that fills me is nearly enough, even though I know I should be doing something else. ~

1

Eva

Once her mother had pressed the doorbell, Eva Coonan knew there was no escape. Her heart was thumping so hard against her chest that she thought she would explode into tears. She willed the door not to open or, if it was going to, to do so faster. They'd come straight from mass and the tune of the departing hymn was still ringing in her ears. She didn't dare meet her mother's eyes. She was convinced that, if she did, she'd be forced to relax and let go of the knot of tension that was keeping her from running as fast as she could from this house and as far away as possible.

The door opened in slow motion and a pair of warm, compassionate eyes smiled at them. Eva put on her act as she always did, pretending to be relaxed and perfectly content with the whole thing, as her mother followed suit. They were shown to a small sitting room. The furniture was nice, but not homely, and it was evident this house was not for living in. The wooden table held a small bowl with pretty pine cones sitting in it, and Eva gazed at them as her mind raced with fear. The lady was Helen, Eva's new therapist. Eva's mother talked to her for a while, discussing timing, payment, the weather and all the other things one usually discusses when meeting one's daughter's shrink for the first time. Eva sat very still and stared around her as her mother often told her she had when she was a baby. Everyone had been amazed back then that she hadn't cried – she just stared at everyone and everything, in complete awe. Eva felt as vulnerable now as when she was a baby. At least then people had recognised her weakness and need to be looked after, whereas now, a fully grown seventeen-year-old, she feared people had more faith in her coping skills than was deserved. She wanted to go home and sit on her mother's lap and cry and sob and be held until she felt all right again, but it was too late. Somewhere deep down inside her, she knew that, eventually, the therapy would help her. It might get worse before it gets better, she warned herself, like a cut forming a scab, or stinging with antiseptic, but it would clean and heal the wound.

The neat garden was visible through French windows. It consisted of a small white patio, with steep steps leading up to the lawn, which was littered with small pink flowerbeds. Eva took it all in, trying to distract herself from the task ahead, wishing she wasn't there, but wishing most of all that none of this had ever happened. She wished her dad was still alive and that she was still the Eva she'd always been. She wished she wasn't here, months later, having to talk to someone about how terrible she was feeling and to admit how weak she was these days. She began to cry, but concealed it from the chattering pair. This was all harder than she'd expected, and the session hadn't even started.

Eventually her mother left, promising to return in an hour and telling her not to worry and that she'd be fine and that Helen would be nice to her. Eva smiled her big bright smile and stood brave and ready for whatever was to come, when inside she was wilting.

They headed upstairs to what would have been a bedroom had the house had been a home. She and Helen sat on the same style of modern, unwelcoming chairs that had been downstairs. Eva noticed a candle burning on a small table in the corner of the room before being drawn into conversation by Helen. Eva knew this was Helen's job, but couldn't help willing her to stop and let her go. Getting here had been ordeal enough for one day.

Helen's voice was soft and kind and flowed through the room, which was completely quiet. Eva listened and threw in words here and there, still pretending to be relaxed, though she was sure her body language and glazed eyes said otherwise. She was trying to take it all in, but she was numb and full of racing emotion all at the same time. All the talk of how she felt, and how life had been since her father's accident, made her withdraw further and further into herself, until the room where she and Helen sat seemed miles away and she was sure that she could curl up inside herself and forget it all.

An hour later, Helen gazed up from her notepad. Her eyes held a compassion which vaguely reassured Eva, but she was glad when the end of the session was announced. She was relieved it was over, but remained withdrawn from it all, so that from the time she left the room and all the way home in the car with her mum and even when she reached her house, she remained completely silent, but for the steady drip of her tears.

The house was unusually quiet that night. Eva ate very little at dinner and didn't join into her mother and sister's conversation at all. After she'd cleared the dishes, she went straight to her room to get ready for school the next day. She lay on her bed and stared at the ceiling. The emotions and thoughts that were racing through her were overwhelming and she thought that the silence was going to make her explode. She crossed the room to her CD player and selected something from her vast collection. The opening guitar riff filled her pale pink room, and she resumed her position on her bed. The lyrics made little sense to her and every note seemed alien. She wasn't the girl who'd left her house that morning. She was vulnerable and weak and the guitar seemed to be aware of this as it slowly exposed her so that she found herself paralysed with emotion by the time the first track had ended.

By track three she didn't know whether to burst into tears or stand up and sing along. Suddenly, there was a knock on the door. It was Sarah, her sister.

'Mum said I was to come and talk to you. Are you okay?'

Much as she wasn't in the mood, there was something about her younger sibling that made Eva invite her in. She sat next to where Eva lay and looked completely lost for something to say. She was fourteen and looked pretty in the blue jumper she'd stolen from Eva without asking. Eva placed her hand on hers.

'I'm fine. Just a bit… emotional, that's all.'

'Well, that music's not going to help. Put on something a bit perkier there, will you?'

Eva smiled. The day she started taking music advice from her sister was never going to come. Eva admired her sister. She'd been much stronger when their dad had died, looking after Eva and their mum. Of course she was upset, but she had talked about it with her friends and seemed to have found some sort of state of acceptance – she was sad, but was getting on with her life and was the same girl her dad had loved so much.

'Do you want a cup of tea then, and we'll have a chat?' Sarah asked, breaking the silence. When Eva paused, Sarah added, 'Or just the tea?'

Eva smiled. She was glad her sister didn't push her into talking. 'I'll be down in a sec and I'll make one myself. Thanks.'

Sarah nodded and left. They both knew that Eva wouldn't be down at all, but the gesture had been noted and, in that moment, the sisters had shared more than they would have in any chat.

Tiredness dimmed Eva's thoughts until the view outside her window was nothing but blackness. She washed and changed and got into bed. She'd half expected to lie there for hours while sleep teased her but never came quite close enough to grab a hold of, but within minutes her hazel eyes closed, exhausted from their marathon of crying that had been an early September Sunday.

2

Zac

Zac frowned as he tried to force the words to come. He'd seen and heard so much already in his life that he was sure this part would be the easy bit. But, as he slumped back into his chair, a mixture of exhaustion and annoyance wafted over him as he realised that lyrics were hard work – harder than he'd thought. A sudden admiration for all those songs out there, no matter how good or bad, filled him. At least those songwriters had managed to say what they wanted, make it all rhyme and fit nicely into a tune, line after line, all making sense and leading somewhere. Whereas the piece of paper he'd been aiming to fill with meaningful choruses and bridges was completely empty, all he had for his debut song was the title – 'Forget'.

Maybe his dad was right and he shouldn't bother with the guitar. It wasn't like he was any good at it. Then again, according to his dad, he wasn't good at anything at all, really. His son, a musician? His father had said he doubted that very much. He was a lost cause, after all, and almost as useless and pathetic as his mother.

Zac winced. Home life wasn't easy for him. He rarely spoke about it to any of his friends, even his closest ones, he was always too embarrassed, ashamed even, about how he lived in such hell compared to them. It sounded like such a cliché, but music was his escape. Whenever his mum and dad were having an argument or the tension in the house got too much, he would reach for his guitar and try and drown out the rows or awkward silence that filled his home. When he started playing the guitar, he wasn't very good. He never had lessons so he was completely self-taught, but he'd kept at it and had improved a lot. Up until now, he had always played music he'd downloaded from the internet or worked out by listening to his large CD collection, but he had decided to try his hand at his own stuff. Maybe then he'd show his dad that he actually was talented. But most of all, he hoped that what he was feeling inside would make more sense to him if it was written down.

He stared, as he often did, at the posters on the dull blue walls of his bedroom. The images of musicians stared back at him. They'd all done it. They'd all managed to make music that would send shivers down the spine of anyone who listened. They'd all been left playing on his stereo as he drifted off to sleep, often close to tears if it had been a bad day. His CDs were stacked up, names facing out, in what had once been an orderly fashion, but time and his wide musical taste had juggled them around.

Desire was always a word Zac associated with music. Girly as it was, he felt that music was something that was needed and that, when it was listened to, touched a person to the very depths of their sorry souls. Very sorry, in his case. He smiled briefly. If he wasn't careful, he was in danger of becoming another moany, depressed Irishman with an acoustic guitar, and there were enough of them out there already.

But they were good, he'd give them that much. Irish musicians seemed to have an honesty about them that made them unashamed of their experiences and unafraid to bare all their deepest emotions just to create a song, usually one of those songs that Zac called 'the ones where you wish you had someone'. There are songs that make you melt, that make every hair on your neck shoot up and send goose bumps racing all over your body, so that you have to close your eyes until everything is shut out but you and the song. And if you're lucky, it's the same for that someone else too. But Zac feared that he had no one. He had friends, but none that knew him entirely and would understand and would make it all go away if they could. This was as much his fault as theirs – if he didn't tell them everything, how could he expect them to look after him and help him through it? But he didn't care. He didn't need anyone. If he did, he'd only be admitting defeat and showing the world that he was weak. But he wasn't. His father told him over and over that he was weak and pathetic and useless, but Zac was to prove him wrong. And he would play guitar until he wrote a brilliant, genius song that would make everyone melt and close their eyes and think, 'this guy is amazing'. And if this song didn't come tonight, or tomorrow night, he'd just have to give it time, because he could do it. And he would do it.

He stared at himself in the mirror, trying to picture himself on stage playing his guitar and hundreds of people gazing up at him. He was a pretty tall guy – his father's rugby build had been passed on to him. He had dark hair that was just long enough to need a cut, and he'd been told he had rich, chocolate eyes. Girls always commented on his eyes and the fact that he had really long eyelashes. He didn't know whether this was a good thing or not, but they'd seemed to think it was.

His train of thought was broken by shouting voices from downstairs. Zac flinched. They were at it again.

'You stupid bitch, I sometimes wonder what the hell I ever married you for.'

'Liam, just relax now, you're getting carried away.'

'Don't you fucking tell me what I am and am not doing.'

'Liam, I'm sorry. I didn't mean…'

Zac could hear his mother's voice begin to crackle with tears. He could just picture her innocent face gazing at his father and willing him to feel even an ounce of pity, or better still, love, for his wife.

'The crying jag won't work with me any more, Nancy. What kind of idiot do you take me for?'

Zac could hear his mother's sobs getting louder and louder.

'I said cut it out!'

Silence fell like a thick blanket on the house. A few moments passed, then footsteps echoed on the floorboards of the hall, out of the house and into the night. The revving of an engine meant that his dad had gone out, probably to the pub or to his club.

Zac paused a moment and then decided to go see if his mum needed a shoulder to lean on or a cup of tea but, when he reached the kitchen, his mum was scrubbing away at the dishes as usual.

'Mum, are you okay?'

She didn't look up from the bowl she was washing and Zac was sure that this was so he didn't see her tear-stained face.

'I'm fine, dear, why wouldn't I be?' Her voice seemed perfectly composed compared to what it had been just minutes ago as she'd pleaded with her husband.

'You and Dad... I heard...'

'Ah, your father's just in a bit of a bad mood. Now, leave me be while I wash these.'

Zac headed back upstairs. His mother had seemed so contained and pretended to be fine, when really he knew she must be broken inside. But she had said nothing. Made excuses for him. Told Zac everything was perfect. Zac was angry, angry at his mum for not showing her true feelings and defending his father. But he realised it was ridiculous for him to be mad at her – it wasn't her that was in the wrong, but the man who was probably off with his posh friends, sitting in comfy leather armchairs and sipping on a whiskey, while everyone around him laughed at his jokes, blissfully unaware of the evil, ignorant man they were associating with.

3

Eva

Monday morning weighed down on Eva. She lay motionless, hoping that if she didn't stir, maybe the world would forget about her and she could stay in the warmth of her bed all day. Of course, reality intruded in the form of a loud alarm clock that rang like there was no tomorrow. She peeled herself from the sheets and flicked on the radio. Through blurry eyes she dressed and put her hair into a high ponytail. Staring in the mirror, she noted that her skin was thankfully in good form today, so little effort was required in that department. She wished she had the energy to put on some eyeliner, but all she could manage was a layer of lip gloss.

She was pretty. She admitted that. Her hair was a shade somewhere between chestnut and hazel, and was quite long. It complimented her hazel eyes well which had diamonds of green sparkling throughout them. Although her skin had been pretty bad growing up, finally it was settling down and despite the odd breakout, it remained calm. Hockey had kept her figure slim, and she didn't tend to complain too much about her body. The lads in school used to tell her how good it was, how hot she was and some of them had expressed interest at one point or another. The feeling had been mutual with only a few of them and although she'd had a couple of boyfriends, it was nothing like the number her friends had had. Especially since her dad's death, she'd lost interest in the whole 'ooh he looked at me I bet he'll ask me out' thing. She rarely bothered putting on make-up for school now, and she never went out at the weekends. She was often invited to the house parties that were usually on a Friday or Saturday night, but she always politely declined. She missed getting dolled up with her girlfriends and getting tipsy and running around someone's house, slapping everyone's ass or dancing along to blaring music. But all that seemed part of the old her. Part of her old life.

And it was true, her life had changed. Things didn't seem to matter any more. The parts of her life she truly valued now were so different to those that she used to deem important. She knew that everyone in school, especially the boys, regularly talked about how she was different now, and that they wished she'd go back to the way she used to be. But Eva didn't care what they said. None of them knew or understood what she was feeling. She could never explain to them what it was like to lose a parent, and how life suddenly slaps you in the face and drops you down so that your perspective on everything is greyer.

*

A month into the school year, she was getting used to the routine of it all again. She knew that many of her friends had thought, and hoped, that the summer would have done her good and that maybe she'd be a bit more upbeat when she returned after the holidays. Little did they know that the summer, if anything, had made things worse. It had been so much harder keeping her mind occupied when she didn't have the ritual of getting up and going to school five days a week. She had no structure for three whole months, which just led to her moping around and thinking constantly.

'Eva, we need to go. Get a move on, would you?' her mother shouted up the stairs.

She gathered everything, and with a peck on the cheek from her mum, headed off to school. It was only fifteen minutes from her house so she had no objection to walking. The Blackrock streets were bathed in pale light and the morning air was crisp as birds sang a song of autumn that would eventually erase all shades of summer. The leaves were transforming into a palette of golden delights, which made the treetops look as if they were alight with a flame that flickered in the morning breeze and danced in time with the thudding of Eva's heart. The footpath ahead of her was full of leaves. Staring at the other side of the road, which was leafless in comparison, Eva crossed over and averted her eyes from the golden mounds she'd left behind. She had spent many autumn afternoons with her father running through the leaves and kicking them into the air so that they danced around as if someone had sneezed them into life. The smell of conkers and late-blooming flowers would fill their nostrils and shrieks of happiness would echo through the fading streets. Eva didn't want to walk through the leaves today. It was too weird, too wrong without her dad there. She knew autumn was his favourite season, and as this was her first one without him, she knew it would be hard.

Turning the corner, she saw a group leaning against the wall and talking in loud, southside accents. She instantly placed the faces as the lads from her year, the jocks (both rugby and hockey), all collars up and high-fives and tanned faces from their latest expensive trip to their family's Spanish villas. They clocked her approach and the conversation stopped.

A chorus of 'Hey Eva, how's it going?' was thrown in her direction. She smiled and joined the group. She liked these guys. They were good to her, even the new her. Although she'd changed, they'd never given up. Whether this was pity or genuine friendship, Eva didn't know, but for now it was enough.

'Basically, right, she was a cracker. Couldn't get enough of me and I wasn't exactly saying no, if you know what I mean!' One of the boys, Cian, boasted about his latest Saturday night conquest.

'Did you get her number?' another voice asked.

'Well, sort of,' he hesitated. 'As in, I remember her putting it in my phone but I can't remember the girl's name, so it's going to be a bit of a kick in the nuts trying to find it!' Cian laughed.

Eva smirked as the guys all high-fived Cian, and as the group headed off for school, she couldn't help but feel comfortable as the six well-built bodies walked alongside her, as if protecting her from the world.

When they got inside the gates she spotted a few of the girls, so they headed over and broke off into various groups, chatting loudly about the weekend or coming up with good excuses for their serious lack of homework. Suddenly, a hand shot into hers and a big kiss was planted on her cheek. It was Cathy. Cathy was Eva's best friend, but Eva was just one of Cathy's many best friends. This was cool with Eva. She didn't expect exclusive rights, and when a girl had as much personality as Cathy, it wasn't surprising that everyone wanted a piece of her. The guys loved her, the girls loved her – and Eva loved her. Much and all as Cathy was the life and soul of the party, she was always a shoulder for Eva to cry on, and had really helped her since her dad's car accident.

Today, Cathy was all excited about nothing in particular, and it was wonderful to watch her flit from person to person, kissing them or tickling them but, most importantly, making everyone around her smile and almost making them forget the grey truth that was the first school day of the week.

The bell broke the eruption of laughter that had ensued from another of Cian's jokes and everyone reluctantly trudged towards their classes. Eva lolled unenthusiastically to English, but was cheered up by a sheet of paper stuck to the classroom door which informed the students that their teacher was delayed in traffic and would be late, so they were all to just go in, sit quietly and wait. At least the first class had been put off, even if only temporarily. Eva walked into the classroom and gazed around for an empty seat. None of her girlfriends were in this class, as she was in the highest English class, and she was the only one out of her friends who actually loved and excelled at this subject. However, today she noticed a collar standing up among the rows of tidy uniforms. It was a guy called Killian. Eva instantly went over and sat beside him. 'Since when are you in this class?'

'Jesus, Eva, thank God you're here. I thought this class would just be full of nerds.'

Eva smiled and was sure a number of heads turned around to shoot the pair some filthy looks! Killian seemed unfazed by their obvious offence and continued, 'I got moved up – apparently I'm actually good at a subject that isn't rugby!'

They talked about their weekends, though Eva went slightly pink, as her quiet few days seemed like hell compared to Killian's mad excursions. But he didn't seem to care. They were always part of the same group but didn't connect much – Killian was very much the centre of the gang and definitely the most popular guy, whereas, especially recently, Eva remained out on the edge. Even before her dad's death she'd never been the centre star – that was left to Cathy.

But all that aside, she'd always liked Killian. He was a nice guy, and now that she thought about it, not the worst looking at all. She knew he was hot from the number of girls that had been with him, or at least who wanted to be. He was definitely one of the best looking in the year. His skin was a warm shade of gold and his hair was fair and slightly lighter at the tips from the summer's rays. He seemed so comfortable just sitting there, leaning against the window. He had a square jaw-line, broad shoulders and a rugged charm about him that was nothing but comforting, since she didn't fancy him. Some people she knew found Killian cocky and full of himself, which was always a possibility, seeing as how he was one of the few people in the school who was actually pretty damn good at rugby, but she found that now that they were just talking one on one, this wasn't the case. He was sure of himself and had all the potential to be an arrogant posh boy with wads of cash and an ego to match, but he was sound and, for someone Eva had rarely talked to before, very easy to get on with.

It turned out the traffic that day was worse than expected and when the bell sounded after forty minutes, Eva and Killian were deep in conversation and were disappointed the class had gone so quickly. They didn't see each other for the rest of the day – Killian got off school at break time to go play a rugby match – but for the next few weeks, English classes were the most enjoyable forty minutes of the day for Eva. She sat beside him, talking or laughing or even sometimes paying attention to the teacher. But no matter what she was doing, she felt there was a bond forming between them and it surprised her to realise that it felt good. Nothing more than friendship, but that was all Eva needed and she was happy to have found it, to have found Killian. She hoped he felt the same.

4

Zac

Sitting at the back of Geography class while some old countryman muttered on in his thick Galway accent about global warming, Zac and Johnny were deep in conversation. Trouble was, they kept getting the evil eye from their teacher, as Johnny wasn't exactly the world's greatest whisperer.

'Anyway… would he ever stop looking over here?' Johnny caught the teacher's glaring eye. 'Yeah, do you have a problem? Yeah, that's right, the greenhouse effect is a pile of…'

Johnny was given a hundred lines. Punishment had never stopped Johnny before, and since he was in the middle of telling Zac about this hottie he'd been with over the weekend, Mr Geography could take his melting ice caps and stick them wherever he felt best.

'So anyway, her name's Cara. And as soon as she heard what school I was in, she was gagging for it. I'm telling you, man, much and all as I hate my parentals, they did do us a major favour sending us here – it's like the best chat-up line ever for birds.'

Zac laughed a little louder than he'd intended and was rewarded with a hundred lines of his own. He didn't really mind, but he was a little jealous as he'd actually have to do them, whereas Johnny would say that he had a very important rugby match and didn't have time to do them, and your man would let him off. That was the way things were. Though he'd rather do a hundred lines than become a rugger bugger any day! Contrary to popular opinion, however, the jocks in his school were actually very sound and he got on really well with them all, even if he didn't like running around with a load of men in a muddy field, chasing a deformed ball.

Geography finally ended and the lads all shot off to the cafeteria for some much-needed grub. That was the thing about going to an all boys' school – the grumbling bellies echoed through the corridors from about ten o'clock onwards, and by the time lunch actually came, the stampede towards the hot food was dangerous. And since half of them practised scrums every day, Zac was at a severe disadvantage.

Eventually, he got a steaming plate of chicken and mash and joined his year. The lads were discussing their afternoon rendezvous.

'So, we get off after next class, don't we?'

'Yeah, match is at three, so we need to get warmed up.'

Zac was at a loss. 'Who're you playing, lads?'

'Ah, you know, the school round the corner. Should be a walk in the park. Mixed schools can never field a decent team, so we should be grand.'

'Yeah, all the lads there play hockey.' A shower of laughs ensued, and looks of utter disgust were exchanged – boys' hockey? Nah, the only way hockey could be played was by girls in short skirts, not by puny guys who couldn't even manage a real game!

The guy beside Zac interrupted the babble. 'One of the lads on their team is on Leinster, though, isn't he? Apparently fairly decent like.'

'Yeah, Killian Lain, he's sound enough, actually. Not a bad kicker, either.'

'But one player's not going to win the match, is he?'

'Lads, it's us, like – what do you think?' Johnny's last comment was followed by a round of high-fives.

That afternoon the team headed off, leaving Zac with his few remaining mates who didn't play rugby, wishing they were anywhere else, even if it was on a muddy pitch.

Last class was Maths and Zac's patience was wearing thin. When his teacher set them an unbelievable amount of homework he was royally peeved and shot him a filthy glare just so his opinion was clearly noted. He was jealous that the lads were getting off this truck-load of sums, but at the same time he didn't feel resentful towards them – after all, the Senior Cup team were mostly friends of his and if they were lucky enough to be good at the sport and got to miss loads of work for it, then lucky them – he'd do the same if he was into rugby. But he wasn't. He hated the thought of how his teachers would react if he strolled into school and said he hadn't done the homework because he'd been practising guitar and writing a few songs.

Of course, his dad had always wanted him to be a rugby boy, and when Zac had turned out to be something completely different, his father's disgust was obvious. That was the reason Zac had been sent to this school – to become the perfect image of a southside jock his dad could be proud of and boast about to all his chums while they played a round of golf in Powerscourt. But Zac was Zac. And his father was not impressed.

Zac did love his school, absolutely. The teachers were good but, most of all, his year was sound and he had so many good friends. He decided he wouldn't bother going to study that night, as he was wrecked, and since the guys wouldn't be there, what was the point?

*

That night at dinner, Zac's mood worsened. It turned out that the busload of maths homework he'd got had been extremely hard and he was sure that his head was about to burst. He kept quiet as he shovelled in his lasagne, but eventually his father broke the silence.

'Zachary, why aren't you at study?'

'I told you, I'm wrecked and all I have is maths homework, so I may as well do it here.'

'But we've paid for study, Zac. Surely it would be easier to concentrate on your Maths in school rather than here, love.' His mother had got her say anyway.

'It's not like I'm going to get the homework done either way. He gave us loads and it's impossible.'

His father was starting to go red. 'Well, if you listened in class rather than wasting your time thinking up chords for your guitar, maybe you'd be getting somewhere,' he spat.

'Is that your answer to everything? Oh, and you'll be glad to hear that all the rugby team got off the homework, so if I'd been a "real man", we wouldn't be having this row.'

'But you're not, are you?'

Zac was silent. He hadn't expected his dad to come out and say that, but he supposed he shouldn't have been surprised.

His dad obviously wasn't finished. 'And while we're on the subject, I may as well warn you – since you're not the rugby captain I'd wanted you to be, you better start focusing on your education. You're in fifth year now, and you're not exactly going to be getting a sports scholarship into college, that's for sure.'

'Believe it or not, Dad, there are other ways into college.'

'Don't push me, Zachary. I'm well aware of how to get into college, but what I'm saying is that you have got to get your act together and knuckle down and do some work for a change, or your mother and I will have to start having some serious discussions.'

'About what?'

'Let's just say we've been hearing some shitty reports from your teachers. They said they're going to keep us informed as to how you're getting on. If we don't hear about some serious improvement, Zachary, there will be trouble. So I'd watch it if I were you and start putting some damn effort in.'

Zac stared hard at his father, as if challenging him to continue, shout even louder, maybe even hit him. But his father ignored him and so the fight was over. One lousy comment about some maths homework and all of a sudden all this comes out.

Zac did concede to himself that he'd been taking things easy and had found it difficult to work hard after Transition Year. And he knew that his teachers knew. What he hadn't known was that his teachers had obviously been in contact with his folks and they were all too aware of Zac's recent dossing.

Zac's mother broke the dense silence. 'Will you have seconds, dear?'

Zac merely shook his head and stood up with such vigour that the chair legs screeched against the wooden floor. He'd had enough, and he had to get out.

'I'm going for a walk.'

Neither parent objected, surprisingly, but simply let him stroll out of the kitchen and out onto the streets of Blackrock. It was cold outside, and putting his hands into his pockets, Zac stiffened against the biting evening air. He was fuming. He was so sick of his dad and his stupid attitude and his constant shouting and dictating. Zac and his mother had no say in anything, as his dad had scared them both out of having an opinion. His poor mum. At least Zac could escape as soon as school was over. He would find an apartment or a dorm in college, even a bus shelter – anything would be better than living under that man's roof. But for now, there was little Zac could do but put up with it and bite his tongue before he made matters even worse. The mile-long stretch of Mount Merrion Avenue seemed to go on forever, and as he headed towards the village, Zac considered calling for his friend, Kev. But his every bone ached and the thought of having to talk to someone was awful. That was Zac – he didn't mind being alone. He wasn't a talker, he was a thinker, and that was the way he liked it. It was something the lads at school often mentioned but Zac usually just smiled. He was glad he didn't go to a mixed school, as he imagined that girls would have pushed him to talk and make him 'get in touch with his feelings and share them with others'. Zac couldn't think of anything worse, and respected the lads' contentment with him saying very little.

The air was getting thicker and as he walked by the various pubs and shops, he began to shiver slightly. There were quite a few people around for a weekday night, and a steady stream of adults filled Main Street, popping into the various pubs for a few scoops after work. The Italian was fairly busy, and a young couple in the window, each munching away on a large bowl of tagliatelle, looked wonderfully happy. The soft lighting of the restaurant seemed so much warmer and welcoming than the dark night air that hung stiffly about Zac's hunched figure. He decided that this was stupid and turned around. He upped his pace and reached home much more quickly than he'd left it, but was actually glad to be indoors again – the glow of homely heat was welcoming, but the realisation of the tension he'd left behind came speeding back to him.

In the TV room, his father sat watching the golf. He looked in Zac's direction as Zac strolled by the open door, but didn't even bother to say anything to his son. Down in the kitchen, Zac's mum was still washing up after the meal, looking tired and hassled. Zac sensed a row had taken place.

'Mum? Did you and Dad have a fight?'

'Not really, love.'

'Mum, come on, it's fairly obvious.' Zac wasn't going to let her cover up for him.

'Well, I just suggested to him that maybe he was being a bit hard on you earlier and that I've every faith that you're working as hard as you can. He didn't agree.'

Zac felt slightly ashamed. He was thankful for his mother's confidence in him, but there was no denying that he hadn't in fact been working as hard as he could and, hard as it was to admit it, part of what his dad had said was true.

'Mum, do you want a cup of tea or something?'

'No thanks, pet. You'd better head up and have another look at that maths, yeah?'

'Yeah, I suppose. Thanks, Mum.'

Zac left as his final words hung in the air. He doubted his mother realised it, but Zac was in fact saying thank you for so much more than she knew. He was grateful for her and was sorry she'd ended up with such a terrible man. He promised himself he'd look after her and wouldn't let his dad bully her too much.

He lay down on his bed, exhausted from the day and from all the arguing. He wished that things were different and closed his eyes in the hope that when he opened them maybe it would all have changed. The only thing was, the moment his eyes were closed, they weren't going to open again, and Zac lilted into a thick, dreamless sleep.

Up here, no one watches me,
The silence sings along in time with my
Memories, or better still, my dreams.

5

Eva

Eva couldn't deny the slight tingles she felt knowing her last subject of the day was English. And it was a double period. She arrived to class, sat down in the back row, plonked her schoolbag on the ground and waited. There was no sign of Killian yet, but he'd be there soon. Eva smiled to herself as she realised that she was turning into such a girly girl – even the thought of some stupid boy was making her heart flutter slightly and she couldn't believe how much her mood had improved in the last few weeks, ever since she and Killian had become friends. But that was the funny thing – they were just friends. So why was she acting like this? Why did she sneak a glance at him across the cafeteria when she thought no one was looking? Why did every inch of her tingle when he touched her, even if it was just a shoulder brushing off hers as they passed each other in a crowded corridor, or the faintest rub of elbows when they sat next to each other at lunch? Killian had never shown any signs of doing any of this purposely, so she knew it wasn't a big deal to him, but was it to her?

Sure enough, as the bell rang to signify the start of class, in came Eva's English teacher, Mrs Lucas, closely followed by Killian's confident swagger. He looked around the class and, when he saw Eva, he smiled and headed to the seat beside her.

'All right, class, since we have a double period, I've booked the video player and we'll be watching clips from various modern adaptations of Shakespeare.'

Mrs Lucas continued talking, but Eva and Killian were already deep in conversation. Trouble was, this wasn't going to sit well with Mrs Lucas.

'If you two intend to continue your endless chatter, I'm afraid supervision is the place for you. However, if you wish to remain part of this class, I suggest you keep your mouths shut and start appreciating the beauty of Mr Shakespeare.'

Eva and Killian glanced at each other, smirked and stared back at the screen, where some eejit pretending to be Hamlet was talking in a rather questionable accent.

When the bell rang, showing the first period was over, Eva was actually enjoying the class, but it was annoying the way Mrs Lucas kept changing the video so that they could 'get a little taste of everything'.

As Eva sat enthralled watching a rather dark version of *Macbeth*, she felt an elbow dig into her ribs. Turning to Killian, he held out a folded piece of paper to her and gave her a wink. She nodded, took the note and opened it with her hands under her desk so that Mrs Lucas couldn't see. Eva's heart was beating slightly faster than usual as she uncrumpled the page.

Whatcha doin dis wkend?

Eva reread it a few times and then penned her response.

Dunno. U?

A moment later, another stiff elbow was injected into her ribs.

Grahams havin a party. Wanna cum? Iv askd him lyk n he sed he wants U der. So do I.

Eva's heart nearly jumped out of her mouth. She'd heard everyone talking about this party and Cathy had kept telling her how great it would be and how Eva absolutely had to come. And now Killian was personally inviting her to it and she thought she'd faint with happiness. But, suddenly, the cold, grey realisation of all that had happened came piercing through her aura of glee. She wasn't ready. All this time, she'd been telling herself that she was ready to go out again, ready to let loose and have fun and forget about how awful she felt about her dad. But she couldn't. Not yet. It was too soon.

As she snuck a glance at Killian as he read the reply she'd written, she felt a small prick of pleasure as she saw his face drop. But this was little comfort to her – she was back to square one again after she had everyone, even herself, convinced that she was changing back and that this butterfly was finally coming out of her cocoon again. But her dad was still dead, and she was still as scarred.

With fifteen minutes of class left, Mrs Lucas announced that she was putting on *Romeo + Juliet*. Eva felt a little cheerier, as she loved this particular adaptation of the play. Mrs Lucas fast-forwarded to the party scene – Leonardo Di Caprio was gazing at Claire Danes through the fish tank and the whole thing just oozed romance. And then, when they kissed and held each other and everything was just perfect, Eva felt something brush ever so slightly against her leg. She stiffened and felt it again, very gentle, but evidently done on purpose. She was too nervous to look down and see what it was, but slowly she began to realise. Butterflies were having fits inside her and her heart was thumping so loud she was sure he'd hear. She didn't know what to do, so she just applied a little pressure from her leg to the one beside it. She knew he'd felt it, as he returned the pressure and both their legs relaxed and melted into each other. Never once did they look at each other. They both kept their gazes fixed on Juliet and Romeo giggling and kissing and falling in love.

Class ended and they both stood up and headed out to the corridor, neither saying a word. When Eva reached her locker, Killian leaned on the one beside it. 'I really would've liked you to come.' He paused, looking straight at her. 'But if you can't, that's cool. Have a nice weekend.'

'You too. And enjoy the party.'

'Take it easy.'

He swaggered off, only to bump into a big group of the lads. They all headed down the corridor, loudly discussing how much they were all going to drink that night. Eva began thinking over every moment to make sure that it hadn't all been her imagination and that he was definitely in on it too. Eventually, she concluded that it wasn't one-sided and that he had both initiated it and responded to her. She felt herself going red and smiling so widely she was sure everyone walking by her was convinced she was gone in the head. But she didn't care. And the funniest thing of all was that all it had been was a bit of a leg rub in the middle of English class. But to her it was so much more – it had been a realisation and a confirmation of something she had felt coming for a while now. She was in love with Killian!

Well, she thought, love was a bit strong, but she did really, really like him. A little voice inside her said that he liked her too, but she didn't want to admit she'd heard it for fear it was wrong and then it'd be even harder for her to be rejected. She felt a smack on her ass and whirled round to see a beaming Cathy.

'Woohoo, weekend at last!'

'I know. It's great, isn't it?'

Cathy surveyed Eva carefully. 'What's got you in such a good mood?'

'Nothing.' But Eva's broad grin announced that she was lying. She just gave Cathy a wink and tried to skip away, but with a firm grasp on her arm she was wrenched back in front of her best friend, who wore a look of utter disbelief.

Then, as if a bright light suddenly went off over Cathy's head, she said in an unnecessarily dirty voice, 'You just had English, didn't you?'

Eva nodded, but was a little surprised – how did Cathy know that was what was making her so unusually cheery? Eva hadn't told anyone how she felt about Killian or how well they'd been getting on, as she didn't want a big deal to be made of it. Plus she was way too shy to have her inner feelings revealed to the whole year – once Cathy knew, everyone else would too. Her puzzled look obviously gave away what she was thinking.

'Don't look so surprised, Eva. I've noticed your perkier mood! So I tried to work out how come you were so much smilier, and judging by the way you and you-know-who have been getting on these days, well, it's not rocket science, now is it?'

Eva laughed and wondered if everyone had noticed. Maybe she was making it really obvious, and if so, had she looked like a desperate fool? She decided that she'd actually been very subtle about it, since she had barely admitted to herself that she liked Killian. Plus Cathy had a sixth sense for this kind of thing, so no wonder she'd figured it out. Cathy ate, slept and drank boys, so she was perfect at picking up on even the tiniest ounce of chemistry. Eva smiled inwardly as she thought of that word, 'chemistry'. It summed up what she felt when she was around Killian – there was a sort of electricity running between them, making every word and movement alive, giving her a little shock of pleasure. She never knew what was coming next – it was fast, exciting, exhilarating. Wow, she really did like him!

She thought about him all weekend and what she'd say to him on Monday. And if he really felt the same way. And if they'd ever get together. And if the next time he asked her to a party she'd go, and they'd score and everything would be, well, lovely! Even her sister noticed a change in her, and when Eva couldn't hold it in any longer, she told Sarah every last detail about English class and all the little things that had happened between them recently. Sarah insisted that Killian was obviously interested. 'It's so going to happen,' she said. Whether this was genuine or just Sarah being nice since it was the first time she'd seen Eva this happy and excited in months, Eva didn't care. She was in love! Well, a little, anyway.

On Sunday night the Coonans' house phone rang. Sarah answered and shouted to Eva that it was Cathy. Eva took the call in her mum's room and was instantly met with screaming down the line.

'Cathy, shut up.'

'He wants to hug you! He wants to kiss you! He wants to marry you!' Cathy sang in an annoying, taunting tune.

'What are you talking about? Was your weekend any good?'

'I'll spare you the details, pet, cause I know you only really want to know about Saturday night!'

'Go on then, spill!'

'Well, turns out Mr Lain has taken a bit of a shine to you.'

The mention of Killian's name got Eva going a bit. 'And how do you figure that one out, then?'

'Well, let's just say he was a bit quieter than usual at the party. So of course when I asked him what was wrong, he told me he had really wanted you to come and how he really likes you.'

'Oh yeah, I'm sure that's exactly what he said.' Eva doubted he would be so open with Cathy, even if it was true.

'No, honestly. Well, that's the shortened version. Basically, we had a big chat about you and he was telling me how close you guys had got this year and how he really liked you but he didn't want to push things too quickly cause he didn't know if you were still all sad and stuff about your dad.'

'He said that?' Eva's voice had gone quiet as she took it all in. This was better than she'd expected.

'So then I was all going on about how you're such a great girl and that it was no wonder he liked you, blah blah blah. And then he asked me if I'd have a word with you and see if you liked him too and to try and get you to come out, as soon as you were ready, because he really wants to score you.'

'Oh, wow.'

'Oh my God, it's the coolest news *ever*, Eva!'

'I can't stop smiling! So it was a good night, then? Did you score?'

'Yeah, Cian and Graham. Bit of a fight there – neither was too pleased.'

'And who do you prefer?'

'Probably Cian – he's so much funnier, but Graham has that whole tall, dark and handsome thing. He's such a good kisser, too. Oh here, listen, my stupid mother is shouting at me to get off the phone. I just thought I'd ring you to fill you in. I'll talk to you tomorrow, yeah?'

'Yeah. Thanks a million for calling, Cathy.'

'Love ya!'

Eva felt like she'd just jumped off a bridge into a warm ocean. Adrenaline was pumping all over her body and she suddenly knew what people meant when they talked about 'that warm fuzzy feeling'. Her mood couldn't have got any better; she was sky high, on top of the world. At times like this, she thought of her dad and was sad that he wasn't there to see her good mood, but nevertheless, she pictured him in heaven looking down on his little girl, making all this happen so that she was happy again. She said a quick prayer for him and went into the TV room to her mum and sister to enjoy a long, leisurely evening of television, as the fire crackled and heated the warm, welcoming room. She was home.

6

Zac

Since the fight between Zac and his dad, the air in the O'Dwyers' house had settled slightly. Zac still tried to spend as much time as possible out of the house or up in his room, just to ensure he avoided another confrontation. In school, the teachers had already begun mentioning the Christmas tests and Zac could have shot every single one of them – it wasn't even Hallowe'en yet and already the festive season was looming. Zac liked the idea of Christmas, but it was never as wonderful at home as he wished. Being an only child was hard and, since things were already tough enough at home without an excuse for his dad to get drunk, eat lots and complain about his family.

The pile of homework seemed to increase every night and Zac found himself still left with hours of work to do even after study. In his view, this was utterly unfair and he kept making excuses to himself so that he didn't have to complete all his assignments. However, his teachers were unimpressed and Zac found himself landed with extra punishment work, which made the load even bigger. His brain was crammed and every night was just an endless quest to get at least half the work done. This wasn't what school was about – why should he have to sit in his room until midnight every night completing some irrelevant essay that wasn't even going to make a difference to his grade, since his teacher hated him anyway? His French teacher was also one of the rugby coaches and, in his eyes, if you didn't have a number on your back, you could kiss any chance of an A goodbye. Zac had to admit that the rugby thing was getting to him again. Every morning he'd come in, exhausted from the late-night homework he'd been forced to do, yet the other guys seemed fine.

'Ah no, the teacher said we didn't have to do it cause we'd extra training yesterday.'

'The match is on that day so he's given me an extra week to hand it in.'

Zac's patience was wearing thin.

It was a Thursday afternoon and Zac's first class after lunch was Irish. He hated the subject as it was, but the inordinate amount of work they'd been set the night before was ridiculous. As the teacher called the role, he asked anyone who didn't have the work done to say so, and he'd deal with them accordingly. Johnny O'Brien's name was called and when he confessed he didn't have it done, the teacher wasn't pleased. He was about to start off on a rant about how homework was very important and that no excuses would be tolerated, but Johnny knew one that always worked.

'But Sir, you said that me and the other lads didn't have to hand it in til Friday since we had that match yesterday.'

The teacher's face changed. 'Of course, Johnny. Apologies. Well done, by the way – you played a blinder! Now, where were we. Ah yes – Zac O'Dwyer?'

Zac paused, took a deep breath and decided the truth was the only option. 'I don't have it done, Sir.'

'You don't have it done? For goodness' sake, Zac, do you think I set homework for the good of my own health? Do you think when I set this work that it's only to be done if you feel like it or can be bothered?'

'But Sir—' Zac tried to protest.

'Don't interrupt me. Listen, I set work and I expect it to be done how I want it and, more importantly, when I want it. I'll deal with you after class. I think a detention or two might do the trick.' He concluded his rant with a final comment, said under his breath so he thought no one could hear. 'Stupid O'Dwyer boy. Always was a waste of space.'

That was it. Something inside Zac snapped in two and he felt himself erupt with rage and hatred for this man and the words he had just said. They had been all too close to something his dad would say and they had cut him so deep that he couldn't control himself any more.

'Waste of space? I'll give you a fucking waste of space. Just because I don't have a big Cup game today, I'm suddenly a waste of space? You narrow-minded dickhead. Whatever, rugby is big in this school, but I am sick of everyone and their double fucking standards. Fuck the lot of you!'

Zac grabbed his bag and stormed out of the class. The classroom was left completely silent with looks of utter disbelief at what had just happened. Zac, the quiet guy, had just shouted his head off at the teacher. Zac, the most decent bloke in the year, had just stormed out of class and called his Irish teacher a dickhead. Things like that didn't happen in this school. The school was strict and rules were not broken. Allowances were made for rugby players or sometimes the nerds, but people never, ever went around doing something like that and got away with it. Zac was in serious trouble.

The teacher looked like he had been punched. He was pale and completely startled. However, the colour returned to his face as he realised that he was the one with the power, and the little pup that had just insulted him was going down.

He excused himself from the room and headed out to the corridor, where Zac's angry footsteps could still be heard echoing through the afternoon tranquillity. Zac was mad. His fists were clenched as his heart pounded against his chest. He couldn't believe what he'd just done, but he was still too furious and wrapped up in the moment to realise how much trouble he was in. At that moment, though, he didn't care – he'd been treated like shit. And no one, not his dad, not his Irish teacher, not anyone, was going to call him a waste of space and get away with it. Zac had spent so many nights trying to grab on to any inch of self-esteem he had; his father had crushed his spirit and made it so hard for him to have any self-belief. And now he was subjected to the same disrespect at school. He hoped his classmates hadn't thought he was giving out to them – they'd never treated him any differently because he didn't play sport – but his teachers had, and this time they'd crossed the line.

Behind him, he heard the voice of his teacher commanding him to stop. But it was too late – Zac could feel the hot tears beginning to fill his eyes and he couldn't give that git the satisfaction of seeing him cry. He headed out to the yard and, before he knew it, he was out on the street. He didn't know where to go, but he didn't care. The further he went from it all, the better – the teacher wouldn't miss him. After all, he was just a waste of space and, right now, he felt like the most worthless person in the world.

He took the bus into town and spent the rest of the afternoon wandering up and down Grafton Street. The street was quiet, the usual buzz muted by the chilly breeze and melancholy chords of a lone busker. It was that awkward hour when afternoon shoppers have given up but evening theatre or restaurant goers haven't yet come out, all high heels and rich, musky perfume. Puddles splashed the paved ground like windows to loneliness. A woman pushed a buggy, and despite her crimson scarf, she still stiffened against the bite in the air. The baby lay, not realising the grey murky air that hung around it and smiled.

A swift gust was forming and, picking up leaves and dirty remains of that morning, it formed a whirlpool of litter and fag-ends.

Zac wandered until he felt so out of place he had to leave. He knew that, at home, he would be faced with one of the most ferocious arguments he'd ever been through, but he'd have to deal with it sooner or later, and since he wasn't achieving anything where he was, he decided he might as well head home. When he got there, he took a few deep breaths before putting his key in the lock.

When he walked in he could sense that the tension in the air was even more awkward than usual. His father and mother were sitting at the kitchen table, his mother with a cup of tea, his father nursing a large whiskey. Both had harrowed expressions. When they heard the door close they both looked up. His mother's look of pity alerted him that she was already feeling sorry for him, as she knew what was about to come. His father instantly stood up and launched into a fit of uncontrollable shouting.

'This is too far, Zachary. What were you thinking? I couldn't believe it when the principal called, that you could do something like this… Cursing at your teacher, causing a scene and storming out of school. What sort of delinquent little shit are you? I'm waiting for him to phone back, they're discussing what to do with you now, but don't think that the fact that I know him will help you – you're on your own…'

Zac said nothing – he didn't see the point. Whether he said he was sorry or angry or upset or even a little proud of his actions, it would have made no difference. He was in so much trouble, he decided to just stand back and take it all in.

'…ashamed, embarrassed. When I left that school I left a wonderful reputation. The O'Dwyer name was one of integrity and honour. But now you've not only destroyed your own name, but that which I spent so many years building up. You're a little shit, do you know that? You may as well have been dragged off the streets and dropped into some…some *public* school for all the difference it's made to your attitude.'

'Easy, Liam.' Zac's mother had noted the increasing redness of her husband's face. His teeth were gritted and he had a look in his eye that screamed hatred, as if he were only seconds from punching his son.

'All my life I have tried to mould you and shape you into something I could be proud of. But today you shattered all hope I ever had for you. When I look at you, I don't see my son, I see an ungrateful little fucker. Today you gave out to your teacher about rugby boys and how they're treated. I'm a rugby boy, Zachary, do you hate me? Because right now I certainly hate you.'

'I'll live,' Zac muttered.

It was too far, but Zac was sick of standing there like he always did, the quiet, hurt little boy he usually was. Trouble was, his dad wasn't impressed by this sudden surge of confidence. But before he could lash into his son again, the phone rang.

His mum answered and her face drained of all colour as she listened to whoever was at the other end. She put down the receiver and avoided Zac's eyes as she announced the news.

'That was the principal. He wanted to ring before Zac's told officially tomorrow at school – he's been suspended until further notice. They're not happy.'

Zac stared at the ground so hard he thought the floorboards would split. He could feel his father's gaze burning into him until he could bear it no longer and looked up.

'Go to your room, Zachary. Don't come down any time soon. Your mother and I need to discuss what to do next. Consider your life over from this point on.'

Zac was more afraid of his father at that moment than he cared to admit. He had so much power and he knew it. He really could ruin his life, and he certainly seemed like he intended to. Zac turned on his heels and headed to his room.

He flopped on his bed and closed his eyes. All he could do now was wait. His fate lay in the hands of the man he despised most in the world and a woman who wouldn't stand up for herself if she was paid to. He was in trouble, and for the first time in a long time, he was scared.

*

Later that evening, Zac was called down from his room to be given his punishment. His mouth was dry and every inch of him was praying that what he was about to experience wouldn't be too bad. His father dominated the proceedings, as usual, but nothing could have prepared Zac for what he said.

'Right, Zachary, your mother and I have been talking about this for some time and we feel that, excellent as it is, the school you're in just isn't suited to you.' He paused, allowing the silence to hang awkwardly before he continued. 'Today you displayed that it's wasted on you. And if you're going to show this by being a disgusting brat, things are going to have to change. You're going to have to start doing some actual work from now on – you're in fifth year now, so this lazy, half-assed approach is not going to be acceptable. It's a proven fact that boys do better academically in mixed schools, and if being a non-rugby player in a rugby school is going to annoy you so much, then I think it's time to say goodbye and shift your ass and that damn guitar to the mixed school down the road.'

Zac's heart was doing ninety and he was sweating with nerves as the reality of what had just been said hit him.

'Dad, you can't be serious?'

His father was calmer than earlier, but it was evident he meant what he'd said and there was absolutely no way he was going to be moved on this one.

'Mum? Come on! At least give me a chance or something, for God's sake!'

His mother was small and timid in comparison to the towering man who stood beside her, but her opinion was the same as his –

obviously she wasn't going to argue. Things were rough enough between them at the moment without her disagreeing with him on this. Zac forgave her for making poor excuses for his father's pitiful argument.

'Your father's right, dear. I mean, this is no time to be giving you chances – you're in the Leaving Cert cycle now and I've heard excellent reports about this other school – Sue's boys go there, you know.'

'But I don't want to go there. I want to stay where I am. I love my school. I was only messing about the rugby thing – I don't really mind if they get special treatment. Whatever, like. They're my friends. I'm really sorry about today – it won't happen again, but I can't just up and leave because you decide you want to screw up my life for no good reason.'

'Oh you can, Zachary. And you will.'

His father always had the final word.

*

Up in his room, Zac was so angry he was close to pounding downstairs and punching his dad square in the face. He restrained himself, but only just. He couldn't believe what he had just heard. His father was actually going to stoop so low as to take him away from all his friends and plonk him in the middle of some poxy mixed school with a load of hockey players where he knew absolutely no one.

Surely he couldn't move straight away – there'd be a waiting list or something. But he remembered with a groan that his dad actually knew the principal very well – they'd been in college together, so surely he could pull some strings and Zac would be there sooner than he could say 'this is possibly the worst thing in the world and I am actually going to cry with hatred for that man'.

Zac debated whether to complain or not, whether to go downstairs and talk it over with his dad and try and make him see sense. But he was defeated. He knew he could never change his dad's mind. His father always had to be right. Zac and his mum had learned that the hard way. And he knew there was no way he could honestly sit opposite his father and be reasonable. Reason was not a factor in their relationship any more. In fact, they had no relationship – he hated that man with every inch of his body. As he picked up his guitar, he strummed with even more vigour than usual, just so that the man downstairs would hear every angry chord.

And everyone's out there and they're all smiling
And they're all living and I am dying,
And he's still shouting and I'm trying to
Forget.

7

Eva

It was a Wednesday afternoon and Eva and her hockey team had a match against an all girls' school from the other side of the city. She was good at hockey, so the team she was on was taken very seriously by their coach, who was working them extra hard as they had a good chance this year of actually doing well in the Senior League. They'd won all their matches so far bar one, which they'd drawn, and they were feeling good.

They had over three hours between school and the match, so Eva, Cathy and a few of the girls decided to go down to Blackrock and have a look around to kill some time. Even though it was a cold day, they decided to walk and treat it as part of their warm-up for the match. As they headed out the gate they noticed a big group of lads just a few paces in front of them. It was the guys, who were easily persuaded to come to Blackrock too.

They all headed off, chatting and having a laugh, as usual. The Rock Road was buzzing as cars collected children from the various surrounding schools. Each frantic parent or minder was eager to get the run over and done with and a sense of urgency fuelled the traffic. With Hallowe'en just over a week away, Eva's friends were trying to decide who was going to have a party and who would be invited. Eva spotted her favourite face and casually strolled over for a chat.

'Hey Killian, how's it going?'

'All right, Eva, how's things? Who you playing today, then?'

'Some northside school. They're supposed to be pretty good, but we'll have a go, sure. Do you not have a match?'

'Nah, I'm injured. Pulled my hamstring in training yesterday, so I'll be out for a few weeks. I think me and the lads are gonna watch your match, if that's all right?'

Eva blushed and told him he was more than welcome, praying inwardly that she'd have a good game.

They spent an hour in Blackrock having coffee in Insomnia and chatting aimlessly before deciding it was time to head back. All the girls were protesting about the lads watching their match, but the guys insisted.

Luckily, Eva had a good game and they won. It was close enough at one–nil, but Eva was proud that she had set up the goal. When they scored, she looked over at the supporters cheering madly and she could have sworn Killian gave her a little wink. Her heart melted momentarily, but it wasn't the time for swooning – there was hockey to be played!

*

Straight after the game her mum picked her up and they headed off to Monkstown for her therapy. This was her fourth appointment with Helen and she felt she had come a long way even in such a short space of time. The session was good but tiring.

'Eva, I want you, in your own time, to tell me about what it was like around the time of your father's death. Did you go to see him? Was he brought to your house? I just want to get an idea of what actually went on around then. Just take it very slowly, all right?' Helen added gently.

Eva thought back to that awful time, and though she was reluctant to relive any of it, Helen's reassuring voice made it easier.

'It was hard,' Eva began slowly. 'He was taken to our house and we put him in the front room. He was lying in his coffin and mum had spent so much time preparing the room so that it was full of candles and lilies and smelled of lavender. Pictures of him dotted the room and it was very peaceful. It took me a while to go in and see him. I knew Sarah had been in earlier that day and spent quite a while with him. I could hear her talking to him and stuff and I didn't know if I'd be able to do the same. But I realised how much I'd regret not saying a proper goodbye, so eventually I just went in.'

Eva paused. Going into the room where her father had been laid out was one of the hardest things she'd ever had to do. Talking about it was hard, too. She took a deep breath and closed her eyes.

'I opened the door and the first thing that hit me was the temperature. Mum had had to turn off the heat and it was colder than the hall and it hit me like a wall. The low lighting made the room seem weak, as if death were hanging in the room and preventing the light from shining properly.' The image became clearer in Eva's mind's eye and she felt the knot in her throat tighten.

'The coffin lay in the centre. The smell of lavender filled me. It was nice. Mum had put a cross above the mantelpiece and lots of candles around the place so it felt almost like a church, like a room in the house we'd never had – it was so different. So strange and new, the walls seemed to ache with sadness. The amount of tears and sad words that those walls had seen and heard! I was glad his face hadn't been affected in the car crash – I don't think I could have brought myself to see his face all messed up. I took a deep breath and looked at him. He really just looked as if he was sleeping. He looked paler, but they'd made him look lovely, really lovely. I made sure to keep very quiet. It sounds stupid, but the place was so still and perfect I didn't want to disturb anything. And I cried on my own but I looked at him the whole time. And I stared at his face and so many things filled me. I wanted to say something. When Sarah had been in I'd heard her saying things. Lovely things, I'm sure. And I wanted to say all the things that filled my mind, but I couldn't. I couldn't bring myself to talk. So I thought the things instead. I don't know if I was saying them to Dad or to God or just to myself, but I felt the moment inside me. And I knew it would be one of those moments I'd never forget. I could pinpoint it as a split second where I felt truly lost and truly found too. That sounds stupid. I'm sorry.'

'Don't be sorry,' Helen soothed. 'You're doing so well. But if you want to stop, that's okay.'

Eva paused, but her words were now flowing from her. 'I cried some more. Then I kissed him. He was so cold, it shocked me. But I looked at him and I said goodbye. That's the last time I saw him.'

Eva began to cry. The memory was still so vivid and she could still picture her father lying there and the feelings inside her. She'd never seen a dead person before, and it had seemed so final. It was then that it had hit her that he was gone. Really, truly gone.

'The removal and the funeral are a blur. The hardest bit was watching my mum. She didn't even cry, Helen. She was too upset. And that made me even more upset.'

Eva's tears kept streaming. This was hard. At the end of the session, Helen asked Eva how things were going in her life in general – school, friends, the usual. Eva thought of Killian and wondered if she would sound ridiculous if she told Helen about him, but concluded that she had listened to so much other rubbish that had come out of her mouth, this wouldn't seem that odd.

'There's this guy that I really like at the moment. And he's being really sound to me. And all my friends are being really good to me recently and it's all just better. I feel better. More like I used to.'

Helen wrote something down and nodded. 'All this sounds very good, Eva. A boy, friends, they can all help a lot with bringing your life back on track. They symbolise normality, which is what you're trying to achieve. Sure, things are never going to be normal without your dad, but what we want is to get things as close as possible to how they were.'

With that, the session was over and Eva felt good. She was sure she looked an absolute state, what with her mascara leaving black rivers down her face, but she loved getting things off her chest and, tough as it had been, talking about the days leading up to her dad's funeral had really helped. That night, though she was tired both physically from the hockey and emotionally from her time with Helen, she felt good. Sarah was up in her room doing homework and Eva decided to make her a mug of hot chocolate. Sarah was grateful, though slightly surprised.

'Any particular reason for this?' she asked.

'Nah. Things just went really well today and I'm just in good form now,' Eva explained.

'How was therapy?' Sarah was careful to note Eva's reaction to this question to ensure she wasn't delving into uncomfortable territory. Luckily, Eva was more than willing to share.

'It was really good, Sarah. She made me talk about the funeral and all that and I was shocked at how I'd never thought about it all properly before now.'

'It's hardly something you forget.' Sarah's voice was low – obviously remembering too. A long silence fell between them and Eva found herself hypnotised by the steam rising from Sarah's hot chocolate. It danced upwards in caressing spirals, distracting her from the ever-fresh memory of her dad's death.

*

Hallowe'en was fast approaching and the two sisters and their mother were heading down to Cork for the break to stay with family. The girls would spend most of the time with their father's sister and family, while their mum would go visit their other uncle, her younger brother, Don. It was a good idea and Eva was looking forward to seeing her cousins. Both the boys were just a bit older than she was and they always had great craic together. She hadn't seen them since the funeral, but they texted loads.

One English class, Killian had asked Eva what she was dressing up as for the big Hallowe'en party. His voice possessed a naughty inflection, and his little wink showed he was obviously hoping her reply would be a Playboy bunny or something equally slutty. Her response wasn't what he'd wanted to hear.

'I'm going to Cork for the week. My mum's staying with her brother and my sister and I are staying with cousins. I won't be at the party.'

Killian's face fell. He was sick of Eva never going out, but he wasn't going to let it show.

'That's so shit. I was really looking forward to you being there.' He stared down at the floor before sneaking a cheeky look up at Eva. She blushed in appreciation.

'Well, I'll definitely come out soon, okay? I really want to, you know. It's just the way things are sometimes, I can't.'

Killian knew what she meant. It didn't make it any less annoying, but he knew it wasn't something he could push. If he wanted Eva, he was going to have to be patient.

*

The week in Cork was fantastic. They got the train down and their aunt was at the station to pick them up. It was great seeing their cousins, and Tommy and Ger had obviously been instructed to keep the girls entertained. They spent the week going to the cinema, amusements and generally having a laugh. Ger, who was just a year older than Eva, brought her to the pub a couple of nights with his friends. She'd been a bit shy the first night but a few drinks had sorted that out and eventually she'd relaxed and had great craic getting to know Ger's mates. One of them was cute and kept her in conversation for most of the evening.

'So, do you have a boyfriend?' he asked coyly.

'No, not really.'

'Not really? What's that supposed to mean?'

Eva didn't know what she meant. Part of her felt some sort of attachment to Killian, which was holding her back. The night passed without her doing anything even remotely scandalous, much to her admirer's disappointment.

Hallowe'en night had been a blast. They'd gone to a massive fireworks display followed by a big bonfire party in the park. Staring into the flames, deep in conversation with Ger, Eva felt a moment of true happiness. She thought of her dad and didn't know if it was the smoke or the memories of building the bonfire with him every year, but Eva's eyes began to water. Only, for the first time in a long time, they were tears of happiness. She missed him, but she knew he was with her wherever she went. Ger looked a bit startled when she launched a hug on him, but she hoped he understood. Eva was so grateful and had a brilliant night staring at the fire and at everyone having fun and thinking of all the fun she'd had with her dad.

By the end of the week the girls were sorry to leave, though the trip had done them good and left all three members of the Coonan family feeling much brighter and lighter inside. It was undeniable the effect Don had had on their mum, they'd always been close and were still very tight. Once they were back in Dublin, it was obvious that she missed her brother, and she seemed to lose some of the spark he'd given her that week. She was still so fragile.

Cathy hadn't been in touch but Eva had been too busy to notice. The night before they were due to go back to school Eva decided to give her a ring.

'Party was a total nightmare. Too many people showed up and

everyone drank far too much. Don't worry, though, Killian was completely faithful. Seemed in a pretty terrible mood, actually. A lot of people had a crap night.'

'You?'

'Well, Graham and Cian again. Whoops! Blamed the drink, though, so all's okay again. Didn't actually intend on getting as drunk as I did, but had my period and you know yourself, you're gone before you know it when Aunt Flo's around! So, how was Cork?'

'Really good, actually. Relaxing. It was nice to just chill out, you know?'

'Definitely. Well, you sound great anyway. Got to go have dinner. Talk to you tomorrow, honey.'

Eva was even happier – Killian hadn't been with anyone else and she'd had a great week. Life was good for Eva Coonan and, with a silent thank you to her dad, she headed to bed.

8

Zac

Half-term felt more like a year than a week. Zac was grounded and had to beg his father to let him even go for a walk to get some fresh air. Though he spent the days doing very little, Zac was drained and withdrawn. He seemed to have gone into shock since he'd been told he was moving schools, and every day it was an effort to get out of bed and feel any enthusiasm for life whatsoever. He'd been banned from using the phone and his parents had taken his mobile from him too, so he felt completely isolated. Half the time, he didn't know whether he felt like screaming or bursting into tears. Zac never cried, but over the past few days he'd seemed so close to it all the time, as if at any moment he'd be pushed over the edge. He wasn't just annoyed that he was moving schools – it was the way it had been done. He'd been treated like scum, and as usual his father seemed to be having a great time wrecking Zac's life. He knew he could still see his friends outside school at weekends or Wednesday afternoons, but just because he wasn't captain of the rugby team or Mr Academic, apparently he didn't deserve to go to the school where he was happy. Suddenly, there were only two ways to be considered a good person in this world – to be clever or to be sporty and he was neither.

At dinner, the table was silent as usual. Liam never asked about how his wife was or how her day had been. He never said a word to Zac. In fact, since the row he hadn't even looked at his son. Until tonight.

'Zachary, I've been making some phone calls and I've set up a meeting for your mother and me with Geoff. He said you should come too. Tomorrow, two o'clock. Wear something decent.'

Zac loved the way his father casually dropped in his new principal's first name, just to remind him that they were old buddies and that there was no chance of him being refused entry to the school. Zac's father confirmed his thoughts.

'Just so you know, I've been on the phone to him already and you're in. Tomorrow's just a formality.'

'They'll probably just want to show you round, give you your locker, that sort of thing. Get you familiar with the place. It should be nice,' Zac's mother said, trying to lighten the mood.

'I doubt it, Mum, but there you go,' Zac sighed weakly.

'Lose the attitude, Zachary. Don't even think about giving your mother and me stick about the move, because it's happening and that's final. And if you think you're going to be clever and purposely do badly in the new school just to prove a point, we'll have to discuss further punishment. Maybe boarding school – or maybe we'll throw out that damn guitar of yours so you won't have that distracting you.'

Zac looked his father straight in the eye and knew that he meant it. His father was very pleased with himself – he'd got Zac good this time.

After dinner Zac helped his mum with the dishes before heading up to his room. He took the notepad from the drawer under his desk and flicked to the page with the lyrics he'd been working on. They were coming along nicely, but the past few days had fuelled him with more ideas. He'd been feeling so much emotion he felt he'd burst unless he put it down onto paper. As he scribbled away, there was a soft knock on his door. He knew it was his mother – she was the only one who'd ever knock before coming in.

'Yeah?'

She closed the door quietly behind her. She seemed a little hassled and was holding something behind her back.

'Hi, love. Listen, as your father confirmed the move with Geoffrey today, I thought, well, since it's official, you might want to let your old friends know. I mean, I know they're not your old friends, they'll still be your friends, but you know what I mean. Sorry, that was the wrong way to put it...'

'Mum, relax, I know what you mean. Thanks.'

She handed him his mobile and the house phone. 'Don't be on the house phone too long, will you, love? It's just your father wasn't too pleased when I asked could you make a few calls, so just go easy.'

Zac stared up at his mother. It was obvious what she was doing and it was so kind of her. She wanted Zac to know she wasn't happy about the move either, that she felt bad for him and was hoping he wasn't mad at her.

'I put some credit on your mobile. I just thought that the next few weeks the lads will all be texting you like mad, to see what all the girls in your class are like!'

She gave Zac a sheepish smile. She was trying so hard, as if waiting for Zac to tell her she was all clear. Zac didn't know how to say it, or how to tell her all the things he was thinking, so he just stood up from his desk and gave her a hug. She was so small compared to him, but as she held him, it was still a hug from his mum and it was nice to know that someone was on his side. They stood there for a few moments before pulling back and giving each other a little smile. She headed downstairs and he sat back at his desk. Neither said anything but the air was officially cleared. They were on the same team, and now they both knew it.

*

Zac held the moment before realising he had a phone in each hand and loads of friends he hadn't talked to in a week. First he turned on his mobile and was inundated with text messages from the past few days.

ZAC MAN WOTS D STORY? NO ONE KNOWS WER U R?

HEY! TEL ME D RUMOUR ISNT TRUE – U BN EXPELLED?

TRIED RINGIN UR GAFF LAST NITE. UR OLD MAN SED U COULDNT TLK? WOT D HEL IS D CRAIC. WB

Zac smiled as he went through about twenty similar messages before picking up the house phone and dialling so quickly he wasn't sure he'd even got the number right. It was as if he was dialling his sanity back. At the other end of the line was a voice he was glad to hear.

'Zac, man, is that you?'

'Johnny, how's it going?'

'Where the hell have you been? Everyone's been talking about you all week. We were going to call round but we didn't want to like get involved in whatever the hell is going on. It's half-term, man, why haven't you been out?'

After about ten more questions, Zac was able to get a word in.

'Johnny, I've left.'

'What?'

'Yep. As of Monday, I officially go to the mixed school up the way.'

'You're not serious!'

Although Zac was afraid to say that he was deadly serious, he explained the whole sequence of events to Johnny, who was gob-smacked. By the end of the story, Johnny was raging.

'Zac, that is not on. I mean, I know your dad's always been strict, but he can't be serious. This is too far. What is he on about the rugby thing? You've never given us stick about it at all and that Irish teacher was well out of line last Thursday – fair play to you for storming out. He can't go around saying stuff like that, everyone was totally on your side. Look, do you want me to call around and tell your parents where I think they can stick their mixed school?'

'Johnny, it's not going to make a difference, they've made their minds up. No, sorry, *he's* made his mind up. She's totally cool, she doesn't want me to go at all. But I'm still going. Getting my uniform tomorrow after meeting the headmaster. This is serious.'

Johnny was speechless. He'd known Zac would be punished for walking out of school – he and the lads had just presumed he'd been grounded for half-term or something, but this was ridiculous. Wait till he told the guys. Zac couldn't leave the school. He was one of his best mates, probably the most genuine of all the guys out of their group of friends. His dad was well out of order.

'Listen, Zac, I have to get off the phone, but I'll give you a buzz tomorrow. I'm meeting up with the lads tonight, heading into town, so I'll fill them in. Take it you're not allowed to come?'

'Doubtful.'

'Well, listen, take it easy, okay? See ya later.'

Johnny clicked off. He hadn't known what to say. This was a small comfort to Zac. At least he'd be missed. But he was going to make sure that he didn't lose touch with the guys. Some of them had been his friends for over ten years; there was no way he was going to stop being friends with them now. It wasn't like he was going to make any proper mates in the new school. Sure, he'd find a few people to talk to at lunch, but his real, true friends would always be down the road, playing rugby.

*

Walking down the street in his brand-new school jacket on Monday morning, Zac was freezing. Winter was making itself known and every inch of him that wasn't covered by clothing was so cold it hurt. He turned a corner and in the distance he could see the gates. They were much scarier now than they had been the day of the meeting and Zac felt his heart quicken slightly. He noticed a number of people all coming from different directions, all heading the same way. A few stopped off in a little corner shop to stock up for the day, but most wrapped their coats and scarves around themselves and stiffened against the biting temperature.

When he got in, he headed to reception, as he'd been told to. A couple of odd looks were thrown his way, but Zac chose to ignore them. He explained to the receptionist who he was and she called to a student who was walking by.

'Show this gentleman to room twenty, will you?' She smiled at Zac and explained, 'Your year is divided into six classes, each with a class head, who will give you your timetable and things and show you where to go from there.'

Zac nodded and headed off with his guide, a younger boy, obviously wondering where Zac had come from and what he was doing there. 'You new?' the boy asked.

Zac nodded, and when the boy finally reached room twenty he merely muttered that this was the room. Zac thanked him and headed in.

School hadn't started yet so everyone was still relaxed. About twenty boys and girls sat around the room on randomly placed chairs – none were facing the desks they were supposed to be at and everyone was laughing loudly at something someone had just said but as Zac walked in, they all turned and looked at him. The room fell silent and everyone looked at each other, wondering who this boy who had just strolled in was, standing there looking utterly terrified. Zac decided he'd go for it and say something.

'How's it going? Eh, I'm new and I think I'm supposed to be in this class.'

The awkwardness hadn't lifted as Zac had hoped it would. Finally, a tall boy with blond hair, obviously the ringleader, announced, 'Right, well, I'm Cian and this is everyone so sit down and tell us who the hell you are!'

Zac was thankful for Cian's words. They seemed to break whatever cloud of tension had hung over the room and everyone relaxed again, either back into whatever conversation they had been having or to listen to what Zac had to say. It felt a bit like an interview, but Zac was slightly pleased that quite a few people had gathered around him. Cian seemed like a sound guy and was being nice to Zac, and since he was obviously popular, everyone else followed his lead.

'So, where did you go to school before now?'

Zac pointed in the general direction of his old school and they all knew what he meant. They all smiled and a few presumptions were made there and then.

'So, bit of a rugby head then, are we?'

Zac smiled but stood his ground. 'No, actually. I don't play rugby.'

'Do you play any sport?'

'Well, yeah, I play soccer or whatever, just messing around with the lads, but not properly.'

'Where do you live?' A shower of giggles followed from a group of girls and the one who'd asked the question blushed profusely.

'Blackrock, just a few minutes away.'

During the course of the interrogation, Zac was repeatedly asked his name and in return he was told everyone else's, though he doubted he'd remember even half of them. The arrival of their class head silenced everyone, though, and Zac went up to him and explained who he was. The head introduced him to the class (which prompted a series of comments, mostly to do with his old school and rugby) and he gave Zac a timetable. The teacher also asked one of the lads to look after him for the day. At this, Cian stood up and declared that he was the man for the job and, with a smile to Zac, he was employed.

At nine o'clock the bell rang and everyone headed off into the bustling corridors. Cian waited for Zac and then told him to follow him. As Zac headed off into the sea of unknown names and faces, he was still nervous, but it had been okay so far and maybe, just maybe, it wasn't going to be as bad as he'd thought.

FORGET

And in the darkness I can only wait,
And in the morning will it be the same?
Will all this help or better still
Help me to forget?

9

Killian

The routine of school had started again and Killian was none too pleased. Getting up on Monday morning had been torture, and he was dying at the prospect of a full day's work ahead. He was late for school as usual and, when he strolled into Geography class, the stupid old woman who was standing in for their usual teacher started giving out to him about the importance of punctuality or some rubbish like that. As he looked around for a spare seat, he saw that there was only one. He headed for it but noticed a stranger sitting in the next chair. Who was this chap? He nodded to him as he sat down and the other guy nodded back. Killian wondered where he had come from until the substitute teacher announced she'd left something in her car and had to go get it. With her out of the way, Killian turned to his neighbour.

'Hey, are you new?'

'Yeah,' he replied.

'Right, fair enough. What's your name?'

'Zac. You?'

'Killian.'

'Oh, right. Eh, do you play rugby?' Zac asked.

'Yeah, why?' Killian replied.

'Some of the lads in my old school said they knew you – Johnny O'Brien, Kevin…'

'Ah yeah, Johnny and Kev, both well sound. Take it you're from down the road then, yeah?'

'Yeah.'

'Do you play rugby?'

'No, not really.'

'Pity. So how come you're here?'

Zac explained about storming out of school, being suspended and having a fight with his dad. It all sounded a bit mad to Killian – the poor guy had been through the wars the past couple of weeks. Killian decided he seemed all right, and if he was as good mates with Johnny and Kev as he said he was, then he must be sound.

Break-time finally came and Killian was knackered as he sat down to a mini pizza from the canteen. Cian and Graham were opposite him talking about hockey, like they usually did. Killian looked around for Zac but couldn't see him anywhere.

'Did you guys talk to the new bloke?'

Cian cursed, stood up and headed out of the canteen.

'He was supposed to be looking after him,' Graham explained to Killian. 'Seems sound enough.'

'Yeah.'

'So, have you seen Eva yet?'

'No, why?'

'Well, you haven't seen her in over a week! I figured you'd be dying to clap eyes on her!'

'Shut up, will you. So what's the story with Cathy?' Killian turned the attention to Graham's love life so smoothly Graham hadn't even noticed, although he did look a bit agitated as he talked about Cathy.

'Ah, I don't know. I like her, but she and Cian are so going to happen and that's grand.'

'Bit gay of her to keep scoring you both – you're such good friends, like.'

'Whatever. I don't really care. I'm kind of into someone else.'

Graham gave Killian a grin and Killian wondered what he was playing at.

'Go on then, who?' Killian asked.

'Just a certain Eva Coonan.'

Killian's face fell but he tried to cover it up by taking a bite of his pizza and pretending he was cool. He had to admit that it wasn't like anything had actually happened with him and Eva – he couldn't stop anyone else from liking her. But Graham cut in on his train of thought.

'Relax, man, I'm only messing. You should have seen the look on your face!'

They started laughing, Killian with relief and Graham in hysterics at how his friend had looked. He was obviously really into this girl.

'What's so funny?' Cian had returned and sat down where he had been before while pulling up a chair for Zac. Killian just shook his head, dismissing what had just been said and noting that the new guy looked totally lost.

'All right, Zac. So, what do *you* think of the girls? Some hot ones, don't you think?'

'Yeah. I haven't really had a proper look yet, but some of them look pretty good.'

'Our year's probably the best in the school.'

Cian joined in the conversation – the female race was his favourite topic. 'Only little Killian here has only got eyes for one lucky lady.'

'Which one is she?' Zac asked, but Killian sat back in his chair trying to look as if he didn't care. On the other hand, Graham and Cian were eager for Zac to check out Eva and eventually they found her standing in the queue for food with the other girls. 'Yeah, she's pretty hot all right,' Zac declared.

The lads high-fived and left Killian feeling embarrassed but slightly proud too. She was hot, wasn't she? Not that they were going out or even scoring yet, but Killian knew he had her and it was only a matter of time before something happened. He'd been so patient, he was guaranteed to get in there and, if he didn't, he'd be annoyed. So many times he felt like telling her to shut up about her problems at home and actually come out for once, but he knew that would blow any chance he ever had of getting with her. He really liked her and, though they hadn't even kissed yet, he was sure that, pretty soon, he'd get to show Eva just how much he liked her.

The rest of the day crawled by, and by the time four o'clock came Killian was thankful to be finished. The hockey boys had training so he was waiting outside for the other guys to come so he could get the DART home with them. Zac passed by, obviously heading home. Killian gave him a nod and told him he'd see him tomorrow and to take it easy. Zac shouted something similar back but Killian wasn't really listening – a group of babbling girls had just come out the door and, as usual, he spotted Eva immediately. She was smiling at the others as they all spoke quickly about something or someone. Killian tried to listen and grabbed the general gist of the conversation.

'I think he's really good looking.'

'He's kind of quiet, though.'

'Yeah, but it was only his first day and, in fairness, he knows no one.'

'He's got really nice eyes.'

As they reached Killian, he decided he'd join in on the proceedings.

'So, we're all after the new boy Zac, then, are we?'

The girls giggled and blushed and told Killian to shut up. Most of them then headed off to the bus or to their lifts home and Eva shouted over her shoulder, 'See ya, Killian. Give me a text or something later.'

'Will do. See ya.' He was chuffed. Eva had told him to text her. He was totally in there; it was just a question of when she'd get over herself and decide she was 'ready' to come out. She'd cave soon.

Just then, the guys he'd been waiting for finally came through the door. He joined them and they headed to Booterstown DART station, all engaged in a deep conversation about O'Driscoll's most recent try. Killian swaggered along Booterstown Avenue, laughing at the idiot who hadn't seen the match in question. As always, Killian was displaying his rather wide knowledge of anything rugby related. He knew he was being a bit cocky, but the other lads laughed along. Killian *was* feeling cocky because Eva Coonan was his and soon everyone would know it.

At home, Killian remembered they'd been set some homework but he wasn't in the mood. He decided he'd go for a run instead. Since he'd injured himself and hadn't been at training he was worried that his fitness would drop. He'd made it onto the Leinster team and he wasn't going to throw that away just because his hamstring was giving him a bit of trouble. He put on an old Nike T-shirt and a pair of shorts and headed out. He lived near the seafront and decided to head up Dún Laoghaire pier. The early evening air was nippy enough but, after a few minutes, he started to push himself harder and he warmed up. The pier wasn't that crowded yet. The sky was turning grey and the thick, woolly clouds had hidden the sun, making the artificial lights the only source of brightness. Killian heard nothing but the steady rolling of waves and the odd clink of a boat. Behind him, Dún Laoghaire was lit by streetlights and shop signs of reds and yellows which illuminated the darkening air.

Killian found a steady pace and stuck to it. The thud of his runners on the hard ground was like a drum and matched time with his pounding heart. It felt good to be doing some exercise and he was happy at how his stamina was holding up. His hamstring was starting to hurt, but he just ignored the pain and pushed even harder. He reckoned he'd be back to training by the following week, which would be a relief to his team-mates, as there were some big matches coming up. He loved playing big games. When he played for Leinster, he was proud to be on the team but, if he was honest with himself, he preferred playing for his school when all eyes were on him. When he made that all-important tackle or, even better, scored the winning try, the sidelines would erupt with cheers as everyone realised that he was easily the best player on the pitch and one of the best the school had seen in a long time. It was great when the girls stayed to watch the rugby matches too. Even if they lost (which they regularly did, seeing as how the level of interest in rugby was low in the school), it was always evident that he was a great player.

He ran even harder as his mind filled with the buzz he often got when playing a match. He couldn't wait to be out on the pitch again and would love to score an amazing try and look to the side and see Eva, clapping and smiling at him and making him feel even better than he already did. She was pretty. He'd always known that. But just recently it seemed she'd been making a bit more effort again and it really showed. She'd kind of let herself go a bit when her dad died, but now she was looking good again. Killian thought about her dad dying and conceded it must have been hard for her. But sometimes it just got so annoying when she wouldn't come out and always used her bereavement as an excuse. She was too wrapped up in being emotional to see that being around people would take her mind off things – and Killian could think of lots of ways of distracting her!

He'd been in such a bad mood when she'd told him she wouldn't be around for Hallowe'en. He'd just spent a whole English class rubbing legs with her and putting on the whole 'nice guy' act, which was so boring, and then she told him she was swanning off for the whole holiday. It was at times like that when Killian felt like giving up on her. Sure, she was nice, but she had a lot of issues going on and was it really worth the effort? Obviously, it wasn't her fault her father had died, but sometimes Killian just felt like telling her to get over it so he could finally score her. He knew that sounded harsh, and the lads were always telling him that if it ever got out to any of the girls that he was saying all that stuff about Eva, he'd be public enemy number one. But Killian knew the girls would never find out and, besides, it was true. Everyone had their problems, so since when did Eva Coonan become so special that she could moan on about hers the whole time?

Killian had reached the end of the pier. He stopped for a minute. His heart was pounding so hard against his chest it hurt. He didn't know whether this was because he'd been running so fast or because he'd made himself angry thinking about Eva. Either way, he took a few deep breaths to settle himself before heading back again, this time a little slower. It was dark already and night was pressing in. The moon's reflection rippled in the sea below. The breeze caressed the top of the water and made the image shudder, as if shivering in the cool night air. Some people were out for an evening stroll, but few went all the way to the end of the pier. They had underestimated the coldness of the air and even the brightly coloured scarves they donned weren't enough protection against the icy temperature.

Killian had steadied himself and conceded, as he always did after thinking about how annoying Eva was (which was very often), that he did really like her and that he shouldn't get so worked up about her. She was a challenge, but that was part of why he was attracted to her. He couldn't give up now, after all the time and effort he'd put in. All the lads knew what an achievement it would be if he got with her and some had even warned Killian that Eva was a long shot and not to be disappointed if it didn't happen – it wouldn't be anything personal. Killian couldn't wait to prove them wrong.

As he reached the start of the pier again, tiredness began to set in and Killian slowed to a walk. His T-shirt was wet with sweat and he was embarrassed when he turned the corner to head for home, only to see a big group of girls walking in his direction. He considered crossing the road but decided it would be too obvious and, besides, what he was wearing pretty much explained that he had been for a run, rather than just some guy who sweated loads. As they got closer, one or two of them nudged the girl beside them and Killian felt good as six pairs of eyes fixed themselves on him. As he passed, they all smiled at him and one of them, a pretty girl with blonde hair and a red coat, held his gaze. Killian gave her a small but flirty smile back and the girl turned away as the others all began to babble at once.

'Oh my God did you see that?'

'He so checked you out.'

'What school does he go to because he is so hot?'

'Oh my God, I know. Did you see the way he looked at you, Katie?'

'I was so nervous when he smiled at me. Total ride!'

As their voices faded, Killian couldn't help but think how he could have any girl he wanted and how lucky Eva was. He just hoped she realised the scale of who she was dealing with and how stupid every other girl in Dublin would say she was for not scoring him yet. Killian smiled inwardly and swaggered home, the words of those girls still echoing in his head.

*

The next morning in school he had a double free period first thing and was still so wound up with having pretty much convinced himself that he and Eva would be scoring the following weekend that he ended up telling the new guy the whole story. Zac had thrown in the odd word and funny comment, but on the whole had just listened to what Killian had to say, which made Killian feel even better about himself. He blabbered on to Zac for ages before realising he didn't want the new kid to think he was totally big headed, so he asked him about his own love life. Zac told Killian that there was nothing to tell at the moment. He said it with such a relaxed manner that Killian was a bit surprised – he seemed like a really nice guy, so Killian was shocked that he wasn't seeing anyone. Either way, he was sure Zac would have a good few female admirers now that he was in a mixed school – the girls were already flirting like crazy with him. Killian told Zac as much and Zac just laughed. He'd seemed a bit taken aback by the compliment and seemed a little unsure whether Killian was trying to tell him to back off. Killian put him straight.

'Here, don't worry, Zac. As far as the ladies are concerned, man, work away. None of us guys are the jealous type and, sure, at this stage we've all been with all the girls so the novelty has worn off. So get stuck in to whoever you like the look of. Except I'd advise you not to go for Cathy – there's already too many guys wanting a piece of her. And then there's—'

'Eva. Yeah, man, I know. There's no way I'd try it on with her. It's obvious you two are going to get together so I'm not going to interfere.'

Yet again Killian was impressed with the new guy and was glad Zac had said it was obvious Killian and Eva were going to get together. It was nice for someone else to confirm what Killian had been telling himself.

The bell went and as Killian consulted Zac's timetable to see what they had next, his smile grew even more. Swinging his bag over his shoulder and telling Zac he'd see him at break, Killian sauntered off to English feeling on top of the world.

10

Zac

The afternoon air was fresh as Zac walked along the streets to the bus stop. The grand white houses of Avoca Avenue were secluded by large trees, naked apart from a few remaining leaves that just wouldn't accept that winter had come.

Zac liked walking. It gave him time away from everyone and everything to think, or best of all, to not think. Only a week into his new school, he felt like he'd been there a whole term. It really wasn't as bad as he'd expected and he was making some nice friends, but now he was on his way to meet up with his real friends. He knew where his priorities would always remain.

Hopping off the 46A, Zac entered the swarm of people. He hadn't been on Grafton Street since the day he'd stormed out of school and it seemed different to him now. The hustle and bustle and incessant hum of people was welcoming beneath the soft glow of Christmas lights. Lists and bags and elbows and scarves all merged into a wonderful painting where colours grew into each other and produced a rainbow of never-ending fuss. Zac walked through it until he was beneath the glowing HMV sign where the guys would appear any minute. Zac gazed around at the others who had appointed the record shop as a meeting point. A rather tired looking man with a navy polo neck kept checking his watch and shaking his head as 'she' refused to turn up. He'd obviously been there a while and the outline of his figure seemed to sag with realisation that he'd been stood up.

Zac spared a thought for the man before being woken up again by a loud voice, calling at him in the most typical of southside accents.

'Well, look who it is, lads.'

Zac was surrounded by seven familiar faces, none of which he had seen in what felt like a very long time. They all greeted him and amidst the bustle of high-fives, shouts and laughter as the wise-cracks began asking about Zac's new school, Zac felt at home again. Johnny broke his trance by announcing they were off to Eddie Rocket's for some proper food and the noisy group headed off.

Seated in the warm restaurant, Zac's interrogation began. He laughed at the level of interest the lads were paying his new school or, more precisely, the female students.

'Are they hot?'

'Have you scored yet?'

'Have you hung out with them much?'

'Do they look sexy in their uniforms?'

Zac decided to put them out of their misery and fill them in. 'Well, my year's probably the best for girls. They're all real sound, and a couple are absolute stunners.'

'And when exactly is the next party your new little friends are going to be having? And more importantly, can we come?' Johnny was quick off the mark.

'I'll see what I can do, man,' Zac laughed.

But secretly he knew the chances were slim – if and when he got invited out with his new friends, he knew that he'd already stand out as the new guy and he didn't want to be seen to be pushing it by bringing along a load of friends. It would also look like he couldn't go out with all his fellow jocks holding his hand, which he didn't want. The thought of the word 'jock' led him to tell the guys about the person in his new school he was most friendly with so far.

'Kev and Johnny, I think you know him from rugby, he's on the Leinster squad too. Really sound guy. Killian Lain?'

'Yeah, of course we know Kill – savage kicker, I have to say,' Kev said.

'I keep in touch with him a bit outside rugby too. He's always in town at clubs or whatever at the weekends,' Johnny added.

'Yeah, major party animal, isn't he?' Kev had a twinkle in his eye, indicating there had been many a good night spent with Mr Lain.

'There are a few other guys I've got friendly with. These two called Cian and Graham. Cian's the funniest bloke you'll ever meet. Both hockey boys, though.' Zac had decided to throw this in to see how the lads would react; it was how he'd expected.

'What faggots!'

'Spot the gays!'

Zac decided to defend them. 'Actually, they're such legends. Total jocks, like – no different to you guys. The ladies love them too!'

The lads didn't seem that convinced, but nevertheless they settled down as they were all served their burgers.

In less than five minutes the plates were spotless. Zac had forgotten how much rugby boys could consume in such a short space of time and had had trouble keeping up with the rest.

'Jesus, I'm packed. Anyone want the rest?' he asked, only to be attacked by seven pairs of hands grabbing for his few remaining chips.

Zac felt as if he was going to burst. He slouched back in his chair, barely listening to the babble of deep voices that surrounded him. He gazed around the restaurant till his eyes reached the door, which had just opened to reveal two very hot girls. Obviously, the guys had spotted them too and started nudging each other and sitting up to get a better look.

'Check them out.'

'One on the right is hotter.'

'No way, check out the rack on the other one.'

'Go up to them.'

'Not a chance!'

'Here, fuck this, you're all pussies – I'll show you how it's done. And if you're all lucky I'll just take the blonde and you faggots can fight over the other one,' Johnny smirked as he started to get up from his seat.

However, Zac's grin silenced them all as he realised he had one up on them. With a wink to his friends, who sat open-mouthed, obviously utterly confused at what was happening, Zac headed over to Lisa and Cathy.

The girls saw him coming over and awarded him with big smiles followed by a hug from each. Of course Cathy gave him her typical big kiss on the cheek and the three began chatting. Her eyes darted over to the table of lads Zac had come from and seemed pleasantly surprised at what she saw. She'd thought from the start that Zac was very good looking, and his friends, who she presumed were from his old school, weren't bad at all. She chatted with Zac a while longer, making sure to toss her hair and flash wonderful smiles at him before heading to the table with Lisa, shaking her hips as she went, so that his friends would see.

And, of course, the lads did see. They'd been watching every move the girls had made, and when Zac returned to the table they all stared at him with disbelief. Zac decided to put them out of their misery.

'That's Cathy and Lisa. They're in my year. Really sound birds.'

The guys didn't know whether to be jealous or to fall to the ground on their knees, thanking Zac for being their link to such beautiful girls – and surely, that was just two of an abundance of hotties. Suddenly, the mixed school was a lot more appealing and they didn't have a clue why Zac had ever moaned about moving.

Relaxing into memories,
Nothing's changed but I am free,
Until I know I want to be alone.

11

Eva

'Oh my God, Eva, you've no idea how hot they were. We're talking like a million times better than Killian, Cian and Graham put together. All seven of them. Plus Zac. What a group of friends!'

Cathy told Eva for the fourth time about seeing Zac with his friends at the weekend as they walked down to hockey training. Eva smiled and shivered. She could already see her breath in the air in front of her. So, Zac has handsome friends? Interesting! For Cathy and Lisa, whose lives were controlled by boys alone, to say they were that good looking was really something.

In fairness, though, she had to admit that the new lad was really easy to talk to. He wasn't at all what she'd expected, coming from the school he did, and was such a genuine guy. That morning, she'd spent the whole break talking to him. They'd been chatting away as usual in a group until someone mentioned the name of a certain band. She'd noticed Zac's eyes light up, though everyone else had just continued on with the conversation. She'd pulled up a chair beside him and asked him about it. It turned out he loved the band in question, an Irish group whose songs were so perfect it made her laugh and cry all at the same time. She'd never met anyone who'd shared such a passion for them, but Zac loved them just as much as she did, if not more. His eyes shone when he spoke of his favourite song of theirs, and he felt completely at ease telling her that it made the hair stand up on the back of his neck at how one song could be so amazing. Eva was impressed. His musical knowledge stretched far beyond that of any of the other lads she hung out with – music was obviously his hobby and she felt inspired after talking to him.

Eva told to Cathy after French class at how sound Zac was. Cathy agreed. 'I always told you he was cool. He's much more mature than our lads, isn't he? Real kind of quiet, but a hundred per cent decent, like. I'd say he'd be great to have a real deep chat with – he'd totally listen to anything you had to say. I might try it sometime!'

'And then ask him for his friends' numbers?'

'Me? Never!' Cathy stuck her tongue out and swirled off to class.

The highlight of the school week came on Wednesday when Cian arrived into school with the news that his parents were away in Donegal from Saturday morning til Sunday evening. This meant only one thing – a party. Eva knew this was her chance to finally get with Killian and her heart was already doing ninety at the thought of it. It wasn't until the end of the school day that she knew she was definitely in though. She was just closing her locker when she felt the warmth of a familiar body beside hers. He was behind her, hair and skin as usual looking as if he'd just been on a long holiday in Spain. He was smiling, but his grin was far from innocent as his eyes displayed that cheeky twinkle she loved. The way he stood just oozed confidence and, with his top button undone so that the tiniest bit of his silver chain was revealed, Eva thought she'd collapse in his arms there and then. She restrained herself and realised she'd become very nervous. Killian seemed to be enjoying watching her girlish discomfort and smiled even more until finally putting her out of her misery.

'So, I take it you heard about Cian's?'

'Yeah, he mentioned something about it to me.'

'And are you going to come?'

'Depends who's going, really.' Eva looked away with a small smile creeping over her flushed face. She was trying to play it cool but was having serious trouble. Killian decided to play along and the pair created a flirty tension that was blissfully thick. He laughed inwardly – he could play these games in his sleep.

'Well, I think Cathy and the other girls are going.' He well knew that hadn't been what she'd meant, but was going to make her spell it out. Eva rose to the challenge.

'Well, that's not really what I was talking about. I mean, I haven't been out with everyone in so long. Why should I come this time? What would make it so good to tempt me?' She spent extra time emphasising the word 'tempt' before looking up at Killian from beneath her wonderfully long eyelashes. But Killian wasn't going to let her win. He would keep her just far enough away so that in the end she would be on her knees trying to get him. Of course, he would eventually give in. But he liked to be in control first.

'I have a couple of things in mind, Eva, but you'll just have to come along and find out, won't you?' He gave her a wink and a final grin that made his face crease up like a bold child, only when he did it he looked so sexy Eva went weak at the knees. He was good at this. Like Cathy, he had a serious talent when it came to flirting. Eva smiled to herself before heading to join the girls, her head lighter than it had been in a while.

*

The next morning on the way to school, Eva had to ensure the practicalities of the party were in order before she could let her imagination run completely wild.

'Mum? There's this party on Saturday night in Cian's house, you know, the one in Donnybrook? Anyway, I'd really like to go. Can I?' Eva looked out the window of the car as if expecting the worst and when she realised that nothing was being said, she thought she'd burst into tears. It was only when she snuck a glance at her mother that she realised she'd been beaten to it. A tiny drop trickled down her mother's face and Eva began to panic – she hadn't meant to upset her. What had she done wrong? Why was her mum smiling?

'Of course you can, love. You go out as late as you want.'

Eva's heart leapt but she was still mightily confused. Why was her mother being so emotional about it all? A simple 'yes' would have done, but her mother was so full of enthusiasm Eva didn't know what to think.

'Mum, why are you crying? If you don't want me to go, I won't.' Eva hoped in the pit of her stomach that her mum wouldn't take her up on that offer.

'I'm sorry, pet. Oh, look at the state of me. No, love, I'm just happy, that's all!'

'What do you mean?'

'I'm happy my little girl's back. I've watched you recover slowly but surely, but I've always known that a part of you was still too hurt to come back. I didn't want to say anything, I wasn't going to push you. But, finally, you're ready to take back another part of you and I'm just so happy.'

'That's really cute, Mum!'

'Ah, be quiet, you! I know I'm a sentimental fool, but I like seeing you happy. You were always quieter than Sarah and sometimes it's so hard to figure out what you're thinking. That's why I think the therapy has helped you a lot. If anything, it's helped you to make sense of everything in your head and, sure, that's half the battle. Of course you can go out Saturday night, and if you want to have the girls over beforehand to get ready or to stay over afterwards, then you're more than welcome.'

'Thanks, Mum.'

A comfortable silence fell upon the car until her mother decided to push her luck and see if there was more to Eva's new-found confidence than she was letting on. Eva smiled as she realised her mother knew her all too well.

'So, any nice young men going to this party?'

Eva said nothing before deciding that maybe sharing just a little of the truth with her mum would be nice. 'Maybe... oh all right, his name's Killian.'

'Hmm, I see. And does this Killian like you then?'

But before Eva had time to come up with an answer that wouldn't lead to more enquiries, they'd reached the school and Eva was hopping out of the car with a grin telling her mother, 'That's for me to know and you to wonder!' Her mother just laughed and stuck out her tongue before pulling away from the school. But all the way home Eva's mother couldn't help thinking about what Eva had said. And wondering.

She found it hard to watch her daughters wrestle with something that no one, not to mind two teenage girls, should have to deal with. These years were tough enough for them – teenage angst and school exams were supposed to be all they worried about, but here they were faced with a tragedy that she herself, a fully grown woman, found impossible to live with. It just wasn't fair. All her friends, all her family, had been so good to her. But all she wanted was him. And that was the one thing she couldn't have. It was only now, after his death, she realised how much she truly loved him and how life without him was really not worth the effort. But she had to stay strong, for the girls if nothing else. But it wasn't easy. Not even close.

12

Zac

As if talking to him in school hadn't been enough, Killian had taken to texting Zac every other night. The conversation generally centred around Eva, though this particular night Killian wasn't as full of praise for her as usual.

SHES WRECKN MY HEAD MAN. I MEAN, TLK ABOUT PLAYIN HARD 2 GET. WHO DOES SHE THINK SHE IS? WHATEVA HER DADS DEAD BT LYK, DOES SHE WANT A MEDAL?

Zac knew that Eva's father had passed away earlier in the year, as Killian had mentioned it a few times as the reason she never came out with them, but it felt so coarse to hear Killian talk about it in such a derogatory way. Zac didn't know what to write back but decided to keep it light. He didn't want to get involved in being cruel about Eva, he barely knew the girl.

WELL SHE DEFINITELY LIKES U. PLUS U NO SHES SO GONNA SCORE U ON SATRDAY SO ITS KOOL.

Zac knew that there was a party in Cian's that Saturday as a few people had asked him if he was coming. He hadn't known what to say. He felt bad about just turning up when he hadn't been properly invited. Although all the people he hung out with seemed to have just assumed they were going, as they were the usual group that went out together every weekend, Zac felt weird just including himself in that group so soon, so he'd decided to leave it for another few weeks.

I SWEAR 2 GOD IF SHE DOESN'T FUKN SCORE ME IM GONA GO CRAZY. ALL DIS NICE GUY SHITE IS DRIVING ME NUTS. O I NEVA ASKED U – TAKE IT UR CUMN 2 CIANS?

Zac sighed and decided to just tell it like it was.

I DONT TINK SO. I HAVNT REALY BN INVITD N I FEEL SO GAY JUS SHOWIN UP.

DONT B STUPID MAN. COURSE UR INVITD. IL MAKE SURE CIAN SEZ SUMMIT 2U 2MO.

NO ITS GRAND. ID FEEL LYK SUCH A LOSER. ITS FINE.

NO U SPA! HE TOTALLY WANTS U 2 CUM ITS JUS IT WUD NEVA CROSS HIS MIND 2 ACTUALLY PERSONALLY INVITE ANY1. DO CUM – ITLL B A LAF.

WEL, IL C. AS I SED I DONT WANA IMPOSE. LISTEN MAN IL CU 2MO. K.

KOOL. TAKE IT EASY.

Killian was being really generous towards him and Zac was grateful. Plus Zac was quite friendly with Cian, so he hoped it wouldn't be a problem if he came to the party. Still, he didn't want to push his luck. The following day, though, Cian sat beside Zac in the canteen at break and explained to him that he was more than welcome on Saturday. Zac was delighted.

After school, they all congregated outside before the bus and DART people headed in their respective directions, while those lucky enough to be getting a lift swaggered off to the comfortable ride home. Soon, only Eva and Zac were left. She wrapped her arms around herself to try and keep the winter out, but it didn't seem to be working. They'd previously discovered that they lived only minutes from each other.

'Take it you don't have a lift then, Zac?' Eva asked.

'Nope: You?'

'No.'

'Right, well, the sooner we start walking, the sooner we get there.'

Eva looked at Zac and realised that walking wasn't going to be as boring as usual – she had a companion, and a sound one at that. They headed off down the freezing street. The cars of parents collecting their little dears were bumper to bumper and no one seemed as if they were going to give in. Zac smiled and decided he'd rather be walking along here with Eva than stuck in a traffic jam. The pleasant silence that lay between them as each stared at the road rage that they passed was broken by Zac's deep voice.

'What else are you up to this weekend then?'

'Nothing, really. I've therapy on Sunday.' Suddenly, she came to a halt. Her face was ghostly white. 'I can't believe I just said that. Shit.'

'It's okay.'

'I'm such an idiot.'

'Relax, Eva, it's cool.'

'No, it's not. No one knows that I go to therapy. Except Cathy. They'd all think I was such a freak if they knew. Especially the guys.'

'No they wouldn't. Don't be stupid.'

'Please don't tell them, Zac. I mean, I like to keep it private. I don't know why I told you, it just slipped out. That never happens. I'm usually concentrating on not mentioning it at all.'

'Eva, don't worry. I won't say a word.'

Eva stared at the ground, but the sincerity in Zac's voice relaxed her and she decided it wasn't that big a deal that she had told him. She began to elaborate. 'It's because of my dad, you know. It's just nice to talk to someone.'

'Yeah, I'd say it is.' Zac didn't know what to say. He wanted to give her a hug and tell her how terrible a thing it was to happen to such a nice person. But he didn't want to make her upset. And yet, he still wanted to show her he cared.

'It must be awful. I mean, I can only begin to imagine what you must feel. Sorry I can't say any more than that, it's just, I'm not going to pretend I know what you're feeling because I don't. But I know it must be hard.'

Eva smiled. No one had ever said anything like that before. None of her friends ever commented on how awful she must be feeling, just about how awful she must have felt. But for the first time someone realised that it wasn't just hard at the time. It was hard all the time, even all these months later.

'It *is* hard. But I'm getting on with things and the therapy is really helping. My sister Sarah, well, she was able to get on with her life so much more easily than me. Not that she wasn't as upset, but she knew that life was going to go on whether she liked it or not. I wasn't that strong.'

'Yeah, but everyone deals with these things differently. There's no right or wrong way – it's too raw a situation for that.' At this Eva began to laugh. Zac was afraid he'd offended her. 'Sorry. Did I say something wrong?'

'No, no, it's not that. It's just, you're so good at this. I can't imagine any of the lads saying any of this. You're different.'

'Thanks… I think!'

'No, it's a good thing. It's nice to find someone who realises that they can't understand what I'm feeling, but that there are other ways to help.'

Zac stared at his shoes. He didn't know what to say. He was glad he'd said the right things, because he really did care. He cared a lot for her even after a few weeks. She was different. Here they were on a cold street in the middle of Blackrock and she had just shared things with him that she dared not tell anyone else. It was this that made him hope that maybe she cared for him too. Obviously she didn't fancy him – she was too obsessed with Killian – but it seemed as if they clicked and that they understood each other in a way that was rare and comforting.

'So Zac, what about you? Your parents still together? All happy families?'

Zac paused. He wanted to tell her about what was going on. She'd been honest with him, why couldn't he do the same? It was just that, however terrible things were between his parents and him, it was nothing compared to Eva's pain and he didn't want her to think that he thought it was. Then again, he wanted to tell the truth.

'Well, my parents don't get on, really. It's my dad, you see. He's bent. He treats my mum like shit and he's not much better to me. But at least I can escape from it all soon. The moment I finish school I'm going to get as far away as possible from him. But my mum is stuck with him. And I'd feel so bad leaving her. They fight all the time like. Literally.' He paused before adding, 'Look, I know it's nothing compared to what you've been through, but it's tough.'

'Of course it is. Don't feel you have to tiptoe around just because my dad died. You have your problems too, and I'm not going to think any less of them just because of my situation. It sounds awful.'

'It is. I mean, home is just so awkward. He rules the place and when he's there the tension is unbearable. Then if he's not there, my mum is too worn out from their latest fight to be herself. I don't have any brothers or sisters so it's just me like. I get really pissed off. Usually I just go up and play my guitar but he tells me I'm terrible at that too and that it's a waste of time.'

'You play guitar?'

'Yeah, acoustic. I love it like but it's hard to enjoy it when he's downstairs shouting up at me that I shouldn't bother cause I'm crap. He thinks I'm a waste of space. That's why he made me move schools. He didn't think I was good enough for his precious rugby school, so he made me leave.'

'Yeah, I never heard what happened there. There were a load of rumours going around.'

'It's a long story. But basically I didn't fit my dad's image of the perfect son – the rugby playing, collars up, get away with murder just because I'm captain of the Senior Cup team kind of guy. But I'm not, and he hates me for it.'

Eva looked at Zac. He felt so relieved to be getting all this off his chest, but it was hard hearing out loud the harsh reality of how little love his father had for him and that he considered him worthless. Eva looked genuinely concerned. She turned to him with compassion in her eyes.

'Zac, just don't listen to him. I'm serious. Never let him convince you that you're a disappointment, because you're not. He's the one who's messed up and you just keep on playing guitar and ignore him.'

Zac smiled and let the silence hang between them. Both had told the other things that they usually kept deep inside them. And they had listened and comforted each other that allowed them to relax and see that life isn't easy, but people can still be wonderful. Even if they'd had it tough, it was still possible because hurt and loss and neglect can mould the best person and give them a strength that they might not have had otherwise.

They reached Eva's estate first and she stopped outside the entrance.

'Thanks for today, Zac. It was really nice. I'll see you tomorrow night.'

'Yeah, cool. And thanks, Eva.'

Both stared at the other until Eva broke the stillness. She walked up to Zac so that their faces were almost touching and then gave him the softest, most warming hug he'd ever had. He hugged her back and they stood there in each others arms, as if releasing all their worry and cares. They both pulled away and smiled at each other again before heading their separate ways.

Zac reached his house within minutes and headed straight for his guitar. Only now, he felt like writing and had just been fuelled with lyrics that would fill a thousand songs. He grabbed a pen and paper and began scribbling away, capturing everything he'd just felt. It was wonderful.

And I'm dreaming and my mind is cloudy,
And she's near me and I pray that when I
Look at her, I never will forget.

13

Eva

In the car on the way over to Cathy's, Eva, dressed in her comfiest sweatpants, closed her eyes as she listened to one of her favourite CDs. Her mother tapped along appreciatively to the music as the lyrics filled the vehicle. And as 'Star Star**' by The Frames came on, Eva was forced to sing along, just quietly so as not to interfere with the already perfect vocals. She loved this song – not only was the tune brilliant but the lyrics were so perfect and she wished, more than any song in the world, that she had written it.

Star, Star, teach me how to
Shine, shine, teach me so I
Know what's going on in your mind,
'Cause I don't understand these people;
Saying the hill's too steep well,
They talk and talk forever
But they just never climb.

And it was true – some people just never took the initiative and embraced life and forgot all the bad things they'd experienced and smiled. But now, for the first time in so long, Eva could see that she wasn't one of these people. She'd climbed the hill, and although so many times she'd felt like just letting go and rolling all the way to the bottom, she'd kept going and, now, she was happy again and the path wasn't as steep.

*

'Hi, baby, how are you?' Cathy squealed as she opened her front door.

'Nervous!' Eva admitted as Cathy let her in and the pair immediately headed upstairs, both intent on making sure that every aspect of their appearance was perfect for the night ahead. Eva plugged in Cathy's hair straightener and sat down on her bed. Cathy had been in the middle of plucking her eyebrows when Eva arrived and returned to her work. The pair chatted and laughed and discussed their numerous hopes and aspirations for the evening ahead. Eva expressed her angst over Killian. Part of her had this dreadful feeling that everything would fall apart. She'd built up her hopes so much that it seemed as if the level of happiness she would feel if all did go according to plan was too perfect. And perfection never happened. She looked to her friend for some comfort, but was met with Cathy's blue eyes staring straight at her, smiling as if she hadn't listened to a word that had just been said. But what she had to say was much more pleasant.

'Eva, it's so nice to be doing this again.'

'Doing what?'

'Getting ready to be going out to a party, hearing you fret about your recent fancy. I've missed you!'

'I've missed you too, Cathy.'

They hugged and quickly realised that they had little time for getting emotional – there were far more important things to be doing!

Finally, they were ready and for the entire bus journey to Cian's, Eva was caught somewhere between exploding with excitement and nerves. The butterflies were doing gymnastics inside her and she couldn't bear it for much longer. Cathy announced that they were at the right stop and, as they scuttled off the bus, there was no turning back. It was a quick stroll to Cian's house and they arrived in no time. As they rang the doorbell, Cathy held Eva's hand. It was as if Cathy could hear her friend's heart thumping in her chest and Eva was comforted knowing her best girl was by her side. Cian answered the door.

'Ladies, welcome. Looking stunning, of course. Come in, come in – nearly everyone's here already, so just make yourselves at home.'

The three headed into the living room and were greeted by a sea of turned heads. They smiled at the crowd of familiar faces and headed into the thick of the people. The party had begun. The first person Eva spotted was, of course, the man of the moment. Killian was over in the corner of the room chatting loudly with some of the lads. He looked hot in his faded jeans and long-sleeved black T-shirt. His hair was gelled to perfection and his skin glowed, as usual. Eva smiled at him and he gave her a cheeky grin and raised his glass. Eva thought she was going to collapse, her knees were so weak, but luckily Cathy grabbed her and announced that they were going to go find Graham and, more importantly, a drink.

In the kitchen, Graham handed over the bottles and took the money off his gorgeous customers. Cathy found Lisa and headed off to dump her jackets and took Eva's too, leaving Eva feeling slightly more naked than she wanted to be, but Graham was quick with a compliment to distract her from covering up.

'Eva, you look well.'

'Cheers, Graham. Not looking too shabby yourself.' He laughed but it was true – Graham always looked good and tonight was no different. His dark hair, dark eyes and sallow skin meant that he was the perfect pin-up, and as he smiled down at Eva with his cheeky grin, she was happy that Cathy had scored him – he was a catch! His mind was obviously on scoring too.

'So, are you going to get with Mr Lain tonight then?'

Eva gave an innocent smile and replied, 'Don't know. We'll just have to wait and see.'

'Well, he'd be mad to turn you down looking like that!' he said. She was about to reply when Graham's eyes stared at something behind her and a wink at his buddy sent Eva's heart into a frenzy. It was him! Graham smiled at the pair and quickly excused himself. Part of Eva wished he hadn't – she was so nervous. She turned around to be rewarded with Killian's sturdy figure looking at her from top to bottom. He was impressed.

'You look good.'

'Thanks, so do you.'

'You drinking?'

Eva indicated the Smirnoff Ice on the counter behind her. 'You been here long?'

'Kind of.'

Another awkward silence fell, but it was okay. Both knew it was the best kind of awkward. They knew what was going to happen later that night and were fraught with anticipation. Eva couldn't stand it any longer and decided she needed to be back where the crowd was. 'Will we head in to the others?'

Killian nodded and she opened her first bottle before setting off. He waited for her to pass him before following her, his hand resting ever so softly on her bare hip so that it sent tingles right through her.

In the sitting room, there was a loud buzz of general enjoyment. Eva wandered in and found Cathy sitting on Cian's lap as they joked about something or someone. Cathy beamed up at her friend and told Eva yet again that she looked wonderful and that Killian was a lucky man. Eva stiffened with embarrassment, only to find that Killian was no longer with her, so it was all right. Cian and Cathy returned to their flirtatious conversation and Eva felt like a third wheel, so she headed off to mingle. Lisa brought a group of the girls up to Eva and they all gave her a kiss on the cheek, insisting she looked great. She smiled politely but wasn't in the mood for talking to them. She'd suddenly realised that she was a little tired and that the knot of excitement inside her wasn't helping. All she wanted was some nice, relaxed company. The shrieks of her girlfriends weren't what she had in mind, so she quickly moved on. Luckily, a familiar face smiled at her through the crowds and she was glad to see it.

'Hey, Zac. How are you?'

'Great, thanks. You?'

'Good. Bit tired, though. I know it's early days yet, but I've been so wired gearing up to tonight that it's taken a lot out of me!'

Zac laughed and Eva noticed that for a good-looking chap he scrubbed up even better. He wore a black polo shirt with a pair of relatively baggy beige trousers. His hair was slightly scruffy but it fit in nicely with the style. Normally Eva didn't like anything but short hair, but Zac's hair was different. On anyone else it would look as if they needed a haircut, but on him it just looked sexy and relaxed.

She chatted to him for ages. He made her smile and as usual she felt at ease, only something was different. Zac seemed slightly more confident now that he was in his own clothes and in more easy-going surroundings, and it suited him well. Maybe it was the beer, but he wasn't drunk, just in great form. Eva had tears rolling down her face with laughter more than once as Zac's sense of humour shone through and made her feel at ease. She was perfectly comfortable telling him she'd been so nervous all day about the party and she still didn't know if people had noticed that she was slightly quiet, as she took everything in. He assured her that people weren't noticing whether she was quiet or not. All everyone had been commenting on all night was how well she looked.

'You do look gorgeous, you know. Killian's a lucky guy.'

Eva smiled at him and felt a soft glow inside her. A good few people had given her the same compliment, but when it came from Zac it meant more to her and she surged her with a new-found confidence. It was time.

She told Zac she was going to get another drink from the kitchen, and as she headed out of the room she caught Killian's eye. She gave him a wink and within seconds he was following her. She opened the Smirnoff Ice as he walked in and tension began to build inside her. He, however, seemed as relaxed and confident as ever and chatted away.

'You having a good night then?' he asked casually.

'Yeah, I am. You?'

'Yeah, I guess. But I can't take my eyes off you.'

Eva grinned. He was saying all the right things. He stepped a little closer to her and she in turn took a step towards him as he asked softly, 'Do you want to go somewhere quieter?'

Eva nodded, as the kitchen wasn't the most romantic of settings, although the thought of 'getting a room' made her mouth go dry. He took her hand and her fingers linked his. They felt so safe there and Eva suddenly forgot all her nerves – she knew she wanted to kiss him. She liked him so much, and he liked her, and everything was wonderful. She realised that her views on how there was no such thing as perfection were at a very high risk of being changed, and assured herself she was soon to find out.

He took her into a room at the back of the house, where the noise from the party seemed very far away, indicating they wouldn't be disturbed. It was quite small and dimly lit and had only a red couch and a computer on a cluttered desk. Neither spoke as they entered the room and, as Killian closed the door behind them with a soft click, the mood was set.

He took Eva gently in his arms and she stared up into his twinkling blue eyes. Still looking at her, he tilted his head ever so slightly and kissed her on the lips. Just once. Eva nearly collapsed as his lips softly touched hers, but she craved more. As he stared at her again with an enticing look in his eyes, Eva leaned into him and he responded. He was a wonderful kisser. He was very slow and his lips were soft against hers. His hands were on her back, pressing ever so slightly so that her chest was touching his. Every inch of them that connected was electric and Eva moved her hands up to behind his neck as he kissed her even deeper.

It was bliss. As they melted into each other, Killian pulled away and looked at her once more. Eva felt her heart sink as the end of the kiss had come far sooner than she would have liked. Luckily, Killian just wanted to get more comfortable.

He sat on the couch and pulled her down beside him. Eva was confused as to how this was exactly going to be comfortable, but he took her legs and put them across him so that their faces were nice and close before they resumed the gentle, intimate kissing that Eva prayed would last for ever.

They were there for what seemed like hours. Killian was very good with his hands and Eva tingled all over. Once or twice, when he did try to move his hands elsewhere, she realised that tonight was nice just as it was and told him as much. Killian didn't seem to mind and his kissing was so deep and so passionate that it was quite enough to keep Eva satisfied. At one stage, they were startled by the noise of the door opening. Both pulled away and stared at their intruder, only to be met with Zac's startled gaze. He apologised and scurried away, leaving Killian and Eva laughing to each other before they continued kissing.

Eva thought briefly about Zac and felt sorry for him – he'd looked so lost! But she didn't care. She was certainly not lost now. She knew exactly where she was and who she was with and most of all what she was doing, and she was happy.

Eventually, there was a knock on the door, followed by Cian's voice announcing that Eva's mum was here to collect her. Eva pulled away from Killian, feeling slightly panicked that her mother was in the house, but she didn't want to end the kiss with such a hurried exit. So she leaned into him again and gave him one final kiss before standing up, fixing herself and heading out of the room, still holding his hand.

Before they reached the hall she slowly took her fingers from his –

she didn't want to give her mother more ammunition for slagging than she already had – and as she gathered up her things and, more importantly, Cathy (who was engaged in a rather deep chat with Zac), Eva headed out into the night with her mother and her best friend, feeling as if nothing in the world would ever take her down from the wonderful cloud she sat on. Up there, the view was staggering and everything seemed to make sense. The night had been amazing and she looked up at the stars where she knew her dad was watching his little girl, and felt that up on her cloud, she was just a little bit closer to him, and it was nice. Maybe even perfect.

14

Zac

Saturday had been a late night and Zac was paying for his sins. The party had been such a laugh and different from any other he'd ever been at. Everyone just seemed so at ease with each other. The boys and the girls mingled freely, not in the usual awkward way at other parties he'd been at where all anyone wanted to do was get their bit and then compare who'd had the best-looking score with their friends.

Zac had talked to plenty of people and got to know many of them better. A quiet guy called Frank had really come out of his shell once he'd had a few drinks and Zac had enjoyed talking to him for a good portion of the evening. He seemed really interested in all Zac had to say and told him they should hang out more.

All the girls had looked brilliant and Zac commented to Cian and Graham how there were so many hot girls in their year. Even those he wouldn't have said were pretty at all in school looked really well. But the only girl that any of the guys were really commenting on was Eva. Cian told Zac what they'd all told him at some stage in the night.

'It's just that we haven't seen her all dressed up for a party in ages and tonight it was just as if we'd all forgotten how hot she can be.'

'Yeah, she does look good.'

'I mean, look at that figure. She's cracking!'

'I know. Trust me, I know.'

And Zac did know – so much more than Cian would have thought.

As soon as Zac had seen her arrive to the party, he had fallen for her, completely and utterly. He tried so hard not to – she was out of bounds as far as he was concerned. She was Killian's and there was no way Zac could change that, but he wished he could. They'd talked for ages that night and, as usual, got on brilliantly. They really clicked. Zac wondered if she noticed it too – surely a click couldn't be one-sided. But then again, it was likely she was thinking about Killian during their whole conversation and her feelings for Zac, whatever they were, never entered her mind once. And when she was laughing at something Zac had said and her eyes glazed over and her wonderful smile lit up her face, Zac knew that he wanted more than anything to be with Eva Coonan.

At midnight he remembered his mother had told him to give her a ring, just to tell her things were all right and that he was getting a taxi home with some of the guys. He went in search of a quiet place to make the phone call and opened the door to a small sitting room at the back of the huge house. And there they were. She was draped across him, he with his arms encasing her, engaged in a passionate kiss. Of all the things he didn't need to see, that was it. He'd reassured Killian all along that he would surely score Eva, but now that he'd witnessed it, it hurt. They'd looked so cosy, as if they were enjoying each other. That was what he wanted, that was how he wanted to make Eva feel.

The rest of the night, all Zac could think about was that image of Eva and Killian, and every time he played it in his head his heart broke just a little more. Cathy noticed that he had become subdued and asked him what was up. He just pretended he had a headache, though he didn't believe she was entirely convinced. Luckily, though, she changed the subject and Zac was able to disguise his pain by telling her he'd be ringing Johnny the following night.

'Oh, he's the guy from your old school? Is he with anyone at the moment?'

'I don't think so. I'll ask him tomorrow if you want.'

'Do. And if you just happen to mention that you have a hot single friend that thinks he's gorgeous, more so the better!'

'I'll see what I can do!' Zac laughed.

But now that he was here on the Sunday, left alone with his thoughts, Zac could think about nobody's love life but his own. The craziest part of it all was that Zac never fell for girls. Not like this. Sure, he'd had a few girlfriends and he'd liked them a lot, but he'd never felt so much for someone, especially in such a short time. His mind was overflowing and he wished he could forget it all. But then again, did he really want to lose the tiny bit of pleasure his memories brought him?

He grabbed a pen and paper and began to scrawl. He crossed out most of what he'd written. Words didn't seem to do his emotions justice, which angered him even more. But slowly things began to fit and after almost an hour had passed, he sat back in his chair and let out a sigh of relief. All he had was two verses and a chorus, but he liked it. The words all meant something to him, and when he teamed them with some rich minor chords on his guitar, he realised he'd finally written a song. He couldn't believe it! He didn't care whether it would do to others what it did for him, for when he played it, it sent shivers down his spine and the back of his neck prickled with emotion as his deep voice stroked every line.

A crowded night,
All the backs faced me,
I should have been stronger,
But it felt so good to be weak.

My brown eyes met yours,
Promises unfolded,
I grabbed you a star,

So you could hold it.
And I won't forget,
'Cause the night, don't taste the same.
And nothingness is holding me,
And it feels so cold,
Please take me away.

*

The following weekend brought another party, this time at Lisa's house, but Zac's dad forbade him from going. Zac would have protested if he'd had the energy, but the thought of another night watching *her* with *him* didn't make it worth the fight, so he spent the evening alone with his thoughts.

I should be stronger, but he won't let me,
But there's a chance she won't forget me.
A flicker of hope, in the weeping night.

15

Eva

It had been another wonderful weekend, spending hours in Killian's arms just kissing and feeling happy, and knowing he felt the same. Eva reminisced about it all for the hundredth time while her open history book reminded her that the test was very important and that she had to do well to show she'd been working hard. But Eva didn't really care, and turned her attention back to thinking about what she did care about. When she was with him, she was happy and she felt like she could tell him anything. She didn't though – her mouth was always otherwise occupied! It had all been perfect. Almost. There was just a tiny part of Eva that niggled at her and told her that all was not right. Eva didn't want to think about it because then she would have to admit it existed, which she didn't want at all. She didn't want anything to spoil her warm feeling that was keeping her in the best of spirits. But soon enough the tiny bit of worry that was etching away at her mind would take over, so it was better to confront it now, while it was still tiny.

She thought back to the spare bedroom in Lisa's house. She remembered her initial discomfort at being in a room with a bed – it seemed to symbolise so much more than a couch. But she realised she didn't have anything to worry about. Things would go at her pace and Killian, being the guy he was, would accept that. But, at times, it seemed as if he didn't. He kept trying things she didn't want, and though she'd just casually move his hand away, he'd try again and again. At one point, Eva even pulled away and looked him in the eye and said, 'Let's just take this slowly, okay?' and then she'd moved in to kiss him again but he wasn't having it. He sat there and pulled away from her and folded his arms in a huff like a child who wasn't allowed to have a packet of sweets until after dinner.

'Killian, what's up? Look, what we're doing, it's enough, isn't it? It feels great. Why ruin it?'

'It's not ruining it. Look, just leave it, okay? Let's go back downstairs.'

He'd left the room without an ounce of affection, leaving Eva sitting on the bed, feeling utterly lost and abandoned. She decided he was just in a bad mood. Maybe he was nervous about rugby or the Christmas tests. It wasn't as if it was anything to do with her. They'd been having such a great time and he wasn't exactly complaining while they were in the room. She decided just to leave it and enjoy the rest of her night.

And she had enjoyed it. With the help of the good atmosphere and some alcohol, she was close to forgetting about the incident with Killian. It should have been easy to erase it from her mind, leaving her only with the memory of the nice time they'd had upstairs and how good it had felt. But somehow, she didn't know if she could remember it as fondly. The memory was tainted and she wished that it wasn't, but she couldn't turn back the clock. She pushed this doubt to the back of her mind. Though part of her knew she had a right to be upset with Killian, she couldn't let the perfection of the moment be lost.

Yet again she found herself walking home one afternoon with Zac, both of them feeling totally at ease in each other's company. However, Eva wasn't at ease with herself in the least.

'You're friends with him, what do you think? I mean, it could be nothing, but he seemed so angry, and I haven't talked to him all week. Do you know something, Zac? Has he said anything to you?'

Zac paused before answering. 'No, he hasn't said much. I know he does really like you. Maybe he just wants to take things further with you. It's the same with all guys, though. Just take it as a compliment.' Zac had turned his face the other way, looking tormented.

'Are you sure? It's just, I do really like him, and I just need to know he likes me back.'

'Listen, Eva, the best thing to do would be just to ring him or something. It's him you should be talking to. Just phone him tonight.'

Zac was right. He was always right. Eva thanked him for saving her, again, and knew that the advice was perfect. There was no point in her talking to anyone except for Killian himself. Then, hopefully, she'd see she'd just been making a big fuss and everything would be wonderful again. And the next time there was a party, he'd hold her and kiss her and she'd have a happy tingle all over her body. Yes, Zac was right. She'd ring Killian and find out for herself.

'Killian, it's me, Eva.'

'Eva, how's it going?' he said flatly.

'Good, thanks. How was the geography exam?'

'Pretty crap. Oh well, don't really care!'

'Yeah... listen, Killian, I just wanted to ask you about something.' Eva's heart was racing, but she knew she had to do it. 'I was just wondering if you're pissed off with me or something because you kind of got in a bad mood with me on Saturday night and I haven't talked to you since and I was worried that I'd done something to annoy you and I really hoped I didn't because—'

'Eva, relax. I'm not annoyed with you. Why would I be?'

'I don't know. It's just, on Saturday...'

'Forget about Saturday. Listen, I don't think anything's happening this weekend cause of the exams, so I was wondering if you want to go to the cinema or something?'

Eva's heart leapt right out her mouth, did a little dance and hopped back in. She felt faint, but for the first time all week, in a nice way.

'I'd love to.'

'Right, well, I don't have an exam tomorrow, so I'll just give you a ring in the evening and we'll see what time everything's on, okay?'

'Cool.'

'Right, see you then.'

Eva couldn't contain her excitement as she sat in the car beside her mum on the way to the cinema that Saturday night. She was nervous and her mother's nosiness wasn't helping.

'So, is he your boyfriend then?'

'No, Mum, he's not.'

'But if you're going on a date, then surely you're his girlfriend.' Eva just laughed, as her mum displayed a serious lack of knowledge on teenage romance rules.

The night was already dark and the glow of soft Christmas lights filled the blackness. She couldn't believe she was on her way to a date with Killian Lain. It was scary, but in the best way, like going on a rollercoaster or some other stupidly sickening ride in Funderland. While you stand in the line, you wish you weren't there and can't believe you're doing something so frightening, and when you get on the ride you're terrified and your tummy feels fit to burst. But then it's over, and the rush is incredible and you want it again and again and you wonder what you were ever scared of.

As soon as she hopped out of the car, she caw him waiting for her. He was wearing beige trousers and decks and a Tommy Hilfiger jacket. His hair and skin were flawless, as always, and as he leaned against the pillar, looking at the people who passed him, Eva couldn't believe he was waiting for her. He was gorgeous and any girl would surely think he was unbearably hot. She took a deep breath and headed over to him. As soon as he spotted her, his face lit up and he leaned into her and gave her a soft kiss. He was good at this! He put his arm behind her and led her in to get their tickets and he insisted on buying the largest bucket of popcorn there was.

Eva was really enjoying the movie and almost forgot who she was with until a large hand crept onto hers and their fingers intertwined. His palm was warm and she felt safe within it. However, it seemed he wanted more. Eva knew that couples always kissed at the cinema, but it was something she couldn't get her head around. They were there to watch a film, they were sitting beside each other, with an armrest in the way, and they were surrounded by a room of people. It just didn't sit well with her.

Whenever Killian tried to catch her eye or lean into her, she made sure to fix her gaze rigidly at the screen so that nothing could happen. They still held hands, but for her that was as far as they could take it in the cinema. She didn't want everyone to stare at them as they kissed. Not that she was ashamed; quite the opposite. Kissing Killian was something she loved doing, she just didn't want to share it with a roomful of strangers. Maybe after the film they'd score, but for now she wanted to just sit, hand in hand, and enjoy the film. She knew Killian wouldn't mind. Well, she hoped so anyway.

When the film finally ended, Eva put her coat and scarf back on and led the way out of the cinema. Outside, the night air was biting and people's breath formed clouds in front of them. Killian zipped up his jacket and crossed his arms, making him look less welcoming than he had seemed earlier. Eva was keen to cheer him up.

'Did you enjoy that?'

'It was pretty crap.'

Eva hoped he meant the movie. She wanted to make him smile again. She wanted to kiss him and let him know how much she liked him, but he seemed annoyed. Her mother had told her to ring straight away for a lift when the film ended, but Eva couldn't let the night end without at least some indication of how she felt for Killian and how much she'd enjoyed being with him. But he really did seem distracted.

'Listen, Eva, I'm getting the bus, so I better head.'

'But…' Eva trailed off. She didn't know what to say. Was it too late? Was the night officially over? She hoped not. She walked with Killian to the bus stop. Killian stood beside her, not saying anything. She could sense he wasn't pleased and she decided to make one final attempt to show him how she felt.

'Killian, I did have a good night, you know.'

'Really?'

'Yeah, really.'

Eva turned to face him and made sure to stare into his eyes. He returned her gaze but it didn't seem like he was going to do anything about it. Eva waited and waited and then, feeling so scared that it would all go horribly wrong, but if she didn't try then it would be even worse, she leaned in and kissed him. It took him a second to respond, but eventually he did. His hands surrounded her and his wonderful kissing was upon her again. She'd done it! All was right again and she felt happier than ever, encased by his warm body. The kiss lasted only a few minutes before they heard the loud hum of a bus pulling up. Killian looked up at the number.

'This is mine. I'll see you.' He strolled to the back of the line of people getting on the bus. Within seconds, the doors were closing behind him and the bus was speeding away.

But something still wasn't right. Eva wanted a final kiss or hug or something so finish it all off. It had felt a little like a last-minute score because they felt they should because they were on a date. But it was still nice and, in fairness, no other kissing opportunities had presented themselves. She'd done all she could and was content with that. Only, she hoped he was too.

*

The next day, Eva had an appointment with Helen and her good mood was still obvious.

'Afternoon, Eva. It's nice to see you. You look well,' Helen commented.

Eva smiled and sat down on the chair. She *was* well, she told Helen, but part of her was feeling edgy.

'And why's that? Do you know?' Helen asked.

'I'm kind of embarrassed, to be honest. I mean, it's just... it's got nothing to do with Dad at all.'

'Listen, pet, I'm here to talk about *you*. Your life, your emotions in general. Whatever's going on at the moment is perfectly relevant,' she assured her.

'Okay, well, I told you about this guy Killian I like. Well, I'm starting to really fall for him, we've, like, scored a few times, and it's been really good...' Eva was a bit shy saying this, but Helen didn't seem affected at all, which made Eva feel at ease to continue. 'I've just been in good form, and I can't stop thinking about him. All my friends have noticed. It's just cheered me up loads being with someone, because I haven't done this in ages, and it feels good...' Eva paused again as the doubts began to creep in. Her cheery front faded and she began to pour out all the things she didn't even understand herself.

'It's just, I've been studying so much and I'm so tired. And I keep thinking about Killian and how much I like him, but then, when I'm with him, it's different. It's still nice, but he keeps... he keeps trying to do stuff that I don't want and I wish he'd stop because he's spoiling it, but then he gets in a mood. So I was all worried and I thought he didn't like me any more, but then he invited me to the cinema last night. And I thought the night was going well, but then he seemed all quiet and stuff and I'm just scared I'll lose him. Because I really do like him, but sometimes he just seems to be pushing me away.'

Helen wrote something down and then looked Eva straight in the eye. 'Look, Eva, if he tries to do anything you don't want, you just say no. And if he keeps trying, say no again. And if he won't listen, then I'm afraid there's no point being with him because he's a shit. He must respect you and take things at your pace. It's the same with every girl – you dictate what goes on, and no means no. But he must know that you're feeling a bit fragile at the moment anyway since your father's death and he needs to realise that.'

Eva took it all in. Suddenly the perfect image of Killian was being torn apart and she didn't like it.

'But maybe he's got stuff going on in his life, too. I mean, it's only happened a couple of times. I'm just overreacting.'

Helen tried to convince Eva that she wasn't, but Eva kept telling herself she was being irrational and that Killian was perfect and she was lucky to be with him. She couldn't start throwing it away because of her stupid doubts.

The session came to a close and, though Eva felt as edgy as ever, she was certain about what she had to do. She had been stupid to think Killian would just wait around for her. He could have any girl he wanted, and yet he had chosen her. Eva owed it to him to do things his way. Next time, she'd let him. All her shyness and conservative attitude when it came to anything beyond kissing would have to go. He was the one who was choosing her and she'd have to prove to him that it was worth his while staying with her. And she would.

16

Zac

The week flew by. Every day was the same – exams in the morning, followed by a trip to Blackrock with the gang for a few hours before everyone began to feel guilty about whatever subject they had the following day. So that they then had to all head home and study, which would fill the rest of the afternoon. At that point, Zac felt he could do no more. It wasn't fun, but it was only a week, and Zac wanted to do well in the tests so he made sure to work hard, hoping it would pay off.

One day after an exam, Zac and Killian were the only ones around so they decided to head to Stillorgan. Killian had his mum's car, so they drove up. The shopping centre was quiet enough as it was still too early for people to be finished school. They went to Eddie Rockets and ordered milkshakes and fries. Zac asked Killian what was up. It was clear Killian had been waiting for someone to ask. He erupted into a long spiel about Eva and how she was annoying him so much recently.

'I mean, last week she's all like, "Killian are you pissed off with me?" And I'm thinking, wow, she's finally noticed. Because I was pretty angry, like, after she was being all tight at Lisa's party. But I decided to say nothing, I wasn't in the mood for her whining on. So instead I thought I'd do the decent thing and give her another chance.'

Zac could feel his face twitching as he tried to conceal the anger that was building inside him. But Killian went on.

'So I invited her to the cinema and, obviously, she like jumped at the chance. But then it was shit. I mean, we didn't even score in the cinema. What did she think I invited her for, to watch some poxy movie? Doubtful! Anyway, all I got off her was a lousy kiss at the bus stop and that was it. I mean, what's the point? And then all week this bird I used to go out with has been texting me, and I've just decided to tell Eva to go fuck herself because she's a tight bitch.'

Zac had to say something. 'Killian, Eva is a really cool bird and she really likes you. So what she wants to take things slowly? It's up to her. It's such a lousy thing to break up with her over.'

But Killian wasn't listening. It was obvious he'd made up his mind and, as the waitress handed them their milkshakes, Zac felt like throwing his in Killian's face and telling him he was an ignorant, self-obsessed prat.

Once they'd devoured their chips, Zac made an excuse that he had loads of work to do and quickly headed home. He couldn't stand listening to Killian any more. He was so full of shit and if he called Eva another horrible name Zac was sure he was going to hit him.

He tried to concentrate on his study all night, taking out his anger by forcing the information into his head to make him stop thinking about Eva and Killian and their whole situation. But he couldn't. Picking up his phone, he sent Eva a message. Just something casual, but it was enough.

HEY EVA HOWS U? CANT W8 TIL EXAMS R OVER. ANY1 HAVIN A PARTY DIS WKEND? DYIN 2 GO OUT! WB ZAC

Soon enough the reply arrived, though it didn't cheer Zac up at all.

HEY ZAC. YEAH I NO, TESTS R WRECKN MY HEAD. DUNNO WOTS HAPPENIN DIS WKEND. I MYT HAV A FREE BT I DON'T TINK IM GONNA HAVE PPL OVER.

HOW COME? U JUST DON'T WANT 2 LIKE? 2 MUCH HASSLE?!

WELL, RITE PROMISE U WONT SAY ANYTHIN, BT I TINK IM JUS GONNA INVITE KILLIAN OVER, AND HAV A QUIET NYT IN, THE 2 OF US.

Zac felt his heart snap in two. Yet again Eva had fallen for Killian and was pandering to his every ignorant need. Zac was so annoyed. Why was she wasting her time on such a loser? She deserved so much better. If she did invite Killian over that weekend, he'd only be after one thing, and Zac feared that Eva might give it to him just so as not to lose him.

It wasn't just that Zac was jealous, even though he was, it was the fact that he was seeing someone he cared about be torn apart and treated like dirt. It was awful. He didn't text her back. He knew it was rude but he didn't care. He had nothing to say except to tell her how stupid she was being and tell her all the terrible things Killian said about her. But it wasn't his place.

The final exam was pretty hard, but no one cared. They were finished, and results were irrelevant. They'd all made it through the tests and were now into the Christmas holiday. Finally, they could think about presents and trees and having fun. Everyone was happy, though worn out from the week.

Everyone headed to Blackrock for the last time and, as they squashed into the biggest booth in Eddie Rockets, they were all relaxed and happy to be there. Zac was wedged between Frank and Killian and since neither was in the least bit small, he found he had little space to move. Cathy was entertaining them all with a story about her and Eva when they were younger, and as everyone cracked up with laughter, Zac smiled fondly at a blushing Eva. She gave him a warm smile back before quickly turning back to Cathy and protesting that she'd told the story all wrong.

After they'd eaten and were waiting outside until the last person had paid, Killian took Zac aside.

'Listen man, I just want to say that I'm sorry about moaning on to you so much recently about Eva.'

'Yeah, it's cool,' Zac assured him, feeling both surprised and uncomfortable.

'No, seriously, you've been really sound. Thanks.'

'No problem. So it's all over with her then, yeah?' Zac asked hopefully.

'Actually, now that you mention it, she's invited me over to hers tomorrow night. Her mum and sister are going to a play or something so we'll have the place to ourselves. Looks like she's finally copped on to herself.'

'What do you mean?'

'I think she's finally realised that if she wants to keep me, she's going have to make me want to stay. So I'm expecting a pretty steamy night. Wish me luck!' Killian gave Zac a wink and headed towards the DART.

Zac was furious. Not only was Killian being horrible about Eva again and getting away with it, but it seemed as if Eva was willing to change herself just to keep Killian. Would she really do something so stupid, casting all her morals aside just to please some cocky eejit who didn't even really like her? Zac shook his head and wondered if she was the person he'd thought she was. The Eva he cared so much for wouldn't do something as stupid as this. He hoped she wouldn't do anything she didn't want to. But it looked as if sooner or later, Killian would hurt her. Badly.

As Zac walked home beside Eva, he couldn't even look at her. She seemed in good form and prattled on about how great it was to have the exams over and how she hadn't talked to him all week, and since there hadn't been a party last weekend, it felt like ages since they'd had a proper chat. Zac agreed and asked her how things were at home.

'Pretty good, actually. I had therapy last weekend, which went all right, and my mum and Sarah are heading out to the theatre tomorrow night. I didn't really fancy going, thought having the house to myself might be nice…'

He knew that she wouldn't have the house completely to herself, and dared to ask her about it, trying to sound casual despite himself. 'Yeah, Killian told me he was going to yours all right for the evening?'

Eva looked at him, obviously a little startled that Killian had told him, but somewhat relieved as it meant that she could talk to him about it.

'Yeah. Well, he asked me out last weekend, so I decided I would invite him over. It'll be nice, though. I'm just going to rent a few DVDs and we'll curl up on the couch.'

Zac knew that Killian's idea of curling up on the couch was far from an innocent viewing of a film. Zac pushed the thought to the back of his head and willed it to go away, but he knew that, for the next two days, all he would be able to think about was Killian and Eva together, doing whatever Killian wanted, and it broke Zac in two.

He said very little all the way home. He couldn't bring himself to pretend to be in good form. He wasn't, and he didn't care any more if it showed. They reached Eva's estate and she told him she might be in town tomorrow, so she'd probably see him then.

Zac got home and collapsed on his bed. He closed his eyes and prayed that when he opened them everything would be different. Knowing it wouldn't be, he didn't even bother to prise his eyelids apart. Every inch of him ached. He couldn't believe he was feeling this way. He never fell for girls, and he'd only been in his new school a few months, but it was enough. He tried to think about all the things he didn't like about Eva and convince himself she wasn't all that great. But she was.

*

The next day in town, Zac met up with Frank, Cian and Graham. He asked where Killian was, but they said they hadn't bothered to text him. Zac wondered what that was all about, but decided he didn't really care. They headed into a few clothes shops, followed by a long trawl through HMV before Zac got a phone call from Kev asking where he was and saying that he and Johnny were in town now. He told them to meet him outside HMV as usual, and within minutes they were there. Zac introduced them all and the six of them headed off to O'Brien's Sandwich Bar in the Stephen's Green Centre for a bit of lunch. The lads hit it off instantly and were quickly engaged in a loud conversation about sport and music and just about everything else. Zac said very little and merely watched as the two groups mingled and faded into each other so that there was no difference. Zac's was just finishing his sandwich when his phone rang. It was Cathy.

'Hey, Zac. Myself and Eva are in town, where are you guys?' Zac winked at the lads and told her where they were, and she promised they'd be there within minutes.

For the first time, Zac saw just a hint of shyness in Cathy. She pulled up a chair beside Frank while Eva sat next to Zac, and Zac introduced them both to Kev and Johnny. There was a brief silence which was quickly interrupted by Cian, finishing the story he'd been in the middle of when the girls arrived. Zac kept catching Cathy staring at Johnny and she seemed slightly more embarrassed than usual when the guys started slagging her off about something. It seemed that even the queen if man-eaters got shy, and Zac decided that it was nice to see that Cathy was only human. The conversation broke off into little groups and Cathy turned herself slightly so that she was facing Johnny. The pair began to talk, and Zac could see Cathy laughing and smiling and tossing back her golden curls at every opportunity. She wasn't one for letting nerves get in her way for too long and the pair got on like a house on fire. Kev and Cian were talking about where the best places in town to go at night were, while Frank was giving out to Graham for being so rude to the waitress who'd just taken their plates away.

'Why did you have to be such a prick?' Frank demanded.

'Here, relax, she's clearly lower class!' Graham laughed. Zac watched Frank's eyes pop out of his head and, not wanting to get involved, he turned to Eva. She was sipping on her hot chocolate, evidently lost in thought. She must have felt him staring at her, as she looked up and gave him a friendly smile.

'Looking forward to tonight?' Zac asked, only this time as a friend, not some jealous fool that fancied her.

'I'm a bit nervous, to be honest. I never told you, but the cinema didn't go too well, so I'm going have to make sure Killian enjoys tonight.'

'What do you mean?' Zac raised an eyebrow, implying that he knew exactly what she would be doing to make sure Killian enjoyed himself. Though it seemed as if Eva didn't know what he was getting at.

'Eh, we're just watching a film and stuff. I just hope I pick a good one and that he has a good time.' She excused herself to go to the loo. As Zac watched her leave, he didn't know what to think.

*

That night, Zac took it easy and was glad of the time to himself. He spent the evening fiddling on his guitar and downloading a few songs off the internet. It wasn't until ten o'clock when he was making his mother a surprise cup of tea, just to let her know he was thinking of her, that Zac heard the shouting.

'Do you know what people would say if they knew that my wife was swanning off to Spain without me? Rumours would spread like wildfire. People would start to believe that I had no control over you. So I can tell you now that you will go to Spain with that tramp Sue over my dead body.'

'But Liam—'

'This issue is closed. This is my house and if you think you're going to leave me with your pathetic excuse for a son while you go off with your girlfriends, then you're more stupid than I thought. I'm not going to pay for my wife to enjoy herself without me. You have duties here and you will not neglect them.'

'Liam, it's a week.'

'Just shut up, Nancy. There's no way you're going and that's final. I won't have it! Do you honestly believe you deserve a fucking holiday? It's not going to happen. And the sooner you realise that and start to appreciate all I do for you and that fucking son of yours… You should be thanking me, not asking for more. Now just piss off.'

Zac heard his mother's hurried footsteps as she ran into the kitchen. She stopped abruptly when she saw Zac. As the tears streamed down her worn face, she tried to smile. But failed.

'Oh love, I didn't know you were in here. I thought you were on the computer. Your father and I just had a row, that's all. I'll leave you to it.'

As she headed out of the room, Zac called after her. 'Mum, I was just making you a cup of tea. Come and drink it.' She hesitated but came back, and Zac could feel his voice start to choke. He hated seeing her like this. 'You're so much better than him, Mum. Just try not to listen to what he says, okay?'

His mother stared at him for a moment before taking him in her arms and holding him tightly against her as if he was all she had in the world. Zac feared that, more and more, he was. His mother was so lonely, and as he sat her down and placed the warm mug in her hands, he was glad that at least he was there, so that he could look after her.

They stayed in the kitchen for almost an hour, just talking and letting each other know, without saying it, that they were on the same side. Zac cursed himself for having been so wrapped up in thinking about Killian and Eva and his own stupid worries, that he neglected what really mattered. But now he realised that he had a duty to take care of his mother and pay her back for all the years she'd looked after him. He was so grateful that he had her and he swore that he would never again forget how lucky he truly was.

Looking away, closing my eyes,
Some guy is breaking all that's mine.
While fate forgets that I am even here.

17

Eva

Just hours before Killian's arrival, Eva and Cathy chatted away on the phone. Eva wasn't impressed when Cathy decided to lecture her about that night.

'I think it's nice that you guys are hanging out together, but what if things go wrong?' Cathy scolded.

Eva was at a loss. 'What do you mean?'

'What if he wants to have sex, Eva?'

Eva knew at some stage the word would be used, but all along she'd tried to convince herself that sex was never going to enter the equation.

'Well, then, it's his choice,' she retorted.

'What are you talking about? It's *your* choice. What's happened to you, Eva? You used to be so sensible. You used to take things slowly with a guy – and I respected you so much for that. I was even jealous that you didn't need to do things you didn't want to, to keep a guy.'

Eva was getting angry. Why couldn't Cathy see that even if Eva didn't want to do these things, she felt she was obliged to?

'But I really like Killian and I don't want to lose him.'

'That doesn't mean you have to lose your virginity to him like the fourth time you score him.'

'Maybe it does. Killian could get any girl in the world, but he chose me. Don't I owe him something for that?'

'No, you don't.'

'But if I don't do this, he'll dump me.' She couldn't hide her anxiety.

'If he makes you do this, then he's worth dumping. He's a wanker, Eva, why can't you see that? He's been playing with you all along, and now he's turned you into something you're not. I miss the old you, who would never have considered throwing away all she ever cherished on some stupid prat. She was better than that.'

Cathy's voice trailed off, and for a moment Eva felt herself give in to her friend's reasoning. It felt good to have finally let go of all the tension and turmoil she'd experienced since she'd invited Killian over. Not that she'd assumed that that was what he'd expect, but she realised that he was a teenage boy, so no doubt that's what he'd want. But Eva couldn't let him go. She was sick of letting things go. She'd already let go of her dad, but being with Killian distracted her from that pain all and made her feel special. And if Cathy thought she was going to throw that away, then she was a selfish cow. She just couldn't bear to see Eva happy. Eva hung up the phone and stormed upstairs, holding back the tears that tried to gush from her tired eyes. She wouldn't let them win.

*

Her mother and sister were already getting themselves dolled up for the theatre. Of course they didn't know Killian was coming over and Eva would make sure they never found out. They headed off, and soon after Killian texted her to say he was on his way. Eva put on the microwave popcorn. She paced up and down the kitchen. She was so edgy that every time there was a pop from the expanding packet, she flinched momentarily. She leaned against a press and took a few deep breaths, and had just managed to regain her calm when the microwave pinged, making her heart leap. Eva poured the popcorn into a large bowl and was just setting it on the coffee table in the living room when the doorbell rang. Her whole body seized up and for a moment she couldn't move. Breathing deeply as she tried to come to terms with the realisation that the moment had come, she went to the door and opened it to the casual, gorgeous figure of Killian. He was wearing tracksuit bottoms and a grey hoodie. His hair was gelled and Eva got a waft of Hugo Boss aftershave. Killian smiled at her and she remained numb. He laughed.

'Are you going to let me in or not?'

Eva snapped back to reality again and apologised with a nervous laugh. She led him into the living room and felt slightly awkward, as there was an emotional recital of the most romantic love songs on the TV. Eva flicked the channel so that The Killers now rocked in the background, and Killian sat down on the plush couch. Eva asked him if he wanted anything to eat, anything to drink, what film he'd like to watch, whether he was comfortable, until finally Killian stood up again and took her hands in his.

'Relax, Eva, would you?'

'I am relaxed,' she fibbed.

She sat down beside him and thankfully he launched into a long and involved story about rugby training and a great try he'd scored. She listened intently, though she said very little. Every inch of her seemed to be concentrating on what was coming next rather than what was going on at that moment. After a while, they decided to put on a movie. Killian chose one (Eva insisted he did, she liked them all anyway), and after fast-forwarding the trailers and turning out all the lights, they settled down. Though there was only a tiny portion of their bodies touching, Eva was very conscious of it and couldn't stop the tingles inside her.

Everything was going well and Eva tried to concentrate on what was happening in the film and, just as a fight was breaking out, she felt his hand on hers. It was gentle, and she willingly accepted it.

Their fingers intertwined and she felt a little more relaxed. She always found holding hands a gesture that signified safety and that someone was looking out for her and cared for her. Killian was doing that and she liked it. Maybe she'd assumed the worst for the night. Maybe Killian, like her, just wanted a nice romantic video session, where they could snuggle up to each other and kiss a little. Maybe everyone had overreacted about what his intentions were. She could hardly see the owner of the hand that held hers so lovingly and softly forcing her into anything she didn't want.

Almost a third of the film had passed before Killian gave Eva's hand a little squeeze, as if to get her attention. She hadn't looked at him once since the film had started and decided that now she'd have to. She turned to him and found him looking deep into her eyes. At once she melted and suddenly they were kissing. Eva wasn't complaining as she was pressed softly into him and she realised how much she loved kissing Killian. He was so good at it and she smiled as she wondered how much practice he'd had. But how could she have ever had any bad thoughts about someone who could be so gentle with her and make her feel so good?

Killian's hands moved downwards, past her hips, and Eva was perfectly happy with this. However, after a while she felt them rise upwards. She wondered where they were off to but the direction they were travelling didn't spell danger – until she realised the zip of her jumper was coming softly downwards. She kept kissing Killian and began to quiver slightly. She wasn't doing anything wrong, she told herself. It was all above the belt and, anyway, he was being so gentle it didn't feel weird. She distracted herself by kissing him even deeper and more passionately and tried to ignore what he was up to.

But before she knew it, her T-shirt was coming up over her head. She had to pull away from Killian for a moment while her top passed over her face. In that instant, she caught his gaze. She quickly looked away, feeling awkward, and as soon as she could she returned to kissing him. Discomfort was beginning to set in but she banished it from her mind, only allowing the clear, simple, good things to filter in – 'You like him, he likes you, let him do what he wants. Would you rather he went off with some other girl because you were frigid?' The answer was no. She wanted him for herself, so she'd have to earn him.

Killian's hands headed south and Eva couldn't help but stiffen. She tried to make the tension go away, but as the fly of her jeans was pulled gingerly down she couldn't help feeling nervous. She closed her eyes even tighter and prayed it would all just be over. Fear was taking over her body and soon she realised she didn't want to be where she was, sitting on her couch in nothing but her underwear as Killian's hands travelled wherever they pleased. She began to feel dirty and wished he'd stop. She felt tears prick her eyes but kept them firmly shut, as if to block out the terrible things that were happening. And as his hand began to push hers down his pants, Eva could bear it no longer. She felt as if she was going to scream. She wrenched herself away from a startled Killian, who was obviously surprised that she had made him stop. He looked at her and she at him, her breath heavy and panicked. Killian read her all wrong.

'Do you want to go upstairs?'

She stared back at him with utter confusion. 'What?'

'Do you want to go to a bed or something?'

'Killian, I don't think—'

'Eva, it's okay. I brought condoms.'

And with that something snapped inside of her. She thought of everything Cathy had said and everything she'd ever held close to her, how she used to scowl when she heard stories of girls her age losing their virginity to someone they hardly knew. And here she was, only inches away from having sex with someone who only wanted her for that one thing. He didn't care for her. He never asked her how she was, never asked her about her dad or gave her a hug and told her she was special. He only wanted the things a dirty slut would give him, and suddenly Eva realised that she was his slut of choice. She was about to sacrifice a big part of herself to him and let him do all the things she so badly didn't want. She was going to go to bed with a cocky, arrogant eejit who only thought about himself and cared about nothing else. Cathy was right. Eva *had* changed. Ever since Killian had come along, she'd become someone different. All she ever did was try and impress Killian, and why? Because he was good looking? Because he was a good person? Well, the latter certainly wasn't true, because he wasn't. He was selfish and so wrapped up in being great that he seemed to have forgotten about being decent. She thought of her dad and wondered if she'd used his death as an excuse to forget all that was dear to her. She hated admitting it, but recently all she'd thought about was Killian. It wasn't just that she didn't like Killian – she didn't like what he'd made her become. But she'd caught herself just in time before she crushed any hope she had of going back to the person she used to be.

'Killian, listen. I'm sorry, but I'm not going to have sex with you. In fact, I'm not going to do anything with you. I still really like you, but we're going to have to slow things down, okay? I'm just not ready.'

Part of Eva hoped that Killian would see sense and agree that taking things slowly was the way to go, and that he liked her so much that it didn't matter how far they went, that he liked her for who she was. But she realised there wasn't a chance in hell of that happening. Killian did as Eva thought he would and began to fill with fury.

'You stupid, tight bitch. I hauled my ass over here and this is the thanks I get? Give me a ring when you've got over your fucking dead father and got down off your high fucking horse, and then maybe, just maybe, I'll reconsider being with you. But at the moment I've had it up to here with trying to be nice all the time and getting nothing in return. So fuck you.'

Killian grabbed his coat and stormed out of the house, slamming the front door behind him with such force that the whole house seemed to quiver. Eva was left surrounded by the silence that remained, broken only by the murmur of the television, and she cried.

They were both tears of relief and tears of pain. She was glad she'd woken up to how much she'd let herself down and how she'd become too wrapped up in Killian to think about anything else. But then again, she had really liked him. And he had made her feel good. She knew she'd miss that part of their relationship, but that would never be the bit she'd remember. Those parting words of his had cut her and poured salt on an already open wound. *Your fucking dead father.* The words resounded in her head as she tried to figure out why someone would be so cruel. She missed her dad so much in that moment and as the tears streamed down her face she wished he was there, with his caring smile and his warm hug that made her feel safe.

She wished she could ring someone who would talk to her and try to put a smile back on her face. She thought of Cathy, but since they weren't on the best of terms since that afternoon, she decided against it. She wasn't in the mood for another fight. She still felt drained from the first one. She considered ringing Lisa, but somehow her friend didn't seem to fit the match of someone who would truly listen and be honest with Eva and take the edge off the pain.

And then his name popped into her head. Zac. The one person who was unfailingly kind to her and never minded listening as she poured out every inch of her heart. She dialled his number and was excited as she counted the rings. She was beginning to feel better now as she realised that soon he would be talking to her, which meant soon her world would be put back into place and she'd smile again. Each ring tickled her impatience but a frown began to creep over her when she realised he wasn't going to answer. Maybe he was out. Maybe there had been a party or something and he couldn't hear his phone. It didn't matter. Either way, he wasn't at the other end of the line and her heart dropped so far it hurt. His friendly voice filled her as his answering machine told her to leave a message. She hung up quickly, unable to leave a message as she didn't want him to hear the sound of her voice cracking. She felt very alone. Her world had seemed so perfect and then slowly but surely it had come crumbling down, leaving Eva weeping.

Eva redressed herself slowly and, soon after, her mother and Sarah arrived home from the play full of the joys and it was a few minutes before they noticed Eva's red, puffy eyes. Eva had considered hiding that she was upset but she realised that hiding things wasn't the way to go any more. She was allowed to have problems and they would surely understand. And they did. Eva's mother's smile quickly vanished as she went over to her daughter and held her.

'What's wrong, love? It's okay.'

It was as if her mum had opened a dam that had been holding back all the emotion and heartbreak that was clogged up inside Eva, and Eva let it pour out as she sat on the couch, holding her mum tightly. She couldn't tell her about Killian, but as her mother stroked her forehead, just as she had when Eva was younger, Eva felt relieved and safe in her arms. Eva admired her mum. However upset Eva was, her mum had had to endure the same pain, and still managed to keep the family going. And she did it with such courage. But as she gazed at her mother now, she noticed tears streaming down her face.

'Mum, why are you crying?' Eva couldn't hide her surprise.

'I think I should be asking you the same question, don't you?' A faint laugh escaped the older woman's lips.

'But I know what's wrong with me. What's your excuse?'

'I don't need one any more, Eva. Life's my excuse,' she whispered.

The look of utter sadness in her mother's eyes made Eva's heart feel a thousand times heavier than it already did. They sat entwined for what seemed like hours, both united in grief and a longing for the world to be good again. They both yearned for the comfort of the man who had once lit up their lives. They thought of him, and each other, and the future and barely noticed sleep begin to creep in until it was too late. Peace at last.

*

Sunday arrived, and although Eva was still weary from the gauntlet of emotion she'd endured the previous day, she was glad to have let go of everything that had been clogged up inside her. As soon as she thought Cathy would be up, she rang her.

'Cathy, it's me.'

'Hey, babe. How are you?'

'Terrible. Listen, Cath, I've been such a tit. I don't know what's come over me recently but I totally haven't been myself. And I know you tried to tell me, but I wouldn't listen and I'm so sorry and...' The words began to pour out of her.

'Eva, it's fine, honestly. I should have listened to you, I was being a bitch.'

'No you weren't, Cathy. You were the only one with some sense. I'm so embarrassed with how I've been lately. You were right about it all.' Desperation began to fill Eva as she realised just how wrong she had been.

'What do you mean?' Cathy was still at a loss.

Eva told her the whole story about what had happened with Killian. Her friend was silent throughout, apart from the odd sharp intake of breath as she tried to take in what was being said. When Eva was finished, right down to the 'stupid, tight bitch', it took Cathy a moment to absorb it all before saying anything.

'Oh my God, Eva. Are you okay? You poor thing! I feel terrible.' Then her pity changed to rage. 'What a fucking wanker. I can't believe... Oh my God, I'm going to kill him. I hate that boy so much. I just want to call him now and tell him if he ever comes near you or any of my friends ever again I'm going to fucking murder him.'

Eva laughed. She didn't care what happened to Killian. Then again, she didn't want a big fuss caused, but this was Cathy's way of doing things and, when it came to it, Cathy probably wouldn't say anything. She'd just tell everyone how much she hated him behind his back and throw him so many filthy looks he'd know exactly what was going on.

They talked a bit longer before saying goodbye. Cathy promised she'd look after Eva and that Killian would regret he'd ever said anything of the sort. She assured Eva that everything was going to be okay now and that she'd done the right thing, words that helped Eva regain at least some of the confidence she'd had before the whole ordeal started. Eva put down the phone, feeling slightly better, but also shocked at how much could change in such a short space of time.

18

Zac

Zac was handed back his maths paper and stared at the nice big B with pride. How had he managed that? He was chuffed with himself. When his fellow classmates all asked what he got, they were impressed. He felt he deserved the good mark, as he had put in the work, and he couldn't wait to go home and show his dad. But then he chided himself for making it seem as if he only worked hard in school to prove a point to his dad, which wasn't true. He did it for himself, and because of that, he was happy.

The week had been pretty quiet and drawn out so far as the teachers gave back and corrected the exams, and generally tried to fill the time until Christmas. Everyone knew there was no point in being there. No one was doing any work now that the tests were over and the whole school was distracted by the buzz of the holidays. A few students had put tinsel and the odd bauble along the corridor so that even when the pupils were going from class to class, they were reminded that December 25th was well on its way, which made the mood seem brighter.

Zac smiled as a metallic decoration he passed caught the light and twinkled like a chandelier. He hadn't seen the guys from his old school in a while, so he was looking forward to seeing them over the holiday and no doubt his new friends would have a party or two along the way!

Something else had brightened up the week, though he hated admitting it. Killian and Eva had both been in very quiet moods and hadn't said a word to each other. Zac sensed that something was up but didn't want to pry. When he and Eva were finally alone as they strolled home, he tried to brighten up the cold journey by making friendly attempts at conversation, but her one-word replies left him little to work with. He decided to just leave it and stared at the frozen world around him. The footpath under his feet was spotted with glittering droplets of ice and his feet slid a little more than usual. He was wearing a hoodie over his uniform but wished he had more layers to keep out the raw bite of the air. Eva sniffed a little as her nose began to drip from the low temperature, but her eyes held an emotion Zac couldn't pinpoint. He knew she wasn't being herself. He decided, as a friend, he was entitled to ask what was up.

'Eva, tell me to back off if you want, but are you all right?' he asked kindly.

She looked at him as if debating whether to say anything or not, but the kindness in his eyes made her doubts melt away as she launched into the eventful account of Saturday night's antics. 'Basically he's a wanker, and he was only ever after one thing. Cathy tried to warn me, but I was just too busy fooling myself into thinking that my life was normal again.' She paused. 'It was so awful, Zac. He actually said the words "your fucking dead father". I was in bits.' Eva avoided Zac's eyes.

Zac felt his heart fill with rage. He couldn't believe that Killian could stoop so low and say those things. Zac's view of him had been slipping over the past few weeks anyway, but this was the last straw. Poor Eva. He felt a rush of pity and affection for her and wanted more than anything to tell her how he felt for her and that he'd never do anything like that to her, that he'd take care of her and make her feel safe and respect every inch of her. But he knew it wasn't the time for him to say anything like that as she was genuinely upset by the whole thing. But it was hard to resist as her personality shone through even more as she told Zac how she felt about what had happened.

'Yeah, I was upset and it felt shit at the time. But now when I think about it, I'm actually happy he did and said all that, cause it made me snap out of whatever twisted trance I was in. I mean, up until then I was bloody oblivious to the fact he was treating me like shit, and that I'd become this person I seriously did not like.'

'But Eva—' Zac started to protest.

'No, obviously I'm not saying it was a fun thing or that Killian should be thanked. I guess I'm just glad that it's all come to a head and it's over and done with now. For good.'

Zac was glad for her too. He was glad to hear her talk and get it all off her chest and as he reassured her that she deserved so much better and would surely soon find someone who would truly love her and care for her, the little smile she gave him with those twinkling eyes created just a tiny sliver of hope in Zac's heart that maybe he would be that someone.

Silence fell between them again and Zac was happy that that was all sorted. It certainly explained Killian's weird mood. Although Zac didn't enjoy hearing about how badly Eva had been treated, it was nice to know that she had finally seen Killian for what he truly was. But Eva had more to say. Her voice shook a little this time and her eyes glazed over as she spoke.

'I'm sorry, Zac. It's just, it's not only the Killian thing. I mean, it's Christmas. And I love Christmas. But it's supposed to be a family time, when you spend time with the people you love. And all of a sudden I have to face the holiday, knowing that I'm never going to see one of the people I love most in this world ever again.'

Suddenly Zac understood and was ashamed that he hadn't thought of it before now. Of course Eva was upset – her first Christmas without her father. This was going to be a tough time for her.

'I just keep thinking back to all the Christmases before now and all the happy memories I had with Dad, but every year I just took it for granted that he was there. I just wish that last year I had known that it was going to be my last Christmas with him because I would have treasured it so much more and told him how much it meant to me to have him there.' She began to cry again.

'Eva, come here. Look, there's no way you could have known he was going to die. But I'm sure he knew you loved him. And I'm sure he loved you too. How could he not? You're such an amazing person. He must have been so proud of you.'

Eva stopped walking and stared into Zac's dark eyes. They had just reached the entrance to her estate and, as their gazes held only inches from each other, Zac knew that there was nothing more he would like to do than kiss her. He wanted to let her know how much he cared for her. But he couldn't. He couldn't use her vulnerability as a way of getting her. Zac looked away and turned his back to Eva, taking a few deep breaths to calm his beating heart down.

'Zac, are *you* all right?'

'Yeah, I'm fine. I'll talk to you tomorrow in school, okay? And if you ever need to talk or whatever, you know where I am.'

He headed off home. He felt bad about just leaving her like that, but he knew he couldn't look at her any longer without telling her how he felt. When someone pours their heart out to you it's hard to just hand it back to them, rather than taking it and making it yours. Tiny flakes of snow began to float down from the sky, swirling around him in the gentle afternoon breeze, dancing by his side so that he wouldn't be as lonely as he felt at that moment.

*

The last day of school was a non-uniform day and Zac threw on a pair of baggy jeans and a long-sleeved white T-shirt with a grey T-shirt over it. When he reached school the first person he met was

Killian, who actually took the time to ask where he'd got his T-shirt as he really liked it, but Zac could only manage a short answer. He knew that if he'd bothered to look Killian in the eye and engage in a proper conversation, he would have ended up getting worked up and telling Killian exactly what he thought of him. Since Zac's talk with Eva, his thoughts about Killian had been confirmed and he knew that Killian was not a nice person, and there was no point wasting time on someone who was so self-obsessed.

Although Eva looked tired, to Zac she still looked good and his heart snapped a little further when he saw her from the other end of the corridor. Zac was about to go up and tell her she looked great, but he was suddenly surrounded by bodies, each with their collars up and their hair gelled. Graham, Cian and Frank were full of the joys and all seemed to be trying to tell Zac something, though the overlap of voices made each one inaudible. Zac pointed this out and, as usual, Cian took charge.

'Listen Zac, we're heading down to the pub tonight to celebrate school being finished and all that. Do you want to come?'

He smiled as the excitement of the holidays suddenly hit him. The thought of going for a few drinks with the guys sounded like the perfect way to start the two weeks of freedom.

'Yeah, I'd love to, lads. Who's coming then?'

'Just the four of us probably, maybe a few others. It's a lads' thing, though, so no girls. You can bring Johnny and Kev if you want,' Graham answered.

'Yeah, I might give them a text.'

Zac was now really looking forward to going out. When it came down to it, no matter how much he was confused or entangled in emotions over Eva, there was nothing going to deny him a night out with all his closest friends.

By ten o'clock, the posse of six guys was well under the influence and spirits were high. A smile hadn't left Zac's face since the final bell had rung earlier that afternoon. There had been no problem getting into the pub. Zac himself had just strolled in without being asked for ID and those who were stopped produced their fakes and no questions were asked. Some of them used older brothers' passports. Some had drivers' licences from varying sources. Zac himself had a Garda ID which had once belonged to Kev's cousin. It had always worked a treat.

The dimly lit Blackrock bar was really getting going and the atmosphere was good and buzzing. As usual, Kev and Johnny had fitted in and were glad to have been invited along. All of them agreed that they should go out together more often. Although the girls were good craic, there was no denying the fun of a proper guys' night out.

It was only then that Zac noticed Killian wasn't there. Not that he really cared, but he was surprised no one had invited him. After all, he was Mr Popular.

'Hey guys, where's Killian?' Zac asked.

The others stopped mid-laughter. A couple of them sneered and the alcohol meant they had no problem explaining to Zac where exactly Mr Popular was.

'Zac, look, we know you've got pretty friendly with him and that, but to be honest… we think he's a wanker.' Cian didn't hold back!

Zac looked from face to face. Frank, Cian and Graham all wore similar expressions, nodding their heads and indicating that they all agreed. Frank explained, 'We didn't want to say anything cause we know you guys are mates, but seriously, Zac, that man is a first-class tosser. He thinks he's just the coolest kid in town, but to be honest, everyone thinks he's an arrogant shit.'

Zac waited a few more seconds before realising that they were all being genuine. Even Kev and Johnny seemed to agree.

'Yeah, man, at rugby he's always so up himself. He's good, like, but he's such a gobshite!'

Zac heaved a sigh of relief. All this time he hadn't wanted to say anything to anyone about his dislike for Killian, as it seemed he was the head of the popular crowd and he feared that dissing him would be a big no-no. But suddenly it was okay to be honest.

'Thank God for that! I don't like him either. I mean, at first he was sound to me, but more and more I've just realised what a complete dickhead he is and I really can't stand him any more. Sure, the way he treated Eva...' Zac trailed off and feared he'd said too much, but it seemed the guys had missed the last statement as they were too busy lining up high-fives for Zac as they congratulated his good judgement.

The atmosphere was electric and Zac felt such a buzz as he and the lads shared laughs, engaged in a bit of dodgy dancing, chatted up some college birds and slagged each other for the rest of the evening.

At one stage during the night, both Zac and Frank were at the bar trying to get a drink. But as Frank turned to his friend, it was obvious there was something on his mind. 'We're pretty rowdy tonight,' he began.

Zac smirked in agreement. 'Yeah, it's a good one, isn't it?'

But Frank failed to meet his high-five and instead began to frown, as if he was trying to come to terms with something.

'Listen man,' Frank mumbled nervously, 'do you ever feel, like, ashamed?'

Zac was completely at a loss, but the serious tone of Frank's voice told him not to make a joke about the randomness of this comment.

He continued, 'I mean on nights like this, all of us here in our Hilfiger and Ralph Lauren, knocking back the pints, being loud, high-fiving every two seconds. We must look like such arrogant pricks.'

Zac had never really thought about it. 'We're just having a laugh. I'm sure the people in here are used to it.'

'But that's the thing, of course they are. All lads our age are the same.'

Zac didn't understand. 'Exactly, so why are you worrying?' He laughed but realised the mood was still tense, as Frank seemed even more agitated.

'Because I don't want to become like another snobby little rich boy who thinks they own the place just because Daddy gave them a hundred bills to spend on pints for the night,' he spat.

'But since when do you care what people think?' Zac asked.

'I don't,' Frank insisted. 'Okay, maybe I do. But it's about what I think, too. I just don't want to let myself down.'

Zac quickly intervened. 'Frank, look, you're being way too hard on yourself. Just because our parents have a bit of money doesn't make us bad people. Plus we're hardly millionaires and, anyway, money's got nothing to do with what kind of person you are. We still have morals and shit, we care for people, care about what's going on in the world—'

'But not enough! Frank interrupted. We think because it doesn't affect us it's not that important. We live in our little Blackrock bubble.'

'Look, man, I just don't agree,' Zac said, a little offended. 'There might be people out there like that, but we're not them. You're a good guy and I think you need to stop beating yourself up just because you're well-off or whatever. It's not a crime, yeah?'

'Yeah, maybe,' Frank conceded. 'But you have to admit, some of the guys—'

'Don't give a shit about some of the guys,' Zac butted in determinedly. 'It's not something for you to get worried about.'

'Yeah, okay,' Frank agreed. 'And listen, thanks,' he added sheepishly.

'No worries,' Zac said, though he wasn't sure what to make of their conversation. He got what Frank meant, but it wasn't something to stress about. Ah well, he thought, to each their own, finally catching the barman's eye and ordering another round of pints.

When they finally stumbled out onto the street some time after one, the laughter and good moods didn't die. They headed to the chipper and when their bellies were full of top-quality battered rubbish, taxis were hailed and each headed in their respective directions. Zac was the only one walking and was glad the pub was close to his house as it meant he could stroll home and bask in the hum that still filled him. He'd had a great time and was thoroughly looking forward to the holidays if there were going to be more nights out like that.

But as he entered his house, slurring the chorus of a U2 song, he was met with a sight that made him come to a halt mid-lyric, and realise that the night was officially over. His father stood with his hands on his hips and pierced Zac's glazed eyes with his stare. Zac's confidence quickly melted away. He didn't know why, but he suddenly felt very apprehensive.

'Zac, what time do you call this? Or are you above following orders in this house?'

'Eh, there were no orders. I wasn't given a curfew. No one mentioned anything about how late I could stay out. It's the first night of the holidays for God's sake. Of course it's going to be a late night.'

'You are some little shit. Thinking you're better than me, thinking that you're too cool to respect me? You're becoming a right cocky little bastard, do you know that? What's the story, Zac? Think you're the shit all of a sudden? Because you certainly seem to have some sort of confidence since you met those hockey bastards.'

Zac couldn't help himself. Maybe it was the alcohol, or maybe it was the fuel of so many months of hatred, but he launched into the most risky, honest speech of his life.

'I'm not cocky, Dad. I've always had friends, plenty of them. It was *you* who was bringing me down, constantly burdening me with the fact that I wasn't anything you wanted me to be. I'm happy now. There's a difference. This is me. I'm relaxed and I have friends and

I've realised what a complete and utter tosser you are and that sooner or later you are going to see that Mum and I don't need you, and we're going to escape and be happy. Without you.'

Zac was short of breath after all he'd said. It had taken so much out of him emotionally that he suddenly felt drained. But for the first time in his life, he saw hesitation in his father's eyes, as if part of him couldn't withstand his son's challenge. Zac had hit a nerve, and it seemed as if his father was having problems coming to terms with what he'd said. Only now, his father didn't try and shout the problem away. He told Zac to go to bed and headed towards the kitchen. But there was a look in his eye that Zac had never seen before, and Zac wondered if his words had actually hit home. He climbed the stairs, triumphant at having told his dad the truth, but at the same time exhausted from the drunken night out. Bed came not a moment too soon.

*

Christmas morning was different. It even bordered on normality. At about ten o'clock Zac and his parents headed into the living room, each equipped with cups of tea, and distributed their presents. Zac's heart jumped when he saw his father smile at his mother when she gave him his present – a Polo Sport jumper and a new pair of golf shoes. Zac's mother smiled back and for a moment Zac was sure that each of them remembered what life was like before the rows and the shouting and the pressing air of discomfort blanketed them. It was as if something of old had been roused and they suddenly were reminded of better times and better love. Maybe it was just the Christmas cheer, but maybe his father would see sense, go to counselling or something to control his anger, and then his parents would go back to how things had been and he could stop living in fear of the next row. He knew he was jumping the gun, but the possibility twinkled in his mind so much that it made the star on the top of the Christmas tree seem dull.

He thought of Eva. Wherever she was, he wondered if she was all right. Today must surely be hard on her and he wished she was there with him so that he could ensure she was okay. But he realised that he didn't need to have her. He wanted it, but he didn't *need* it. For now, he was safe in the knowledge that for the first time in a long time, he'd had what could have easily passed for a family Christmas, and the flicker of hope that his family would become happy burned like a candle in a broken night.

But I'm guilty too I know,
I forgot that hope would dance still slow,
Even when I thought the dark remained.

19

Eva

The two weeks of holidays were a continuous cycle of laziness. Eva slept in late and talked on the phone to Cathy and Lisa, giggling away at their stories. Many afternoons, she found herself curled up in front of the fire, still wearing her pyjamas, feeling quite alone. All around her tinsel sparkled and the television spoke of joy, but she wasn't there. She wanted to be, to immerse herself in holiday cheer, but it was useless. There was only one thing she wanted that Christmas and the gap it left was killing her.

On one day of the holidays, she had rooted out some old pictures of her dad. She stared through blurred eyes at each one, at a split second of his life preserved in her hands. But she couldn't draw any comfort from the images. They only represented what she couldn't have. She felt wretched. Her period had arrived that morning, the cramps were terrible and all she could think of was how lonely she was, how much she needed him and how far from a Christmas mood she was. It could have been any time of the year for the state she was in, and she couldn't help feeling that the bright lights and joyous tunes were wasted on her.

Twice over the break, the Coonan women decided to make a trip to Dún Laoghaire and walk the pier. It was cold, but they wrapped up and braved the weather. Little was said between them. All three were clearly deep in thought about the same person, yet none spoke their minds aloud. Eva thought it sad that the three women were each focused on the same thing but were too scared to unite and actually speak about it. But the bond between them was still evident and the knowledge that whether they were talking or not they were there for each other was something. They needed to appreciate this now more that ever for, if anything, Eva had learned that life can change so quickly, and each moment must be cherished for she had no way of knowing how long it would last. She stared out to the horizon and was glad to be there, in the crisp afternoon air.

The last weekend before school started again, they'd all gone down to Cork and, as usual, the time with Don had done their mum a power of good. She seemed refreshed and appeared willing to embrace the New Year. Eva promised herself she would too. She was glad when school arrived. At least she'd had time to really think and focus on things. She felt much more content in herself than she had done for a while, knowing she had a clear picture of who she was and what she wanted.

The first day back at school was lazy. No one, including the teachers, wanted to be there. The majority of the classes were spent comparing stories of the break and Eva enjoyed hearing about what everyone had been up to. She hadn't seen many of them at all and had only talked to Lisa and Cathy. Now she was once again surrounded by all her friends and felt good listening to each of their accounts of the weeks off. Some had gone away. Skiing seemed to have been 'the thing to do' and Eva was one of the few who hadn't graced the slopes.

The biggest surprise of the day, though, came at lunch-time. Eva had just left the canteen when a familiar voice caught her just as she was heading into the ladies. 'Eva, hold on, can I have a word?'

Killian's voice seemed to have a touch of sincerity which surprised her so much that she had no choice but to turn around and hear what he had to say. He held something in his hand and she wondered what was going on. They hadn't spoken since the night at her house.

'Listen, I just wanted to give you this.' He handed her his Leinster under 18s jersey, with his number on the back. Eva was confused.

'What's this for?'

'Christmas present, I suppose. It's just, we did have some nice times. I'd meant to give it to you when we were together but I forgot. Just take it. But don't tell everyone, okay? I'm scoring this other bird now and if she finds out, she'll want one too!'

Eva couldn't believe her ears. Who did he think he was, giving her a present to remind her of their time together when he had treated her in such an unforgivable way?

'So give her this one, Killian, because I certainly don't want it!'

'What?' Killian was at a loss.

'You heard me. I don't know why the hell you're giving me this. You treated me like shit, and all of a sudden you want to, like, end things between us on a good note? Was this before or after you started bitching about my dead father cause, to be honest, I'm more than a little confused.' She thrust the jersey back into his hands.

Killian was shocked at the anger in Eva's voice and instantly tried to defend himself. 'I was just trying to be nice. But if you're going to be like that—'

'How else would I be, Killian? I don't think you realise how much you actually hurt me. I just can't get over the fact that you'd be so arrogant as to try and give me this. Whatever, just leave me alone.' Eva even surprised herself at how hurt she still was.

Killian stood for a moment in disbelief before heading off. Eva was left standing there, still wondering exactly what had just happened. It had been weeks since she and Killian were together, and yet now he wanted to give her his jersey, something which meant something to him, even when she hadn't. It was the kind of present you gave to someone when you were going out, not when you had been and now hated each other's guts. Eva felt drained and headed into the toilet for a quick time out, catching her breath and still reeling from it all.

Later that day, when she was told Cathy about the incident, her friend was furious and wondered why he had done such a thing, though she was much more cynical than Eva had been.

'Probably feels guilty and wants you to keep quiet about how shitty he treated you. Bribery, like! Also, he wanted an excuse to tell you he had a new girl on the go. Oh, and he probably wanted you to wear it so that people will see it and know that Killian Lain was with you. Kind of marking all the pretty girls he'd conquered!'

Eva smiled, but didn't bother joining in with her friend's tirade. She just wanted to forget about the whole thing and promised herself she was never going to be upset by it again. Then again, she wasn't going to suddenly forgive him and change her opinion or conclude that he was a nice guy. Because he wasn't, and no collared top with a number on the back was going to change that.

After school, as Eva walked home with Zac, she told him about the jersey. He had a similar reaction.

'What the hell? Why did he do that?'

'I don't know. He said it was a Christmas present and that he'd meant to give it to me when we were together but he never got around to it. Oh, and then he said not to go around saying it because he's with some new bird and she'd want one too!'

'Typical asshole. It's still really weird, though!' He gave a little laugh, which made Eva feel nice. She really liked Zac's laugh. He had this gentle way about him that was so soothing and comfortable to be with. He was relaxed and decent and made her feel safe. Cathy and Lisa had commented on a similar feeling, but Eva had a suspicion that what she was feeling was slightly different. She dared not touch that subject, though, and distracted herself from it by asking Zac about his Christmas.

'It was pretty good, actually. I was kind of dreading it in a way because Dad always spoils it, but this year was different for some reason. He seemed to be in a better mood and I didn't hear him and mum fight once. I think things might be sorting themselves out,' he told her.

'That's brilliant news,' Eva smiled.

'Yeah, but I could be completely wrong. Though I just have a feeling that something good is on its way and that everything at home is going to work out.'

They'd reached Eva's estate and she turned to face him. She looked straight at him and smiled and they both held each other's gaze but, for the second time, Zac snapped out of the stare and quickly turned away, before saying goodbye and headed home.

Eva wondered what was going on. She had wanted to hug him but he'd left so suddenly. Maybe he was annoyed with her. Maybe he just didn't want to hug her. She wasn't sure, but she hoped that whatever was going on would pass. She loved hugging Zac. He was taller and broader than her so that he enveloped her with his arms. He also smelled nice and had no problem holding her very close.

Eva's house was empty when she got in and she spent the next few hours listening to some music and doing her homework. Even though she didn't have much, it took a lot of time, as she kept taking breaks to listen to music or just think. Was Zac mad at her? She couldn't think why he would be. Maybe it was because she hadn't stayed more in contact over Christmas, but then neither had he. She couldn't put her finger on it and eventually she couldn't take it any more. She dialled his number.

'Hello?' His voice was wonderfully rich and casual. Eva smiled to herself.

'Hey, Zac, it's Eva.'

The voice at the other end perked up. 'Oh, heya, how're things?'

'Good, thanks. Listen, Zac, I was just wondering… are you pissed off with me?'

'No, not at all. Why?'

'It's just, you seemed pretty quiet when we were walking home today and I thought you might be angry because I never saw you over Christmas and then you didn't give me a hug goodbye and it's not the first time and I figured you must be mad.'

There was silence at the other end and Eva feared that she had in fact hit a nail on the head. She could hear Zac taking a big breath before replying.

'I'm honestly not angry at all. Not that I didn't want to see you over the holidays, I did, but I knew you'd be busy and I was too. As for the hug, I just find it weird sometimes...' Zac's voice trailed off.

'What do you mean? Seriously, Zac, just tell me cause I don't like things being not right between us.'

'I don't know. It's, well, we're just friends, and you just broke up with Killian and I don't want you to think I'm, like, trying anything on or... it's just weird.'

Eva said she understood, but she didn't and, when she hung up, Zac's words still ran through her mind as she tried to figure it out. Of course she knew they were just friends. And what had Killian got to do with anything? She didn't get it and hoped she hadn't said or done anything to make Zac think that she thought he was trying to make a pass at her. Maybe all the talk of Killian and how he'd made her uncomfortable and tried to push her to do things she didn't want had scared Zac off. Maybe he thought she wanted him to back off. But she didn't. She cared for Zac and she loved being affectionate with him – not in a sexual way, she just felt nice when they hugged each other or were close. She didn't want to lose that.

The following weeks were pretty uneventful until one Wednesday at the end of January the first round of the Senior Cup was being played. Since the odds were against Killian and his team-mates, most of the school was being bussed off to Donnybrook to heckle as much as possible in a vague attempt to encourage their team to achieve a seemingly impossible task.

Eva and all her friends were going to support the team and they were glad they did. Naturally the team lost, but they sure as hell put up a good fight. The final score was 20–30 and Killian's boys actually deserved to go through to the next round. The atmosphere in the stands was amazing. The other school was a crowd of wannabe rugby heads from Wicklow who tried all the usual chants before they made sure to slag off their hockey school opponents for full effect. Though, with the scores equal at half-time, it seemed the jocks were quaking in their Dubarrys and realised that the hockey school had a lot more in them than expected.

Eva and her friends weren't disappointed that the game was lost. It had always been assumed that would happen, but what hadn't been expected was that the Wicklow team would be given a run for their money. Eva cheered extra loud as her school's team walked off the pitch and made sure that when they eventually came out of the changing rooms she said well done to each of them. She couldn't see Killian around, though, and even though she felt sorry for the other lads, part of her couldn't help but feeling slightly happy that he hadn't won. She told herself not to be so bitter, but after all he'd done, she couldn't help it. She eventually spotted him, only he wasn't alone. He had his arm around a curly-haired brunette who wore a brown uniform and was caked in make-up. So this was the new bird! Wonder if she got the rugby jersey, Eva laughed to herself, and hoped that the girl was a complete idiot so that both Killian and she deserved each other.

The loss meant that that Friday night would be a big party for the fifth and sixth years to mark the fact that the rugby team was out of the league. The venue was Killian's house and, even though Eva wasn't keen on going there, she knew that the place would be packed with her friends and all the sixth years, so hopefully she could avoid the host at all costs.

Killian spent the night trying to drink away the fact that they had lost the match and, even though his new girlfriend and her friends were all standing in a corner looking totally out of place and talking to no one, he made no effort to alleviate their obvious discomfort. Cian told Eva that he himself had tried to talk to them, but apparently they weren't very friendly.

'They were all typical brown-uniform snobs who gave me shitloads of attitude so I told them to fuck off and sort out their fake tan!'

Eva laughed and was glad Killian had found himself a pleasant new girl. But it seemed that in his drunken state he wasn't content with Miss Fake Tan at all. He took Eva aside just before midnight to have another quiet word.

'Lishen, Eva,' he slurred. 'I just wanna shay that you look reeeeally hot and I'm shorry I made you cry. Sho can we have shex now?'

Eva couldn't believe her ears and had to try hard not to cry. Instead she just headed quickly out of the room, grabbing Cathy as she went. The pair went straight to the bathroom, just in time, for the tears had just begun to pour down Eva's face.

'That wanker is never going to change. I hate him so much, Cathy.'

'He's such a prick. I swear to God I'm going to go down there right now and tell him that if he comes near you again—'

'Cathy, no. Just leave it. Please?' Eva couldn't bear more confrontation. She managed to stop crying.

Cathy soothed, 'Listen, chicken, if you want to leave, that's fine. I'm not having that great a night anyway. I have the worst cramps ever and everyone's just so drunk.'

'Thanks, Cathy. But it's okay, I'm not going to let that bastard win.' A new wave of determination had come over Eva and it felt good.

'Yeah, exactly – fuck him. We'll sort out that lovely smudged mascara of yours and then go downstairs and flirt outrageously with the sixth years. That'll show him! Have you seen Sam tonight? He's such a hottie!'

Eva laughed out loud and had to admit that although there was a shortage of good-looking guys in the year above them, the few in existence were of a high standard, and a good flirt was just what she needed. She headed downstairs, make-up reapplied, and a fresh confidence surging within her.

The rest of the night passed swimmingly, and Eva was in convulsions as she talked with the sixth years. After a long chat with them, she went off to find another great guy. Zac was talking with some of the sixth year girls, but once she caught his eye he came over straight away.

'I've been looking for you. Are you all right?'

'Yeah, I'm grand. Why?'

'I saw Killian taking you aside earlier and I was just worried about what he said.' Zac sounded genuinely concerned, and when Eva filled him in as to just what had been said, he looked fit to burst.

'What the fuck? I hate that guy so much. Do you want me to say something? I'd bloody love to have a word with him and tell him just what I think of him.' Zac's fury was building.

'No, Zac. Thanks, but just leave it, yeah?' Eva was firm.

Zac was pretty drunk, but in a nice way, and Eva spent the rest of her night just sitting on the couch talking to him. The later it got, the comfier they made themselves until, eventually, Eva's legs lay across Zac's lap and his hand rested gently on her bare calf. She was a little surprised. Every time his hand moved on her skin she felt her heart stop for just a split second, and hoped that he wouldn't notice as she tensed up slightly as her body tingled with excitement. What was happening? Zac was her friend. It was so weird for her to feel like this, and yet it didn't feel weird at all. It was nice and exciting and Eva felt as if she was going to burst. Zac, however, just continued talking to her and didn't seem to be making a conscious effort to make her feel anything, but it didn't matter. Purposely or not, his finger kept moving along her leg, sending her heart into a flutter of enjoyment.

The night ended and Eva got a taxi home with Cathy, who was staying at her house, and Zac. For the whole journey, she tried to figure out what was going on. The second Zac got out of the taxi, she exploded into a flurry of thoughts and words and hoped that Cathy could make sense of it all, because she certainly couldn't.

'It's so weird, Cathy. I mean, it's Zac. We're such good friends, but his hand was on my leg and it was, like, major tingles. And he was kind of rubbing it, just a little, but I don't know if that was on purpose. But things have been different recently. I mean, we never hug goodbye any more and it's weird cause we're so close. And he was so sound to me about the Killian thing. He was really upset about the way I was treated, you know? It's just really weird.' Eva talked and talked all the way out of the taxi, up her driveway, into the kitchen and even as she made Koka Noodles for the pair to munch on after their night out.

Cathy listened to every word and by the time Eva was finished, she knew exactly what she was going to tell her confused friend.

'Do you not think it's obvious?'

'What? What's obvious? That's what I'm asking you.' Eva felt exasperated.

'For goodness' sake, it's blatantly obvious that you fancy the pants off Zac!'

Eva looked up from her noodles and stared at her friend to make sure she wasn't messing. But Cathy was deadly serious.

'It's the classic case of falling for a close friend. Which is so cool. You guys would have the perfect relationship. You're already so close and now that you like each other you're going to go out for ages! I'm really glad. He's such a nice guy.'

'Whoa, Cathy, do you not think you're jumping the gun a bit there? Suddenly Zac's my boyfriend? Where do you get that from?'

'Eva, come on. You fancy him so much and he's liked you for ages too. Of course he's going to ask you out.'

Eva's heart gave a little leap. Did Zac really fancy her? Or maybe her friend was just saying this to cheer her up. Either way, it had set Eva's heart thumping again.

'Why do you think he fancies me? Has he said anything to you?'

'No, but you can totally tell. You guys spend so much time together.

And don't give me that friendship crap, it's more than that! The way he looks at you, the way he talks about you – he's so into you it's perfect!'

Eva thought she would burst. Not only had she decided that she fancied Zac, but it seemed that the feeling was mutual. It was all too much and, as she sucked up her noodles, sending juice flying all over her top, she decided she couldn't take it all in there and then. She headed to bed, and as Cathy lay beside her under the duvet, Eva thought briefly of Zac before conking out into a thick, exhausted sleep.

20

Zac

The following weekend it was Cian's eighteenth birthday, the first of all of them since he was particularly old for the year, so the gang decided to go to a nightclub in town on Saturday night. Once again, Zac had found it easy to get in and the girls had little problem getting past the bouncers. The club was crowded and the low lighting and neon strips on the walls made the atmosphere exciting. The guys headed straight for the bar and as he ordered his first pint, Zac had to keep telling himself to stop looking at Eva because she would notice him staring. He couldn't help it though. Although he thought it every time they went out, she looked so well and he knew it was a risky business her being in the club, as surely there would be an endless string of guys chatting her up. Zac hadn't a hope. Even though he'd been thinking that tonight he could tell her how he felt, he knew that she'd probably be too preoccupied to notice him. As she danced to Britney's latest hit, her short black shirt swayed in time with her hips and Zac felt his heart snap as he watched the first of Eva's fans chat her up.

He snapped out of his trance just in time to hear Cian announce that his parents had bought him a Volkswagen Polo for his birthday.

'Savage, isn't it? Insurance cost a bomb, but lads, we finally have our own pimp-mobile!' he boasted.

Everyone laughed, clearly chuffed for Cian, who'd never looked so pleased with himself. The only person who didn't seem impressed was Frank.

'That's a lot of money, though, isn't it?'

Cian didn't follow. 'Yeah, and?'

'Wouldn't it have been cheaper to just get insured on your mum's car? She barely uses it.'

'Dude, I don't think you follow – I have my own car now!' Cian gave a hearty laugh, truly believing Frank hadn't understood what he'd said.

'He just doesn't get it. Total waste of money,' Frank muttered under his breath, but no one heard him, they were too busy fighting over who was to be official shotgun passenger. Frank rolled his eyes, clearly unimpressed, and headed to the bar to get a drink.

Later on, Zac was getting in a round of pints, and while he waited for the barman to serve him, a pretty blonde came and stood beside him. Zac gave her a quick look and decided she was definitely hot. She caught him looking and obviously decided the same of him and gave him a big smile. He returned the smile and turned back to try and catch the barman's eye. No hope, though. The girl wasn't finished, though; she caught his eye again and announced that her name was Lara and she was a first year Arts student in UCD. Zac smiled and realised that she obviously thought he too was finished school and was very pleased with himself. He introduced himself and told her he was in Trinity studying Law. Lara seemed impressed and told him she'd spotted him when he'd walked in the door as he was so good looking. He blushed and returned the compliment and they began to talk.

'So, what school were you in?' Lara asked casually, though her composure changed slightly when Zac answered her question.

'Oh my God, I know so many guys from your year in your first school and they're all so sound. You know Barry and Walker and all them, obviously?'

'Oh yeah, obviously!' Zac smirked as he lied. The names rang bells, but since anyone she mentioned had been two years above him in school, he'd never exactly been friends with them.

'So why did you move? It's kind of taking a step down, isn't it? Don't the guys in that other school play hockey? It's a bit weird, don't you think?' Lara cringed at the thought. Zac laughed and quickly moved on, asking where she'd gone to school. Her answer was as he expected, and as she launched into a spiel about how much she missed school but how good it was that they all 'totally' kept in touch, Zac found himself transfixed by her beauty. She was very sexy and as she stared at him from under her long eyelashes, Zac felt good.

'So where do you live then, Zac?' Lara took a tiny step closer.

'Eh, Blackrock. You?'

'Oh well, that figures. Killiney. It's so nice out there, I totally love it!'

'Yeah, there's some savage gaffs out there. Kind of far out, though, don't you think?'

'I suppose it's a bit of a pain, especially on nights like this when you have to get a taxi all the way home from town, but I love this club, so it's worth it.'

'Yeah, it's good craic all right. Here, do you want a drink?' Zac had finally got the barman's attention, so he figured he'd spare Lara the trouble of trying to do the same.

'Thanks, vodka and lime please.' Over her shoulder Zac could see the guys looking for him with impatience at their lack of drink, but eventually Graham spotted him and nudged the lads, each of whom gave him a big thumbs up, encouraging him to get stuck in and signifying that they'd get their own pints in! Zac just laughed, and having bought the drinks, returned to the conversation which was beginning to turn into a total flirting session. As time passed, Zac noticed Lara was using all the oldest tricks in the book and he had to admit he was intrigued.

'So, Law in Trinners. That's super hard, isn't it?' she asked.

'It's good, though. I like the challenge, you know?' Zac had to try hard not to start laughing as he launched into a very intellectual description of his course and why he liked it. The thought of studying Law had never even crossed his mind, but Lara was lapping it up and Zac couldn't help embellishing his story.

'I'm so jealous. Arts has such a good social scene, but you seem so passionate about your course, when for me it's, like, whatever!' Lara took another step in, and Zac realised just how close together they were, as their bodies were touching. She reached downwards and Zac felt a lump rise in his throat. His mouth was dry but as she produced her phone from her bag and asked for his number, he relaxed with a little laugh. But in that moment, he felt something on his hips and realised it was a pair of hands. He swung around only to be faced with Eva's wonderful eyes smiling at him, though not in an entirely convincing fashion.

'Hey, Zac. Having fun?'

Suddenly, Zac realised he hadn't seen Eva since the start of the night and had assumed she was off with that other guy. But now here she was, staring at him as she always did and he was mesmerised once more. And he realised that there was no point trying to convince himself that Lara was a patch on her, because she wasn't. There was only one person in the whole club that he wanted and she was standing right beside him, her auburn hair flowing down to her breasts.

'Listen, Lara, it's been really nice talking to you, but I'm going to hang out with my friends now,' he told the other girl.

Lara wasn't impressed and threw the filthiest of looks at Zac. 'Wanker,' she muttered as he headed away.

Zac felt bad. He'd led Lara on and she'd talked to him for half the night and got nowhere, but he didn't care. He was with the girl he loved, and even if Eva didn't know it, it was still enough for him.

Eva didn't seem herself, though, and Zac asked what was up. At first she was reluctant to tell him, but eventually she murmured, 'I'm sorry for tearing you away from her, Zac. I feel like such a bitch. It's just, I don't know, when I saw you talking to her for ages and the way she was throwing herself at you, I got... well, basically I got jealous. Sorry.'

Eva looked up at him with sheepish eyes as if expecting him to give out to her for taking him from the flirty blonde, but the realisation of what she had just said washed over him and left him stunned. He knew that his moment had come. This was the perfect time to tell Eva how much he cared for her and that what he felt was much more than friendship and that he really wanted to make a go of it. He took a deep breath. The first syllable had barely left his lips when Cathy came running up to Eva, looking very concerned.

'Eva, oh my God, your sister just rang me. She said she'd been trying to get you but your phone must be on silent. She's really scared, Eva. Your mum is in floods of tears and screaming and stuff and she won't stop and poor Sarah doesn't know what to do.'

Zac watched as the colour drained from Eva's face as she took a few moments to comprehend what had just been said. She looked at Zac as if looking for support.

'Eva, you better go. I'll get a taxi with you if you want. Just don't worry, okay? I'm sure she's fine.'

'It's fine, I have Cathy. I'm so sorry,' she apologised.

She grabbed Cathy by the hand and sprinted out of the place. Zac was scared for her. It really sounded like things were bad. This was the last thing she needed and he couldn't believe that her life was taking another bad turn. It just wasn't fair.

Fed up, he found Frank and Cian and told them he was going home. There was no use trying to have a good night now when all he'd be doing was worrying about Eva. All he wanted was his bed.

Almost there but another trap,
Pulls me down and kicks my back,
Forget the little boy who wants to love.

21

Eva

As she stepped out of the taxi, Eva insisted to Cathy for the thousandth time that she wanted to go in alone. This was something she needed to do by herself, difficult as it would be. She bid her friend goodnight and headed up her garden path with a lump in her throat.

Sarah had left the door on the latch so Eva just had to push the front door open before running into her house. The first voice she heard was Sarah's.

'Please, Mum. Look, Eva will be here soon and we can just sit down and talk and it'll be okay,' Sarah pleaded.

'Why would I want to talk to her? I don't want to talk to anyone. When I do talk to you girls, all it does is remind me of how shit a monther I've become.' Her mum's voice was angry and loud and choked with tears. Eva heard a crash of something being thrown and she knew she couldn't just hover in the hall and listen. She couldn't leave her younger sister to deal with what was happening.

Pushing the door of the kitchen open, Eva's heart was hurting her as it throbbed in her chest. She stared at the scene before her and couldn't believe her eyes. Sarah was sitting at the kitchen table, head buried in her hands. Her mum was standing at the window, arms folded, looking wretched. Her face was a blur of make-up and puffy redness, while her hair was wild and tousled. Shards of broken glass and crockery littered the floor and Eva knew that the crash she'd heard hadn't been the first. It was like something from a movie. That split second was a perfect image of just how destroyed their household had become, even all these months on.

'Mum, it's me,' Eva tried.

'Go away,' her mother spat angrily.

'But Mum—'

'I said go away, Eva.'

'Mum, please, it's okay, I'm here. Please just give me a hug.'

'Don't touch me!' her mother screamed, pushing Eva's arms away. For the first time, they looked into each other's eyes and Eva saw just how frantic her mother was. There was something in those eyes that warned Eva that this was worse than she ever could have expected. Her mother broke their stare and began to shout.

'I can't do it anymore. I jus can't. Life is shit, nothing's the same. I wish it would all just fuck off and leave me alone. I just can't take it!' she screeched.

'Mum, please!' Eva felt her strength draining out of her, only to be replaced by terror. 'I know it's hard, but you'll get there.'

'No I won't. I've tried and tried but it's not working. I've tried forgetting, I've tried remembering. But nothing fucking works. He's gone and I'm too tired to try any more.' She trailed off into a silent sob.

Eva panicked and raced to try and find a way to get her mother to stop this. 'Mum, what about God? You pray, don't you? Ask Him to help you through this.'

'God? What the fuck would I want with Him?' Eva's comment had obviously had the opposite of her desired effect. 'He got me into this fucking mess. I've gone to church every Sunday of my life, and this is how He repays me? Well, fuck Him. Fuck you, God!' Her voice was so loud it reverberated through the kitchen. She pulled her hair and stamped her feet and wailed like a child. Sarah looked at Eva and she knew that there was nothing either of them could do. The two teenage girls were way out of their depth trying to deal with this. But who could help at this hour? Eva had almost forgotten what time it was, but glanced quickly at her watch and saw it was after two o'clock. What could they do? She closed her eyes, and even though her mother had started to scream and wail again, limbs flailing and words of hatred spitting from her, Eva concentrated on trying to think of a solution.

'Don!' she announced.

For the first time, her mother went completely silent and still, as if she'd seen a ghost. Sarah, on the other hand, jumped up from where she sat, her eyes holding a new trickle of hope.

'Yes – Don. I'll ring him straight away. Mum, he'll want to talk to you, okay? That'll be good, won't it?' Sarah coaxed before reaching for the phone and dialling frantically.

Eva stood rooted to the spot, willing her uncle to pick up the phone. The room was silent with anticipation, save for her mother's heavy, erratic breathing. Moments passed. Eva was convinced there wouldn't be an answer, that he'd be out or asleep. But just when she'd given up, Sarah squealed.

'Oh Don, thank God. I'm so sorry to ring you at this hour. It's me, Sarah. We need your help. It's Mum. She's having some sort of breakdown and nothing Eva or I say is working. Please, Don, talk to her.'

'Girls,' their mum said, sounding calmer than she had all night, 'I think I'll take this call upstairs. Don't worry about the mess, I'll sort it tomorrow.' Though she was still crying, it was as if even the knowledge that her brother was at the other end of the phone had been a massive relief to whatever had been destroying her that night. She slowly trudged upstairs and once her voice was faintly heard from the bedroom, Sarah put down the receiver, praying that somehow Don would make it all okay.

The kitchen was silent after their mum had gone. Eva suddenly realised how tired she was; every inch of her was drained. But with a glance at her sister, the two of them set about restoring the kitchen to some sort of order.

Eva didn't know how long they worked. Not a word passed between them, as if they were too busy praying the phone call was going well to talk. Eva crouched on her hands and knees, picking up the larger chunks of glass, wondering just how much had been broken. She worked slowly, not wanting the job to end, for then reality would want her back. Each piece of glass glistened in her hand before she dropped it into the plastic bag.

It felt like she was picking up the broken pieces of her mother, each one delicate and brittle. She stared at the one in her hand and smoothed her finger against its rough outline.

'Fuck,' she muttered, blood beginning to pour from her fingertip. Her trance broken, she went to the bathroom to run her hand under the tap. It began to sting, and even though it wasn't that bad, Eva began to cry. Her cries became heavier and louder and soon she was sobbing. One parent was dead and the other was broken. Eva shook as she let every single tear pour from her tired eyes until there was a knock on the door.

'Eva, it's me. Are you all right? Can I come in?' Sarah whispered.

'Yeah.' Eva pulled herself together. The last thing Sarah needed was another sobbing woman on her hands.

'Look, I just checked on Mum, she's asleep. Don must have sorted it. I reckon she was just exhausted too. The amount of screaming she did must have tired her out!' Sarah gave a weak smile and Eva was once again blown away by her strength.

'How do you do it, Sarah? You're so brave. How can you not just give up sometimes?'

'Because I know that's not what Dad would have wanted.'

The words hung in the air and Eva knew that, however strong her sister appeared, it didn't change how much she, too, had been hurt by his death. Eva wrapped her arms around Sarah, not wanting to ever let go. She buried her face in her shoulder and closed her eyes and, just for a moment, believed that everything would be all right again.

22

Zac

The following day, Zac waited until the afternoon to call Eva and see how she was. She said very little but the broken tone of her voice spoke volumes. She asked him if he would mind going down to Blackrock just for a walk or a bite to eat to take her mind off things. He gladly agreed and, as he waited outside her estate for her, he hated himself for thinking that what they were doing vaguely resembled a date. Now wasn't the time. He would make sure he didn't turn into a narrow-minded, ignorant fool like Killian.

Eva walked slowly towards him, but then ran the final few yards and wrapped her arms tightly around him and burrowed her head into his chest while he held her. But she didn't cry. She told him she couldn't. She said she'd seen enough tears last night to last a lifetime and she was damned if she was going to shed any more.

As they walked through the quiet streets, Eva told Zac that she didn't want to talk about her mother or anything that had happened the previous night, although at times it seemed she began to pour out just some of what she was locking up inside her.

'It was awful, Zac. She was wailing and sobbing and screaming about how she hated God and hated herself and her life and how nothing was the same now Dad was gone. And at times she was just so upset she moaned and held her head in her hands, and at other times she would get so angry, she'd start screeching and throwing things and pulling her hair. I was really frightened, Zac. And there was nothing we could do. Sarah and I just stood there watching, paralysed with shock. We tried talking to her, hugging her, making her tea, but she didn't want it. All she wants is him and that's the one thing she'll never have,' she quavered.

Zac stared at Eva's deep hazel eyes and saw a fear he'd never noticed there before. As far as Eva was concerned, this was just the beginning of a long road of pain.

'My uncle did warn us that eight or nine months after my dad's death was going to be the hardest, but we never expected this. My mum's very close to her brother. Eventually, when nothing else would work, we rang him and gave the phone to her. He calmed her down straight away. It was half two in the morning but, within minutes, she was calm. He's wonderful with her.

They were always so close growing up, since it was only the two of them, so I think they've always had a bond. Last night really proved it. He's got such a good way of talking to people – a bit like you, I suppose!' she smiled at him.

Zac looked at her with surprise but she insisted it was true with a warm smile that touched him and, for the rest of the day, even though nothing more was said about it, Zac was safe in the knowledge that she was glad he was by her side, and for him that was enough.

*

A week on, Zac and Eva were doing exactly the same thing again, wandering together through the streets of Blackrock, only this time Eva had just the tiniest bit of hope in her eyes as she spoke.

'Mum's started seeing the same therapist I go to. Basically she said she'd been getting more and more upset recently and last weekend it just all erupted. Helen said she should talk to someone about getting some pills or something to help her sleep so she did that yesterday. She didn't say much but Sarah and I reckon they gave her anti-depressants, so hopefully they'll do the trick. My uncle is coming up next weekend to spend some time with her, so that should help her too.'

Eva then quickly changed the subject and the rest of the afternoon disappeared in the blink of an eye. Zac knew she'd stayed far longer than she'd intended, but she didn't seem to mind and they were both so relaxed that it didn't matter. As the day began to fade, she dropped a bombshell that Zac hadn't seen coming at all.

'Look, Zac, there's something I've wanted to tell you for ages but I didn't know how. I was so close to saying it last weekend but then I got the call from Sarah and everything just fell apart. But it's killing me and I just have to say it.'

Zac's mouth was dry as he anticipated the words he'd waited so long to hear. But they didn't come. He stared as Eva tried to get out all she'd prepared to say but couldn't.

'Eva, let me go first. There's something I've wanted to say for quite a while too, but I was so afraid to mention it. So many times I thought it was too late but now I've realised that it's better late than never when you're feeling what I'm feeling.' He took a deep breath and stared straight at Eva before uttering the sentence he'd wanted to for so long.

'Eva, I think I've fallen for you. I know we're good friends and I never want to lose that, but I'm feeling much more than friendship and it's brilliant and I love being around you and everything about you is just perfect. And I don't care any more if you don't feel the same way because I just had to tell you that I think you're amazing and I care so much for you, more than you know,' he burst out.

They stared into each other's eyes, listening to the beat of their hearts before Eva gave him a warm smile.

'I feel the same,' she confessed. 'Ever since the rugby party at Killian's, I've known that I want to be more than your friend, and the way you make me feel is so incredible that I never want it to go away. I really like you, Zac.' She looked at him, her eyes full of happiness.

It was the best feeling Zac had ever experienced in his entire life and he was completely lost for words. He wanted to kiss her so much but he knew that he couldn't. Something inside him told him he couldn't, he willed the feeling to go away but it wouldn't. His brain filled with the thoughts that he was just taking advantage of her vulnerable state, and most of all, that it wasn't really that long since she'd broken up with Killian and he didn't want to look like he went around stealing other guy's girls as soon as they were done with them. Plus, he wanted to take things slowly – that was why this was going to work.

'Eva, call me a loser, but I really want to just take this slowly, yeah? I don't want to rush it, cause then I might miss something!'

'Zac, you really do amaze me sometimes! Slow is good with me,' she assured.

They talked a little longer until it was time to part, and as Zac watched her as she began to jog home, he couldn't believe it. He liked her, she liked him, and they both knew. Zac was on cloud nine, his stomach was in a knot and he knew that everything was going to just get better and better from now on because the person he cared for more than anything felt the same way, and soon, life would be sweet.

Just out of reach like the slivered moon,
Let me have my perfection soon.
Before I forget she's looking over here.

23

Eva

'It was horrible. Even thinking about it now makes me want to bury my head and make it disappear. She was distraught. You could see her heart breaking. And I know it's terrible, but I was so upset that she was like that because it made me upset and I'm just coming to terms with it myself. I know it's really selfish and I'm sorry, but it hurts,' Eva explained.

Helen smiled and nodded and told Eva that what she was feeling was perfectly natural. She wasn't sure if that was the truth or just being said so she wouldn't be even more upset; she didn't want to find out. The session was drawing to a close and as usual Helen asked her if there was anything else going on in her life she wanted to talk about. Eva thought of Zac and found it impossible not to share just some of the joy she was experiencing, though she wasn't really feeling it to the full yet. Her mother was her top priority now and her heart would have to hold on for a while. But at least she knew that the feeling was there and that it was mutual, and that in itself was plenty. She told Helen everything about Zac – how he made her feel, how he made her laugh, the things he said. Helen jotted something down in her notebook and began to grin. Eva asked what she was smiling at.

'He really does sound wonderful, so don't be afraid to enjoy it. Of course, you have to focus on what your mum is going through, but it sounds like Zac will help you through it, so don't feel you can't let him into your life.'

Eva decided to take Helen's advice and not be scared to let Zac into her life. Not that he wasn't already in her life, but now he was in it as something else, not just a friend. The potential for something much deeper and even closer than what they had was there.

*

On Wednesday, a fresh February afternoon, Eva and the girls had a hockey match, the semi-final of the league. The team they were playing had a good reputation and everyone knew that the winner of this match would probably win the whole thing. The match was in Marley Park and busloads of supporters were sent to cheer the girls on. Eva was nervous and found the surrounding crowds intimidating. As she and Cathy ran side by side around the pitch to warm up, the blur of flags and painted faces and screaming mouths seemed to be closing in on her and she inwardly prayed that they'd win or, if not, that she herself would play well. She didn't fancy making a fool of herself in front of so many people.

By half-time, there was still no score, though both teams had come very close. Eva had had a shot on goal that looked promising, but the goalie's boot got there just in time to stop the goal.

Ten minutes into the second half, Lisa had the ball and was making a nice run up the pitch. Eva screamed to signify she was open but doubted she was heard – the screaming fans were making such a din it was impossible to make sense of any voices on the pitch. But it seemed Lisa had heard her, and in a flash the ball was on Eva's stick as she charged towards a large defender, pulling the ball to her right just in time to dodge her. She was in the circle. All around her were opposing colours and there was no way she could get a clear shot. She began to panic and everything seemed to be dissolving into slow motion as she willed a space or gap to appear so that she could put the ball in the back of the net. And then, as if answering her prayers, a girl in the year below her made a run towards the goal, stick outstretched, with a defender close on her tail. Eva slapped the ball to her and as soon as the younger girl sent it between the goalie's legs, Eva found herself up in the air, jumping for joy. The sidelines erupted. Eva was ecstatic, and after giving the goal scorer a big hug, she returned to the halfway line to restart the game and make sure their lead wasn't lost.

A few times, the other team was close to getting their own score, but tight defending all around made their efforts fail every time. Eva's school cheered ever louder as the full-time whistle neared and, although the other school tried to keep their spirits up, it was hard when they were beaten down by a chorus of 'What's the score? What's the score?'

As soon as the referee raised the whistle to her lips to end the game, Eva's heart leapt and within seconds the whole team was upon her, laughing and smiling and generally feeling thoroughly pleased that they had secured such a good victory. It had been tight, but well deserved, and the whole school displayed their pride in the team with a barrage of congratulations.

As Eva came off the pitch and gave her mum and sister a big hug, both telling her how well she played, a familiar face caught her eye. She ran up to Zac, completely forgetting how sweaty and tired she was; she knew he wouldn't care. She leapt into his arms and he willingly caught her and spun her around.

'Well done!' Zac said. 'You guys played a blinder and you totally deserved it.'

Eva was chuffed and gave Zac a quick kiss on the cheek before she was attacked by Frank, Graham and Cian, all of whom were sporting school flags as capes and loudly singing 'When the Saints Go Marching In'. Eva jumped around with all of them for a while before returning to Sarah and her mother to head home. As she walked towards the car, her mum's arm around her, Eva saw someone swaggering in the opposite direction. It was Killian. When he passed them, he didn't say anything except 'well done', but something about the way he said it displayed a sincerity that surprised her. Eva's mum asked who he was but Eva just shook her head. She doubted her mother would appreciate knowing that that was the boy who had tried to have sex with Eva in her house a few months ago.

The next day in school everyone was still on a high after the match, and with the final just a week away, posters of encouragement were already lining the corridors, instructing every student that they simply had to come watch the final as the league would be theirs!

That Friday was Valentine's Day and, as Eva listened to Lisa listing off all the gifts that had been waiting on her doorstep that morning and how Graham was taking her out for dinner that night, she was glad to be reassured that romance certainly wasn't dead. She hadn't known whether to get Zac anything or not and had decided that he wasn't really a teddy bear or a chocolate kind of guy and had simply sent a card to his house. But the post usually didn't arrive until midday, so it was no surprise that Zac didn't mention it in school. She wondered if there would be a card waiting for her when she got home, but told herself not to be disappointed if there wasn't. They hadn't even gone out together yet, never mind being at the stage of buying each other gifts. Cathy had received a text from Johnny asking her to be his Valentine and Eva swore she had never seen her friend so excited. At lunch-time Cathy planted a big kiss on Zac, exclaiming that he was the nicest guy ever for introducing her to Johnny. Eva smiled as she watched them, but her mind was already distracted with the thoughts of what lay ahead for her. Her uncle Don was arriving that night to visit, her team had a very good chance of winning the hockey league on Wednesday and then midterm would be upon them the following Friday. And, of course, Zac was still lurking in her head like a glow-worm keeping her every move warm.

*

Eva had to walk home after hockey training as her mother and sister were off collecting Don from the airport, and Zac had headed off straight after school. As she entered her house, she noticed something sitting on the hall table, an envelope addressed to her, slightly thicker than an average one. Ripping it open, she found a black card with a red heart on the front. She smiled as the butterflies inside her started to do a jig and when she opened the card she found out what had been adding to the bulk of the envelope. A CD. She was confused but the simple inscription on the inside of the card explained everything.

Dear Eva,
I wrote this song when I thought of you.
Be mine.
Zac x

Eva was dying to know what was on the CD and what exactly Zac had written when he thought of her. She rushed into the sitting room and put on the disc and was instantly surrounded by lyrics that made her want to cry. Not only were they beautiful, but they had been written about her, which made the song a thousand times more special.

A crowded night,
All the backs faced me,
I should have been stronger,
But it felt so good to be weak.

My fingers met yours,
Promises unfolded.
Grabbed you a star

So you could hold it.
And I won't forget,
Cause the night don't taste the same.
And nothingness is holding me,
And it feels so cold.
Please take me away.

Eva was in tears by the time the final chords had softly dripped away and she knew in that moment that she truly was in love. She hadn't even kissed Zac, but what he had just given her was so much more precious than anything she'd ever received. To know exactly how he felt and to hear it sung in that deep voice to such a wonderful tune gave her love a soundtrack.

Eva played the song over and over until she was interrupted by the arrival of her family. She threw her arms around her uncle. Don was over six feet tall and was wearing a smart pinstripe suit that made him appear every inch the typical businessman, but Eva knew that he was nothing like his slick exterior he presented. She was happy to see him, but it wasn't Don's presence that made her beam, but the look on her mother's face. Her eyes smiled again and sparkled in admiration of her younger brother, making her once again look like the woman Eva hadn't seen in so long and had sorely missed.

Her mum had prepared a roast and the four of them sat around the kitchen table, a buzz of conversation steadily flowing through the room. Don spoke about his life in Cork – his apartment, his job and most of all, his girlfriend.

'Pity she was away last time you guys came down. We've been together over a year now. I'll bring her up soon, it just didn't seem appropriate last time I was here and, well, I haven't been the most frequent visitor,' he grinned sheepishly. They all smiled but Don continued, obviously ashamed that he hadn't been around more. 'Guys, I really am sorry. I kept making excuses about how busy work is, or how you all had enough on your plate, but I know now that I was stupid. My brother-in-law dies and I just turn my back? That's not how our mother brought me up to be.' He threw a little wink at Eva's mum and continued with what he was saying. 'But I'm here now. And I promise I will do everything I can for you guys. You all mean the world to me.'

Eva and Sarah left the two adults to talk for the night, and as her sister headed off to do some study, Eva stepped out into the evening air and she felt a skip in her step as she got closer to her favourite boy. The song had been so him. Listening to every chord was just like having Zac beside her and she knew that it had been the best Valentine's present in the world.

She called to his house and they decided to go for a walk. As they ambled through the dusky light, she felt a gentle hand on hers and as it hung there for a moment before their fingers intertwined, she thought of the song and was on a cloud of happiness.

'Zac, thanks so much for the CD. It was amazing,' she said, trying not to blush.

'I'm glad you liked it. Thanks for the card,' he smiled down at her.

Eva was embarrassed at the thought of the stupid Valentine greeting she'd written to Zac in comparison to what he'd said to her in the song. They strolled hand in hand through Blackrock Park and the night sky became dappled with stars. Eva felt good. She knew her mother was at home being looked after by Don, and here Eva was with someone who would look after her too. Zac led her down to the lake where they watched the ducks move silently through the water, which reflected the moon like a pool of rippling light. A soft breeze blew and the only sound was the faint hum of cars on a nearby road. Time stood still, and Zac's song still played in Eva's ear. She turned and looked at him, though he was still gazing at the trembling water. His dark hair and eyes made him seem mysterious, but Eva knew every inch of him, and loved each inch individually.

He turned to her and stared at her until Eva felt her heart stop. Her breathing stopped too as she stood rooted to the spot. As his head leaned into hers and she closed her eyes to the world, she was in heaven. His lips met hers and electricity ran through Eva so that her whole being sparkled. She leaned into him and he held her so close she could feel his heart thumping in his chest. It lasted only a minute, but Eva knew she would never have a minute of such pure pleasure again in her life. And as they strolled homewards, their hands still tightly intertwined, Eva could have sworn a shooting star passed overhead, letting her know her father was up there, watching his little girl fall in love.

24

Zac

The following Wednesday, the nervous buzz that filled the corridors was both exciting and scary. The girls on the hockey team all wore their kit and whenever he passed one of them, Zac made sure to give them a smile. They all smiled in return but were clearly shaking inside at the prospect of the game that afternoon. The team left at break time to spend some time together before the match. After school, Zac, Cian and Killian walked up to the shop as they had an hour to kill before the bus left for Marley. Zac wasn't happy that Killian was there but, as he'd just tagged along, Zac just spoke to Cian all the way there. However, strolling back to the school with a chicken roll each, the conversation suddenly turned to Eva, and Zac was surprised that the way Killian was talking about her actually made him quite awkward.

'So, Zac, what's the story with you and Eva then?'

He gave a little laugh in the vague hope that he could change the subject so that Cian wouldn't realise what had been said, but his friend had ears that were wired for gossip like this and was quick to establish what was going on.

'Eh Zac, what's this?'

Zac was just about to say 'nothing' when Killian dropped a bombshell that Zac had been hoping to keep quiet for a while longer.

'Has no one else noticed what Zac and Eva have been like around each other recently? It's blatantly obvious she wants to get stuck in and I was just wondering if Zac had taken the plunge yet.' Killian tried to sound casual, but Zac noticed a slight nervousness to his voice. He also wondered how Killian had noticed what was going on.

'So, how's that going, then? And why didn't you mention any of this to the rest of us?' Cian seemed a little hurt, but was still keen to know the details. Zac realised that he was going to have to share at least some of the truth.

'I told her I liked her. Luckily she said she liked me too, so that's cool,' he muttered.

'So have you scored her yet?' Cian moved to the important stuff straight away. Zac hoped that his little smile would be answer enough for his friend.

Cian gave Zac a high-five and laughed loudly, saying that he knew there had been something going on. Killian, on the other hand, went quiet and Zac wondered what the story was there. He figured that Killian thought Eva was strictly reserved for a handsome rugby jock who could show her off to all his friends and wear matching Dubes with. But Zac knew that Killian was sorely mistaken and there was so much more to Eva than he would ever know.

The atmosphere in Marley was thick with screams and chants half an hour before the game even started. Zac settled himself on the sideline beside Graham and Frank and had been instructed to tie a school flag around him and to shout extra loud.

'In Dublin's fair city, where the girls are so pretty, I first laid my eyes on sweet Molly Malone…' they sang.

The sideline increased in volume by the second and, as far as cheering went, Zac and his friends certainly had the edge. The opposition was from an all girls' school, which meant the majority of their supporters were girls, and therefore their cries were easily overpowered by those of the mixed posse on the other side. The whistle sounded to start the game and from start to finish the real competition was between the supporters. On the pitch it seemed the mixed school were teaching their all-girl counterparts a thing or two about hockey. Zac kept his eyes on Eva for the entire game and she was playing a blinder. She secured the team's third goal with a half an hour still left on the clock and also set up the fifth and final score of the match.

They won! But they didn't just win, they thrashed their opponents – 5–0 was a score to be proud of and the whistle blew to signify that the match, and the whole league, was over. Instantly Zac, his friends and the rest of the school flooded onto the pitch. Cheers and clapping and shouts of pure delight issued from everywhere and Zac had to admit he was forced to spare a thought for the other team as he watched the players collapse into friends' arms, tears streaming down their tired faces. But he knew that there was no way the other players could ever believe they deserved to win it after the five goals they conceded.

Zac could see Eva, but every time he made to go up to her, she was grabbed by yet another adoring student, telling her how well she'd played and issuing congratulations. The team headed to receive their medals and when the winning captain made a speech, every sentence was followed by an eruption of cheering from the proud fans. As she called out each member of the team in turn as they received their medal from a posh-looking official, Zac made sure to give an extra-loud shout for Lisa, Cathy and, of course, Eva.

It was just before he got on the bus with the lads that Zac saw Eva standing alone, looking around her. He walked towards her and, as soon as she spotted him, it was obvious she'd been looking for him. He threw his arms around her and she buried her head into his chest. He stayed with her a minute before someone shouted that the bus was leaving. He promised to ring her later and headed back to the lads, who boarded the bus full of very pleased students, all feeling patriotic towards their school after the spectacle of hockey they'd just witnessed.

*

Zac's father announced that, the following Friday, he was taking Zac's mother to Galway for the night. Zac wondered whether his father had suddenly found his romantic side after all these years. The story became clearer when he discovered that three other couples were going too and it was actually a golfing weekend. But either way, the fact that his dad was bringing his mum was significant, and more importantly, it also meant a chance for Zac to have a party!

Once half eight came on the night of the party, it seemed that everyone arrived at once. Jack Johnson was the CD of choice in the background. Zac had lit a few candles, and as the gang filed into the living room, he knew it was going to be a good night. Everyone was in great spirits as the thought of the midterm break sat comfortably in everyone's mind. Cathy especially was on a high and fidgeted even more than usual. Zac knew she was impatient for Johnny to arrive and hoped he was extra late just to tease her. He sat back in his sofa with a can of beer, Lisa to his left and Cian to his right, everyone engaged in their own conversations, while he watched them all and smiled. At nine o'clock, the doorbell rang and Cathy was finally put out of her misery. Zac answered the door to Johnny, Kev and four other guys from his old school who he'd stayed in touch with. They sauntered into the kitchen and were met with a few questioning looks. After they'd put their beer in the fridge and made for the sitting room, Zac introduced them all to his new friends and soon barriers between the two schools quickly melted away. He noted that Killian had arrived, and though he wasn't best pleased about this, he wasn't going to let it bother him in the slightest – he was there to have fun and nothing was going to affect that.

Zac spotted Cathy heading over to Johnny and enjoyed seeing her turn on her fantastic charm and woo Johnny there and then. She herself looked great in her denim skirt and black tank top, with her blonde hair curled round her face.

Zac chatted to his old friends, enjoying hearing how everyone was and what had happened since he left. It was nice to think of the old days, but he was also proud as he spoke about his new school and new friends. The guys were particularly impressed with Zac's posse of new female friends and Zac found them staring around quite a bit. They were slightly taken aback when Eva came and sat on Zac's lap and Zac made sure to give her a kiss on the lips just to show the guys how much fun a mixed school could be.

Midnight came and went and everyone had mellowed down and congregated in the living room, feeling relaxed and comfortable in the company of good friends. Zac was feeling completely chilled until the lovely girl on his lap decided to make him entertain his guests.

'Zac, why don't you go get your guitar?' Eva suggested.

She gave him a wink as she knew he never played for people, but the chorus of support her comment had received made it seem as if he had no other choice. He tried to back out but everyone was intent on a good singsong, and since Zac had never mentioned that he played guitar, all were keen to here him play.

Zac gave in and headed up to fetch the guitar. At first he was shy, but he realised that the more his fingers moved over the hard strings and plucked familiar tunes, the more people began to sing along and forget that he was the source of the music. He played old tunes and new ones, the classics like 'Brown Eyed Girl' and 'One' receiving the most enthusiasm, as there wasn't a person in the place who didn't know all the words. Killian kept shouting out for 'Wonderwall' and eventually Zac gave in, though Killian's rendition of it was completely tuneless as the shouted lyrics slurred into one another. Eventually people became impatient with him.

'Killian, you're shit. Shut the hell up, would you?' Cian shouted out, much to everyone's amusement, but Zac doubted that Cian expected the reaction he got. Killian's face turned red and he stared around the room of smiling faces with disgust. His words spilled clumsily out of his mouth and, even though he was drunk, there was no denying the malicious venom with which he spat out all he had to say.

'Look at you all… fuck…fucking puffs. "Oh Zac play another shit song on your guitar so we can all clooooose our eyes and look gay." The state of you! And as for you, Cian, why don't you just…just fuck off with your bum chum Graham and play some hockey. Faggots!'

Zac was not going to have this eejit ruin his party and tried to intervene. 'Killian, man, take it easy, will you?'

But Killian was having none of it. 'Bolox off, Zac. You and your poncey guitar, and your stupid poncey friends – yeah, that's right, Johnny, you're a cunt! Think you're so great because of the school you go to? You're all cunts. The party was shite, Zac, so you and Miss Tight Bitch can go on scoring. I don't care. I'm out of here.'

He grabbed his jacket and stumbled out of Zac's house, leaving the place completely stunned and disgusted. He was an absolute tosser. Silence hung in the air, but Cian quickly broke it and brought back the good atmosphere.

'What a fucker! Never liked him anyway. But enough of that, what about a bit of Coldplay, Zac?' he suggested casually.

'How about 'Yellow'?' Zac asked.

The party resumed, everyone relaxing back into the comfortable mood they'd enjoyed before Killian's outburst.

By three o'clock, people began to leave. By half past, only the small gang Zac had invited to stay over were left and he locked the front door, knowing he'd said his last goodbye of the evening. Lisa and Graham took the couch downstairs, Johnny and Cathy took the spare bed, Cian, Frank and Kev shared Zac's parents' bed, and Zac shared his bed with Eva. They were both tired, but there was always time for a quick cuddle. Kissing her and pressing her to him, Zac's hands ran all over Eva's body, feeling every inch of her. She too let her hands explore and Zac was wild with pleasure as they became more intimate than they'd ever been before.

Eventually, they wrapped their arms around one another and fell sound asleep. Zac couldn't remember the last time he'd slept so well and knew that he owed it entirely to the beautiful girl who lay at his side.

The next morning and for the rest of the day, everyone wandered around Zac's house like zombies, somewhere between consciousness and sleep. Sitting around his kitchen table, they all agreed the previous night had been a great success. Kev and Frank headed off to the shop and came back with a bag full of sausages, bacon and thick sliced bread while Cian declared he was the chef for the day and prepared the meanest fry they'd ever tasted. Zac munched on a rasher and wondered how even after such a late night, Eva could look so good. Her hair was tied in a messy ponytail and her pale pink pyjamas made her look utterly loveable. She and the girls helped tidy up the house but luckily it wasn't that messy. People had made sure not to wreck the place and for that Zac was grateful. The television commentators were building up for the day's Six Nations rugby matches but Zac had the volume switched off so that they could all enjoy the blare of Frank Sinatra that filled his house. Everyone sang out 'Come Fly with Me' and, as Cian attempted to swing dance with Cathy, Zac was thankful for his friends.

When his parents arrived home at half past six, they were both tired too but seemed to have had a nice time. Zac was glad for them. When they asked him what he had got up to he merely replied that he had rented out a DVD and taken it easy for the night. They accepted this without so much as a raised eyebrow and Zac was thrilled to know that his plan had been flawless and the whole event had truly been a night to remember.

If I woke up here right now,
The broken truth would rip me through,
But I would still remember and smile somehow.

25

Cathy

St Patrick's Day arrived which meant, the final of the Leinster Schools' Senior Rugby Cup, and Cathy was unbelievably proud of Johnny when his team won! Soon after the victory, a big group of them headed into town to celebrate. The club was hopping and the atmosphere was amazing. All Cathy's usual crowd went as well as guys from Johnny's year. He and the other lads who were on the Leinster team weren't drinking, as their coaches had forbidden it, but he was still in flying form, the cup victory still fresh in his mind. He and Cathy hit the dance floor and she was in convulsions as she watched her boyfriend's Usher impersonation crash and burn. As usual, there were plenty of girls staring her out of it and talking loudly about her.

'Is she going out with Johnny O'Brien?'

'Yeah, I think so. What is he thinking? I mean, do you know what school she's in?'

'Obviously. You can tell. I guess she is kind of pretty.'

'Yeah, but that's not the point. How does he know her if she goes to that mixed school?'

'I heard Johnny's best friend Zac moved there this year so I think they all hang out together. Did you not see her with him on Wednesday after they won the cup? She was all over him.'

'Oh shut up, let's just dance. We don't need those stupid boys.'

Cathy looked at Johnny having listened to the conversation between the girls. Their voices had just spat jealousy and as Cathy held her man even closer she realised how lucky she was to have him.

The last couple of hours were a bit of a blur in Cathy's mind and the last thing she could fully remember was Johnny deciding that since he wasn't drinking, she should have even more. He teamed up with Zac and both placed their girlfriends at the bar and plied them with shots until they begged for mercy. The four of them fell into a taxi and as Cathy and Eva stumbled into Eva's garden, leaving the guys to continue on to Zac's, Cathy was hit with yet another fit of the giggles. Eva couldn't find the right key and the more she got confused, the more Cathy found it the funniest thing in the world. Eva put her finger to her lips and told her friend not to make so much noise, but the more she tried to hold in her laughter, the more she felt it tickling her down in her toes and surging up through her body until she erupted with giggles. Eventually, Eva gave up trying to find her key and joined her friend sitting on her front lawn in hysterics. It had been such a great night and this was the perfect ending. Cathy stared at Eva and through the drunken hue she still knew that she was lucky to have such an amazing girl as a best mate and decided to tell Eva as much. Eva just laughed harder and told her friend she was drunk, but Cathy knew that, alcohol or not, Eva was the best friend she could have.

Cathy didn't actually remember getting into Eva's house but, when she woke up the next morning in her friend's bed, she knew they must have made it. Her head was pounding like a thousand bongos banging out some unfamiliar rhythm, and her mouth tasted putrid. Eva was still sound asleep beside her, snoring slightly, her clothes from the night before still stuck to her sleeping frame. But then, to make matters worse, Eva's phone rang. The polyphonic sound hurt both their heads and as Eva woke and answered it, Cathy knew instantly by the tone of voice that it was Zac. After a brief conversation, Eva hung up and announced that the lads wanted to go down to a café in Blackrock for a nice big breakfast roll, and they conceded it probably was a good idea to shake off their hangovers.

The two threw on their clothes, Eva didn't care what she looked like. Cathy, on the other hand, was a little more wary of Johnny seeing her with no make-up, and applied a little concealer to the bags under her eyes, followed by a thick coat of mascara and clear lip gloss. Eva dared not tell Cathy that despite her best efforts, she still looked wrecked. It was bright outside and the light stung Cathy's eyes as she limped along with Eva, their feet sore from the ridiculously high shoes they'd worn out the night before.

The lads were waiting at the entrance to Eva's estate and Cathy gave Johnny a quick kiss and took his hand as they headed down the road. The lads thought they were great as they slagged the girls about their hangovers. Even though Zac had been drinking, he hadn't come even close to the same level of giggling frenzy as the girls. Both boys talked in loud voices and kept tickling the girls until they were begged to stop and consider the state of their stomachs.

'Four breakfast rolls to go, please,' Johnny ordered. Even the thought of a sausage made Cathy's tummy turn but, when she was handed her roll, wrapped in greasy paper and smelling of wonderful fried food, she knew that somehow she would manage it. The two couples headed to the far side of Blackrock DART station to the beach and, taking off their shoes and socks, walked along the shore. It wasn't a popular beach, no long stretches of glorious sand, mostly pebbles and rocks, but the waves and sea air were enough for them that morning.

No one said very much as each concentrated on chewing their steaming rolls. Cathy found that she was in fact ravenous and once she'd finished her own she polished off the end of Eva's too. Gazing at the calm sea that rolled gently beneath the bright sky, she felt utterly content. She loved just laughing away with Johnny and realised that they were actually very alike. It was unusual for Cathy to find a guy that held the power in their relationship, as usually she had the guy chasing after her. But with Johnny, she found that he was the one wearing the trousers and she was the adoring girlfriend, which excited her and kept her guessing. On paper they certainly were an ideal couple – both good looking, popular, well dressed. She was on the team that won the Senior Hockey League and he was on the winning Senior Cup rugby team. They were perfect. Cathy smiled as she imagined what it would be like if they were in America. Johnny would be the quarterback on the football team, and she would be head cheerleader. It was such a cliché, but that was the thing that Cathy liked about her relationship with Johnny – it was textbook. Surely everyone looked at them and saw the classic prom king and queen couple, and it was this that Cathy had been looking for, for so long. Now that she had it, she vowed she was never going to lose it.

26

Zac

Before their relationship went any further, the time had come for Zac to meet Eva's mum and sister. She'd talked to his mum a good few times, but it was decided that the first Sunday of the Easter holidays, Zac was coming over for dinner. He was more nervous than he thought he would be. He felt ashamed admitting it, but he didn't know what Eva's mum would be like, what with all the stories he'd heard about her being in floods of tears and constantly upset. But, as she welcomed him into her home, Zac decided not to form any opinions just yet.

Sure enough, the night was a success. It felt good to be in some way accepted into the family. He felt a bit on trial as Eva's mum started a long series of questions about his old school, why he moved, what he wanted to do in college. But he answered as honestly as he could and relaxed into their company.

After dinner, he and Eva went to the sitting room. She had a glint in her eye which Zac knew by now meant she had some juicy gossip to share. She needed no invitation to begin.

'Oh my God, Zac, this is big. Promise you won't say anything? But I'm sure he'll tell you soon enough,' Eva said excitedly.

'Who?' he demanded.

'Shut up, would you, and listen! Cathy rang me this morning and we were just talking and stuff. And I asked her about how she and

Johnny were. So she was like "He came back from the rugby trip yesterday" and I was like "Did you see him?" So she tells me that her parents were out to dinner last night so she had him over and guess what.'

Zac shrugged his shoulders but he knew what was coming. He didn't want to burst Eva's bubble as her eyes glistened with excitement as she told him her fresh, top-secret gossip.

'They had sex,' she breathed.

'No way! I suppose I kind of saw that coming. That was her first time, wasn't it?' he remarked.

'Yeah, obviously. Was it not Johnny's?'

Zac paused and wondered whether to tell the truth or not. Maybe he'd told Cathy that she'd been his first, but in reality Zac knew she'd been at least the third or fourth notch on Johnny's bedpost. Of course, it meant a lot more than that, but Zac wasn't utterly convinced that having sex with someone was as sacred to Johnny as it was to Cathy. He knew he could tell Eva the truth anyway.

'No, it wasn't. Second or third, I think. But that doesn't matter. It's really good that they felt ready to do it. They obviously really like each other,' he admitted.

'That's the thing, though. They haven't said "I love you" yet.' Eva was troubled.

'But you don't have to to sleep together,' he pointed out.

'Yeah, but the thing is, Cathy loves him but she doesn't want to say it because she says she knows he won't say it back,' Eva confided.

Zac knew she was right. Johnny wasn't the 'I love you' type. Not that he doubted that Johnny really liked Cathy; he wouldn't be going out with her otherwise. But Johnny wasn't the kind of guy that went in for anything overly serious, and love wasn't something that would cross his mind for a long time. What was worse was that Johnny wouldn't realise what a big deal saying 'I love you' was to girls. And then a thought struck Zac that both surprised and appalled him. He hadn't told Eva he loved her. How had that happened? He'd felt it for so long, it just seemed to be a given between them. It was blatantly obvious they were in love, but here he was thinking to himself how important it was for girls to hear the actual words, and he hadn't officially told Eva how he felt. He opened his mouth to say it but realised it would be too forced. She'd think he was only saying it because they were talking about Cathy and Johnny. It wasn't right, and Zac wanted it to be right.

But he was nervous. Not only was it going to be hard to say it, but what if she didn't say it back? She hadn't told him she loved him after all this time, so maybe she didn't. What if he said it and she looked at him and smiled and then turned away? And then he'd know that his words hadn't made things better, but had created an awkwardness that up until then they hadn't had.

He deliberated with these thoughts for a few days but eventually decided he had to do it. The next time they were alone, walking as usual through the park at night, Zac knew the time had come. He stopped walking and pulled her to him. She stared at him, bewildered. Zac stared into those wonderful eyes and knew in an instant that it was going to be all right. Why was he so scared? He was only telling her something he'd known and felt for so long. With a sigh of relief, he poured out the speech he'd been composing all evening. 'Eva, I've got something I want to say. And it's weird because it's something I've felt for a very long time, but it never occurred to me how much better it would be if I actually said it.'

Eva stared at him, a blank expression still on her face.

'Eva, I've never felt this way about anyone in my entire life. You're so special to me and you're the most incredible person I know. Look, what I'm trying to say is… I love you.' Zac swore that the words oozed from his lips in slow motion and boomed through the silent streets. Eva looked at him, and for an awful second he thought he saw doubt in her eyes. But another emotion filled her and Zac recognised it as happiness. She opened her soft mouth and Zac's world stopped as she replied.

'Zac, I love you too.'

He kissed her and she kissed him and as her body melted into his he knew what love was. It raced over every inch of him until he was tingling with pleasure. Nothing else mattered. The world was only there for them, and for as long as Eva was at his side, Zac knew that he would never be sad again for she was his first love, and he hers.

Echoes sweet and hope pronounced,
Remember this, remember me,
When darkness falls into the sea, once more.

27

Eva

Eva felt like a child again. She wanted to take off her shoes and run through the streets shouting 'Zac O'Dwyer is in love with me' at the top of her voice, but sense got the better of her.

The first person she told was Cathy. She'd phoned her up and told her to meet her in O'Brien's Sandwich Bar in Stillorgan half an hour later for a BLT and a good chat. Eva walked up, her iPod blaring out happy songs while she smiled at everyone she passed.

'Hey, baby. You're looking great,' Cathy exclaimed, kissing Eva and heading to the counter to make her order. Eva was fit to burst, but waited patiently. It wasn't until they were both sitting down, sandwiches and tea ready to be devoured, that the topic of the day was finally addressed.

'So why exactly did you drag me up here? It's lovely to see you, but I feel like wrecked, so this better be good,' Cathy announced. Eva had to admit that Cathy did look a little off colour, but she was too excited to feel guilty about hauling her up for this chat.

'He said it, Cathy,' Eva blurted, unable to contain herself any longer.

'Whoa there, who said what?'

'Zac. Last night. He said it – he said "I love you",' Eva whispered the last words, not wanting to taint their perfection.

Cathy didn't even bother to swallow the fresh bite she'd just taken, but rather screeched through a mouthful of bacon and bread, 'Oh my

God, Eva, no way! That's so exciting! No wonder you're glowing.' Cathy's reaction was just what Eva had been hoping for and she lapped it up.

'Oh my God, It was the best feeling in the world.'

'That's so cool. I mean, you're both obviously crazy about each other. I presume you said it back?' she asked plainly.

'Of course. I mean, it's true – I do love him!'

Cathy squealed with delight and for the rest of the chat both girls were an abundance of energy and excitement.

'So does this change anything? I mean, wow. This is serious. You guys are serious. How do you feel?' Cathy wanted details.

'Honestly?' Eva asked.

'Honestly. Come on, spill.'

'It feels amazing. I didn't realise three little words could change so much, but they do. I thought I'd felt it all along; I've loved him for a while now. But no – this feeling is a thousand times better than anything. This is it!' Eva couldn't stop the words from pouring out of her.

'I actually can't remember the last time I saw you like this. I'm so happy for you, pet,' Cathy said sincerely.

It made Eva think. Here she was, her mother struggling to cope after a breakdown, her father dead, her emotions all over the place – yet this aura of joy was following her around and she knew that no matter what life had in store for her, she'd be okay. She hadn't felt this way in so long. It felt good.

On the way back from Stillorgan, she decided to text Zac, just to let him know he was on her mind.

HEY U. JUST TXTN 2 SAY IM TINKIN OF U, AS USUAL! LOVE U. XX

Eva smiled, turned up her iPod and practically skipped home. She really was smitten. Only seconds later her phone vibrated with a reply.

LOVE U 2 EVA. ALWAYS

Eva's heart tumbled inside her. Love was the best feeling in the world and she never wanted it to slip away.

28

Zac

Those three words didn't lose their novelty and, even weeks on, saying goodbye after a night in the pub with the gang, Eva's words still sent vibrations through Zac.

'I love you.'

'I love you too,' he echoed, watching until she was safely inside her house.

Zac headed home, his head musky with beer and romance. But when he opened his front door he knew that something was wrong. The light in the kitchen was on and he could hear a faint noise coming from another room. His parents had been at a dinner somewhere, so maybe they'd only just got home. But he knew that his father hadn't been in very good form heading out, so a late night on their part was doubtful. Zac's mind was cloudy as he pushed open the door of the sitting room. The light was out and the only source of illumination came from the window, where the streetlight tried to make the shadows clearer. He spotted something small and shaking in the corner of the room and knew at once that it was the source of the noise. He turned on the light, not knowing what to expect, and wished he'd been prepared for the sight that met him.

His mother lay huddled on the floor, clasping her knees to her, sobbing silently. Her face was a blur of make-up and blood which ran from a series of cuts on her forehead. Her cheek was swollen and turning a shade of sky blue. Her clothes were ruffled and there was a tear in her jumper. Zac couldn't speak. His whole world stopped as he gazed at the wretched sight of his mother.

'Mum, what happened?' he croaked.

But she wasn't going to talk. She just sobbed and shook, struck with terror at whatever had happened. Zac's mind raced as he tried to figure out why his mother was like this and who was responsible. But a tiny bit of him already knew the answer and all he needed was confirmation before he stormed upstairs to confront his father.

'Did he do this to you?' he asked angrily.

Zac's mother shook and more and tears mixed with blood to form red rivers down her harrowed face.

'Mum, answer me, did he do this to you?' He shouted the words again and again until finally the sobbing stopped and the shaking stopped and a small voice came from the broken figure.

'Yes. But don't bother…'

It was too late. Zac boiled with anger as he headed to his parents' bedroom. He wrenched open the door and stared at where he expected his father to be. But he wasn't there. Zac searched the room, then checked the other bedrooms. Nothing. He was fuming. Back downstairs, he demanded that his mother tell him where his father was. He regretted being so angry with her, but he couldn't help it. His mother begged him to sit down.

'Zac, he's gone. I don't know where. But I can guarantee you it's somewhere with alcohol and we won't be seeing him again tonight.'

Zac couldn't accept that. He couldn't accept that someone would just destroy someone else like this and then disappear into the night and leave them wailing, alone, wet with blood and tears. His mother stared at him with the saddest eyes Zac had ever seen. It helped him to pause and realise that there was more to do. He sighed. This was no use. He needed to calm down before he upset his mother even more. He made her a cup of tea and fetched the first aid kit. Between sipping the hot, sweet liquid and allowing Zac to tend to her cuts, she told Zac the whole sorry tale, pausing every now and then to try to come to terms with what had happened.

'As you probably noticed, your father wasn't in a very good mood today, and I suppose he figured the best thing to do was to drown his sorrows at the dinner tonight. I guess he just had one too many,' she murmured.

'Mum, don't even think about making excuses for him,' Zac exploded.

'I'm not. Trust me, not this time. Well, once we got back here he was still in the mood for some more wine, and I suppose I had a good few glasses on me as well. Foolishly I thought that this would be the perfect time to talk to him about something...something I've been considering for a while.' Zac's mother took a deep breath before continuing. 'I told him that I wanted to see a marriage counsellor. To sort out our problems, you know?'

Zac stared at his mum. He hadn't being expecting that. She sensed his surprise and explained her reasoning. 'Oh, Zac. I know it's hard for you to understand, but as much as I hate your father at times, I love him too. I can't help it, you can't control these things. But I'm so unhappy right now that I thought counselling might be a way of bringing us all together as a family again. A fresh start, since your father's temper had been better these past few months. But what I failed to see was that in reality, his rage was just building up until he had an excuse to vent it. And I gave him that excuse,' she said sadly.

'But why would he use you wanting to patch things up as an excuse to hit you?' he asked her, perplexed. He willed his head to stop conjuring up images of his father hitting his mother, but he couldn't. His father's face, red and raging, and hitting his mother over and over again, pounding and crushing her timid frame. Zac began to cry.

'I don't know why, Zac. I've given up trying to figure out what goes on inside that man's head. He just kept shouting and hitting me.

Saying that there was nothing wrong with our marriage, that I was just being selfish and I was a terrible mother and a waste of space,' she poured out.

Zac was feeling a myriad of emotions – pity, hatred, fear, anxiety, all mixed together to form a cocktail of despair. Suddenly the future seemed like the scariest thing in the world.

He spent the next hour nursing his mother, stopping the blood, trying to stop the pain. But he realised how tainted life was. His mother had calmed down, but in the soft light he could still see her sobbing beneath her frozen exterior. His mind raced with questions.

'What will you do, Mum? Are you going to report him to the police? He'll be arrested, you know. I'm sure—'

'No, Zac. No. It was a once-off,' she protested.

'But Mum, you can't let him away—'

'I know, Zac. And I won't. Once was enough and, trust me, I will never look at that man again. We'll sort out something. I'm sorry to put you through this.'

'Mum, please just ring the police. He can't get away with this. You mustn't let him.' Zac's voice was broken and choked with pain. His whole body throbbed at the thought of his father getting on with his life as if nothing had happened. It was sick.

'Let's not talk about it now, dear. I know what I have to do, all right? I'll think about it properly in the morning, look into getting a barring order or whatever. But it's late, Zac, and I'm exhausted.'

Zac gave up. She'd had enough. They could talk in the morning. She hugged him and told him it would all be okay before slipping up to bed. Zac sat there in the silence as his mind raced with questions. How could he have let his father do this? While he was down in the pub laughing with his friends, she was lying on the ground, begging her husband to stop. Zac willed it all to go away, but it wouldn't. Her blood was pouring down her battered face and all the while Zac had been sitting in the pub, chuckling about how life was good.

It was all too much for him to take in, and as Zac felt his eyes grow heavy as he lay back on the sofa, he thought of how just a few hours ago he had believed that life was simple, that loving Eva would take care of everything. But not this. This was something that even love couldn't override and, though Zac tried to think of Eva and her eyes, and how he felt when she kissed him, he knew that things would never be the same. His life had been snapped in two and his heart was bleeding. It was agony, and Zac wanted it all to end. He didn't want to say goodbye to Eva, but life seemed as if it would never be right again. Not even close. Love had been good, but it wasn't enough. Not any more.

Her eyes may stare but mine will cry.
Pray that I won't forget the times
When life was better, golden like the truth.

29

Eva

Every day Eva looked into Zac's eyes and didn't recognise the person she saw. April arrived and passed, and still there was no longer the sparkle of amazing tenderness or brimming personality, just a grey void of pain, and it hurt to even look at him. Zac had talked about it a little, but Eva knew that he was keeping a lot inside him. There was no way she could push him – he was so brittle, and it scared her.

Eva had wanted him to come over to hers on Friday night to watch a DVD or something but, as he had every day that week, Zac just wanted to head straight home and stay there. It seemed he wasn't going to leave his mother alone in the house any more.

Although being alone sounded like a very good idea, Cathy insisted that Eva come to her house on Saturday night. Lisa was going too and the three of them were apparently going to have a much-needed girly night so that they could catch up. The chat was light and Eva felt herself begin to remember what it was like when she had her two best friends and nothing else mattered. How things had changed. They danced and laughed and ate and laughed some more. All three were tired but in flying form and their personalities clicked as they had always done. But for the first time, Eva felt slightly separated from the other two – life seemed so simple to them. All she had been through and seen over the past while had changed her so much that she felt quite different.

Cathy settled down to a nitty-gritty gossip session and shared her big news with Lisa. Eva, of course, already knew that Cathy and Johnny had had sex, but in fairness had been very surprised when she found out. She expected a similar reaction from Lisa, but her response wasn't what she'd predicted at all.

'Me too! Oh my God, I'm so glad I'm not the only one. I thought you guys were going to think I was such a slut. Yeah, Graham and I did it a while ago. Nothing special, is it? But it's cool to be able to say you've done it,' she giggled.

Cathy agreed. 'Yeah, I know. Because remember virginity was like such a big deal? It's such a relief to have it out of the way. And I know it's not that good the first time, but trust me, the more you do it, the better it gets,' she enthused.

The conversation continued, the two girls comparing things Eva would have rather not heard about – about their first times, if it hurt, how many times they'd done it, all the juicy details. Eva sat there feeling totally out of place. Eventually Lisa turned to her.

'Eva, how come you and Zac haven't done it yet?' she demanded.

'I guess we're just not ready. We've talked about it, but we're happy with how things are at the moment. Plus we've both got a lot of stuff going on at home, so it's not really on our list of priorities,' she said quietly.

'You don't want to get stuck in a rut, know what I mean? That's for old people – you want to have a bit of fun,' Lisa urged.

Eva started to get mad. 'Lisa, you have no idea about me and Zac. We don't need to have sex to enjoy being with each other. That's not what it's about.'

'Surely you must be bored?' Lisa's voice had a nasty streak that Eva didn't appreciate. 'Boring isn't fun. I know both of you are steady kind of people, but too much steadiness in a relationship is just a recipe for boredom,' Lisa scoffed.

'My relationship with Zac isn't boring – it's the most amazing thing in the world,' Eva retorted.

Lisa wasn't going to let her win. 'It can't be amazing without sex. Anyway, it must be bad if you're making stupid excuses for not doing it.'

'What do you mean?' Eva felt her blood begin to bubble. Lisa may have been her friend, but she was pushing her now.

'Well, I mean, saying he has stuff going on at home. Give me a break!' Lisa sneered.

That was it. Eva wasn't going to put up with any more. 'For your information, Lisa, Zac is having a shit time at home. Not that I have to prove anything to you, but since you're being such a bitch I don't think you'll mind hearing that his dad beat the crap out of his mum a while ago and Zac came home and found her. She was a nervous wreck, her face was in bits and he was scared. Zac's mum got a restraining order against his dad, whose fecked off somewhere. Meanwhile, Zac is trying to persuade his mum to bring him to court, but she's too upset to think about it at the moment, seeing as how she's still covered in scars from her husband's fists. So believe it or not, Zac's mind isn't really too wrapped up in getting me into bed for the moment.'

Eva spat out every angry word and was glad to see the colour drain from her friends' faces. She was disappointed at having had to tell them so much detail to make them see her point, but at least now they'd realise that there was more going on in people's lives.

Silence lay awkwardly on the three girls until Cathy said, 'Listen, Eva, we'd no idea. Poor Zac, he must be in bits.'

'Yeah, Eva, I didn't know. I shouldn't have said those things. None of it matters compared to that.' Lisa seemed to finally get it, but this was little comfort to Eva. She was already crying and, as the two girls put their arms around her, she found that she was letting out tears that had been bottled up for weeks, and now that they were free, they flowed without end.

'It's just I miss Zac. Usually he'd be the one I'd talk to when I had a problem, but he *is* the problem, so I can't go to him. He's just not there any more. Since the whole thing he's completely changed. Not that I blame him. What he's dealing with is mind blowing, but I miss him so much. And I need him too. It's almost my dad's first anniversary, and Mum's not getting any more cheerful, and it just seems like I've no one left,' Eva sobbed into Cathy's chest. It felt good to let go and forget about trying to be strong. She let it all rush out of her.

'Eva, you have us, you know that,' Cathy assured her.

'Yeah, we're sorry if we haven't been there for you, but we are now, so you don't have to feel alone for one more minute,' Lisa added.

Eva looked up at them and was somewhat comforted by the knowledge that they weren't going anywhere.

*

A few nights later, Zac rang Eva for the first time in what seemed like ages. Even in school he'd been distant and Eva was delighted to hear his voice.

'I miss you so much, Eva. I've piles of homework tonight, but tomorrow after school, can we hang out?' he asked.

'I'd love to. But I'm not coming into school tomorrow.'

'How come?'

'I'm going to mass.'

'What?'

Eva took a deep breath. She didn't want him to think she was trying to compete with him when it came to problems, or trying to steal his thunder. But there was no denying what was going on in her life too, so she told him.

'It's my dad's one year anniversary tomorrow, so we're having a special mass for him and then going out for lunch.'

Eva waited as silence lingered at the end of the line. Finally Zac spoke quietly. 'I can't believe I forgot. What an asshole I am. Jesus,

Eva, I'm so sorry. Of course it's his anniversary. I wouldn't mind but I know the date and all. I've just been too wrapped up in... I'm so sorry.'

'It's okay,' Eva assured him.

'No, it's not. There you were, apologising for being ignorant when dickhead here completely forgets about everyone else. I'm so sorry.'

Eva told him not to worry, she was glad that he had phoned and that they had talked about what was happening.

*

The next day Eva found herself still quiet with pain as they left the church. The priest had said such wonderful things about her father, and the more she thought about it, the more Eva couldn't believe it had been a year since she'd last seen him. It felt longer. Like a lifetime. So much had happened since then and she hated to think that everything that had taken place in the last twelve months had been without him.

After talking to family and friends in the pub afterwards, Eva's mother told her daughters that she had a table booked for the three of them in Roly's in Ballsbridge. The girls happily escaped the babbling hum of people and, as they tucked into a tasty meal, Eva noticed a look in her mother's eyes that worried her. Was her mum going to cry? She hadn't at the service, so maybe she'd held it all back until now. Sarah looked up from her plate of pasta and noticed the same grey veil on her mother's face. Eva waited for someone to speak, but no one did.

'Mum, are you all right?' Eva asked anxiously.

'No. No, I'm not,' her mother responded.

'What's wrong?' Sarah's voice was panicked.

Eva's mother opened her mouth to speak and Eva braced herself for what was to come, though what was said was a thousand times worse than any crying fit, and infinitely more unexpected.

'Girls, I've something I've wanted to tell you for a while. I just wanted to wait until things were all finalised and I'm afraid you're not going to like what you hear. But just let me finish before you start interrupting, because it's hard enough for me to say it as it is.'

Eva and Sarah looked at one another and sensed that something was really up. The tone of their mother's voice was unfamiliar and seemed to be prophesying bad things. Eva's mum looked from daughter to daughter.

'As you know, I've been having a hard time of things recently. Not that I don't doubt you two have too, but I've been doing a lot of thinking and I realised things have to change. Every moment of the day, the only thing I can think about is your father. Whether I'm alone in the house, or out with friends, I can't escape his memory. Not that I want to, but it's so hard, girls, living every moment of your life knowing it's not reality.'

Eva's mum took a sip of her wine and Eva noticed her hand shaking as she placed the glass back on the table.

'So I've been talking to people. Mainly Helen, our therapist, and your uncle Don. And although we've agreed that it's my problem, there are ways I could help make it even just a bit better. I need to escape! Escape from the place in my life when your father was here, and find a new place of my own. Life has to move on.' She paused. 'So I've decided to move. Well, I've decided we all should move. The house, the area – it's doing us no good living in the same four walls we shared with your father. I can't bear it any more. I see him and I hear him and I want him back so much. I know you girls lost your father, but he was everything to me. I loved him so much and gave my all to him and now he's gone. I have to go, girls. *We* have to go. Of course there's the question of where we go. The further the better, I say! And then Don had a suggestion, and for the first time in so long, something felt right. It just clicked and I knew that everything would be all right again.'

Eva could hear the faint rumble of her world as it prepared to fall down all around her.

'Girls, we're going down to Cork. Permanently. To your uncle Don. I've been looking at property and Don has been organising things. He's put your names down for schools and he says there are some really nice ones in his area. I know it's going to be a big move, but I really need this. You know how close I am to my brother and I really do believe that being with him and getting away from all this will help me with things. What do you think?'

A thick blanket of shocked hurt fell upon Eva and she found it hard to breathe. She wanted to shout and scream and tell her mum that there was no way she was moving. The scale of it was too vast to even register with her, but all she knew was that it was terrible, impossible. She opened her mouth to speak but found that even looking at her mother made her want to erupt with rage. She looked at Sarah and shook her head, stood up, grabbed her coat and bag and headed out of the restaurant. As she raced out the door in despair, she could have sworn she heard her sister asking whether she should go after her, but her mother just replied, 'Leave her, Sarah. Just let her go.'

30

Sarah

'Eva, please just sit down,' Sarah urged her sister.

'Sit down? How the fuck can I sit down?' Eva shouted, and Sarah conceded she was probably right. She herself was numb and, although she wasn't ranting and raving and pacing the room like Eva, she was just as upset. How could this be happening? They'd spent an entire year trying to get their lives back on track, back to some sort of normality, only to be told that just as things were picking up, it was all going to be taken from them and moved to the other side of the country.

'I mean, I know I sound selfish, I'm sure I do. But I know you don't want to move either. And that's two against one. So maybe she's the one being selfish. Oh for fuck's sake, I can't take this.' Eva was frustrated. Throwing herself down on the bed, Sarah watched her stare at the ceiling, hot tears swelling up in her eyes.

'I'm being horrible, I'm sorry. I just can't believe it,' Eva's voice wavered as she tried not to cry.

'I know, Eva. Don't apologise. We're in this together, remember?' Sarah soothed. She knew that a lot of the time she played the role of the older sister, but most of the time she didn't mind. 'We're just going to have to talk to her, try and persuade her not to move,' Sarah explained rationally.

'You know she won't change her mind. You heard her, she's talked to Don. It's all sorted,' Eva sighed.

'Don't think like that. Look, tomorrow, after school, we'll sit her down and just tell her plainly why this can't happen,' Sarah said.

'You're right. Thanks. Sorry,' Eva said before going to bed.

Lying under her duvet, Sarah realised that there really were two sides to this story. She could see why her mum wanted to leave; a fresh start, living near her brother in a place that didn't remind her every single minute of her husband. It did have its advantages. But then again, the girls had their lives here in Blackrock. Everything they knew and loved had always been in Dublin. Sarah didn't want to leave that – all her friends, her school. No. It wasn't going to happen. She hated the thought of fighting with her mum at a time like this, but she had to put her foot down. She knew exactly what would happen. Eva would panic and get upset, her mum would cry and beg, and as usual she would have to mediate. She rarely minded being the most level-headed of the three women but, ever since her father died, it was like she had been promoted to head of the house. The youngest of them all was now unofficially the one who was expected to look after everyone.

But what about her? Who was there to look after her? She'd never seen a therapist. She didn't have an amazing boyfriend to turn to. Her friends were all she had, and even then they didn't understand what she was going through, partly because she never let on. Now that she was expected to be strong, it was all she could be. Every day she wondered what it would be like to just give in and be minded for once. But she feared that if she did give in and fall, there would be anyone left to catch her.

Sarah tossed and turned, thinking, as she did most nights, about how she had to remain calm, for everyone's sake. But soon, unable to fight exhaustion, she fell asleep.

The following evening, the three women sat down to the most important discussion they'd ever had, each knowing the outcome would change their lives forever.

'Okay, Mum,' Sarah said, taking the lead as usual. 'Obviously the three of us need to talk. It's probably just best if you stay quiet and listen to what Eva and I have to say because we've been thinking a lot since yesterday and it's only fair that you hear our opinions.'

'That seems fair,' their mum agreed.

'Right, you go first then, Eva,' Sarah suggested and her sister launched into a speech which Sarah sensed had been much rehearsed.

'Basically all I want you to do, Mum, is look at things from our point of view. I get why you want to move. Of course I get it. But realistically, it's so much easier for you. Next year's my last year in school, all my friends are here, Zac's here. Sarah's friends are here too. We both adore our schools. I mean, basically what I – what *we* – need you to see is that our lives are here. It's been hard, but we've worked at regaining some sort of normality since Dad died, and for the first time I think it's working. It still hurts, but we're happy. Happier than we've been in ages. And the reason is because we got on with our lives. The lives we love. So please, Mum, I'm asking you, don't take that from us. Everything's changed so much already, don't make us adjust again,' Eva finished, with tears in her eyes. Sarah smiled at her, realising how hard it was for her sister to say all those things, but she'd said them well and Sarah hoped the girls were beginning to convince their mother why they couldn't go. Their mum showed very little expression and Sarah couldn't tell how she was reacting. Her mum took a sip of water and placed the glass slowly back on the table, as if taking her time to let things sink in.

'Okay, me next,' Sarah piped up, anticipating the good response her idea would surely receive.

'Right, well, I agree with everything Eva said. I'd hate to leave. I know I've longer left in school than her, but this is my home. But then obviously I was thinking about your reasons for wanting to move, Mum. And they make sense. So it seems a shame that anyone has to lose out. Why can't we all be happy? We deserve a bit of happiness after all we've been through, don't you think? So I came up with a plan. I thought that maybe Mum could go, like she wants to, but Eva and I could stay here.'

Sarah heard a sharp intake of breath from her mother, so she continued hurriedly to explain her plan in full.

'I could stay with Megan, Eva could stay with Cathy. At the weekends we could go down to Cork. Then, Mum, you could visit us every few weeks. The train fare is so cheap, if you didn't feel like driving. And then maybe after a year or so, you'll realise, Mum, that Cork was good for you, but you're ready to come back home. You could just rent the house while you're gone. Basically, what I'm trying to say is that none of us need to sacrifice what we want. It can work,' Sarah finished brightly, waiting for a cheer or a clap or something to congratulate her for the speech, which she felt had gone extremely well. She waited in vain.

'It's my turn now, yes?' her mum asked weakly. Sarah nodded and braced herself for what was to come.

'Right. Well, firstly, I want you to know that I love you both so much, you know that. And everything you guys just said makes perfect sense. How do I know that? Because I've been wrestling with the same thoughts for ages now. Despite what you think, this wasn't just some rash decision. I've gone through it a thousand times in my head, weighing up the pros and cons, looking at it from my perspective, Eva's perspective, Sarah's perspective. I'm not trying to ignore what you two want. That's the last thing I was aiming for. But for the first time in so long, I need to be just a little selfish. For my own sanity. Can't you see that? I don't want to wreck your lives. I don't want you girls to hate me. I couldn't bear that. But I need to go. I have to go.' She began to cry.

'We know that, Mum. We get that. But what Sarah was saying is right – we can all win,' Eva tried, on the verge of tears herself.

'No. I'm sorry, but no. How am I winning when I have to leave behind the two people I love more than anything? How could I move to Cork and have no one? Sure, Don would be around. But I've already lost your father, girls. Don't make me lose you too. I don't think I could face it. You're all I've got.' Their mum broke down, her face streaming with desperate tears.

Sarah looked at Eva. She was pale and her silent tears flowed slowly down her face. That was it. Both girls knew it. How could they bring themselves to abandon their mum? She needed them. She'd been through enough. Losing her husband had nearly destroyed her; the last thing she needed was to lose her daughters too. They couldn't do that to her. They'd have to sacrifice so much, but didn't they owe her that? She'd looked after them all their lives, and now that she needed them, they couldn't turn their backs. Their consciences had defeated them and as the sisters looked into each other's eyes, they knew they were moving to Cork, and that was that.

31

Zac

Eva rang him on Wednesday night in floods of tears. He knew she must be feeling down what with the anniversary mass the day before, and she cried and cried. But when she didn't stop he wondered if there was more to it than he knew. And then she told him. Just like that. Nothing could have prepared him for what she had to say.

'But Eva, no! You can't go, you just can't. Have you tried talking to her? What about school? You can't just leave. Eva, I need you. You just can't.' Zac couldn't even put together a sentence without it being interrupted with yet another reason why it was simply impossible for Eva to move.

'I mean, you've got your exams next year… oh, fuck school, what about your friends? It's such a hard time for you and she wants to just take you away from the only things keeping you going? Sorry, I know she's your mum, but this is fucking ridiculous.' Zac's anger began to build. He just couldn't get his head around why her mum would be so selfish.

'Did you say no? Come on, you must have told her you weren't going, put up some kind of fight?' Zac asked.

'Of course I did. We had a family meeting earlier and talked it all through, but it's final, Zac. We're going,' Eva said softly.

Zac put down the phone and wondered how he was still standing. He felt as if he was going to collapse. And why wouldn't he? Through all the sadness of the past few weeks, he'd been held up by the knowledge that Eva was his and she loved him. But now that was going too. He couldn't even bring himself to consider how much that would hurt. It couldn't happen, it just couldn't.

The next day, the minute he saw her walking through the corridor, he knew he had to talk to her. He grabbed her and took her into a corner.

'We need to talk,' he demanded.

'I'm on my way to Maths. I'll find you at lunch,' she replied.

'No, I have to speak with you now. Eva, it's killing me,' he pleaded.

'Where do you want to go?'

'Out of here. School, I mean. Down to the park or something. If we go now no one will notice. Eva, I can't last another class without knowing at least a little more than I do. Please?' he begged.

'Let's go.' Eva grabbed his hand and they headed out a side door. By walking round the back of the school grounds and out a back gate, Eva and Zac were free to the world.

They walked in silence until they reached a nearby park and sat down on an old bench. Zac looked at her but realised it was too painful, knowing that all too soon he wouldn't be able to see her.

'Eva, this is crazy. Why is your mum being like this? I mean, I know she's really messed up at the moment, but does she not see what this is going to mean for you and Sarah?' he burst out.

'Of course she does and, trust me, she feels terrible. But she's convinced that this is the only choice left for her and, to be honest, I can kind of see where she's coming from,' Eva said wearily.

'What?' He couldn't believe his ears.

'Well, come on – what else is left for her here? She needs a fresh start and I actually think it will do her some good.'

'But why all of you? Why can't she just move and leave you guys here with friends or in boarding school or something? Just let you finish school and then see where she's at?' he exploded.

'But Zac, I can't just let her go to Cork alone. Don't you see? She needs me and Sarah,' Eva said flatly.

'But I need you too.' Zac stared into her eyes and Eva's face held a look of pain that made him turn away. It seemed as if her mind was made up.

'Zac, I need you too. And I love you. But there's nothing I can do,' she whispered. 'I don't want to leave you – you've got to know that – but I would have thought that you of all people would understand. She's my mum. Sarah and I are all she's got. Imagine your mum was moving away. Would you stay behind and let her off on her own? After all that's happened to her? No. I have to do this for her, Zac. She's already lost a husband, there's no way I'm going to abandon her too.'

Zac knew she was right. He also realised how similar their situations were and hated admitting that if it was his own mum heading for somewhere new, he wouldn't be able to bring himself to let her go alone. But the thought of Eva leaving was still too terrible to even contemplate.

'How long?' he asked, his voice a monotone.

'What do you mean?'

'How long until you leave? Properly, like.'

'Mum said July. Then at least we'll have August to sort ourselves out before going to our new school,' she said sadly. 'Zac, it's only Cork. I'm clearly going to get the train back up here every weekend.'

'Do you mean that?' Zac wondered, but Eva was adamant.

'Yes, of course! I don't want to go, but I have to. But nothing's going to change, not really.'

'Will we be okay?' he asked tentatively.

'I'm not letting go if you aren't?'

'Of course I'm not. Forever, remember?' he reminded her hopefully.

'Forever,' she reiterated.

Zac took a deep breath and knew that although he felt angry, he couldn't stay that way. If all he had was less than three months, there was no way he was going to waste a second on being in a bad mood with Eva. Their time was sacred now and he intended to savour every moment.

*

On Sunday, Zac and Eva had planned to spend the day together. They had a vague idea where they were going and when she arrived at his house they headed off. They got a bus they wouldn't have normally taken and when they ended up quite a distance from home, somewhere in Wicklow, the adventure had begun. In reality, all they did for the afternoon was walk. They were in a large forest and covered a great deal of ground for the time they were there. But it was so much more than a walk. It was a chance for the two of them to be alone, together, away from everyone else and, most of all, away from their worries.

It was refreshing to be out of the city. Zac was glad to see Eva enjoying herself. He watched her make her way through the sunlight that broke through the trees' curling branches. Every time her face was illuminated, Zac fell in love with her all over again. Her hair was up and the line of her neck was perfectly curved as her eyes sparkled in the afternoon air. She smiled at him and her face created a picture of joy that lit up even the remotest corners of Zac's heart. She leaned into him and placed a kiss on his ready lips. After being together for so long, Zac and Eva had the art of kissing perfected. Both knew exactly what the other liked, but there were always new techniques which kept the flame blazing. Zac took a step backwards, Eva still kissing him, and his back met the firm reassurance of a tree. With a sturdy backdrop, Zac was free to let Eva melt into him and he basked in the amazing rush of hormones that took over his body. She let out a soft groan of pleasure and Zac was fit to burst. He ran his hands all down her back, to her bum and anywhere else he pleased, all the time pulling her closer into him. She rubbed herself against him and Zac's mind was swirling as the kissing got deeper and more urgent. Zac kept up the pace before relaxing again into a slow, sensuous kiss that made him feel incredible. Every time her lips met his and her soft tongue timidly made its way to his, Zac's chest heaved and he drew her tighter into him.

Almost an hour had passed. The emotion and soothing reassurance of passion was a combination that neither Zac nor Eva ever wanted to lose. But, as the air got slightly chillier, both knew that they didn't have all day. They pulled back and stared at one another with utter satisfaction and awe at how each made the other feel. Eva summed it up perfectly so that Zac knew that they were both in agreement as to how the past hour had felt.

'Wow!' she whispered, before kissing him softly once more.

Zac was about to lead the way out of the trees, towards the path to the bus, when he had an idea. Bending down to the dirty ground he located a sharp stone and began to work. Eva stared at him with wonder, not entirely sure what he was doing, but as the letters of their names were slowly scratched onto the rough bark she understood.

ZAC & EVA. ALWAYS

Zac stared at his work and then at Eva. Her face was lit up with delight and her eyes had a glow that thrilled Zac. 'So even when you're gone, this will always be here. On this tree, where we spent such a brilliant afternoon. The memory is etched here—'

'Always.' Eva finished Zac's sentence before kissing him once more, taking his hand in hers and making her way between the tall bodies of wood and lush foliage to where the sun shone at its fullest.

The night was pitch but golden light
Pours through the trees, so that I might
Remember not to forget her smile.

32

Eva

In school the following Monday morning, Eva thought about when the best time would be to tell everyone the news. She wanted to tell them all at the same time, to save her having to go through it over and over again. Once was enough. But she also only wanted to tell her close friends. They were the ones who she was truly leaving behind and they deserved to know first. She had told Zac to tell all the gang that she had something to tell them and they had all congregated in an empty classroom at lunch-time.

Eva watched as the last of the group closed the door behind them. She stared around at Frank, Cian, Graham, Lisa and Cathy and held Zac's hand in hers very tightly. She didn't want to do this. By saying the words and hearing them echo through the musky classroom, she would be erasing all doubt in her mind about the move going ahead. It was so official, so final and so scary. She feared most of all that maybe one of the gang would be upset that she hadn't told them earlier, but she'd told Zac to act like he'd only found out the day beforehand. This was mainly for Cathy's benefit. There was a chance she'd be angry with Eva for not telling her in private as soon as she knew, but Eva didn't have the energy to think about the politics or the correct way of breaking the news. The news itself was enough to be worried about.

The air was thick with apprehension and a mist of chalk dust. The old desks were aligned like soldiers ready for battle. The memories of foolscap pages sailing through the Friday afternoon air and stern gazes from Sir or Miss filled Eva once more and she ached at the thought of all this being much more than a history classroom but, for her, history itself. The room resonated with the fidgeting of nervous kids who longed for the bell to sound and set them all free, like a swarm of bees to the summer air. Eva gazed at the walls at posters of ancient heroes, their faces worn through time and effort. A small window allowed sunlight to filter in and catch the blizzard of dust particles which danced through the expectant air. She didn't want to leave. She wanted to stay and bask in the familiarity she had built up these past school years. Even as she sat in a school test, willing her mind to pour out all she'd learned, she knew she had been sure of at least one thing – it was her school and it was where she belonged. But now she found herself surrounded by staring faces, willing her to say what she had to. There was no prolonging it any more.

'Guys, I know this is a bit weird, but I wanted you all to come here because there's something I need to tell you. Something big.'

'Are you pregnant?' Cian was ever the joker and Eva couldn't prevent a small smile edging across her trembling lips. But the feeling didn't touch the knot in her stomach as she continued.

'No! Jesus Christ, no! Look, as you know, it's a year now since Dad died and although I'm slowly coming to terms with it, my mum really isn't. She's decided that being in the same house and the same place brings back too many memories of him… so we're moving.'

Her audience seemed unaffected. The thought of moving house was no big deal whatsoever. Eva knew she'd have to elaborate on the scale of the move.

'We're moving to Cork. My relations live there and my mum and her brother are really close, so she's enrolled me and Sarah in a new school we're heading down in July,' she explained.

Although it seemed the atmosphere couldn't have intensified any more, it did. Every one of them held their breaths, not knowing whether they'd just heard what they'd heard or if it was some kind of joke. Silence hung for almost a minute, and it became clear that there was no humour involved. Even Cian had lost his usual happy expression. Each one looked distraught and Eva noticed a tiny tear trickle down Cathy's face.

'You can't leave.' Cathy's voice was weak, barely more than a whisper. Eva looked at her and had to look away again quickly so that she herself didn't allow the ocean of tears that was inside her to gush out.

'I don't want to go. It's just, I have to. For Mum. But guys, it's not the end. If you think about it, not a lot's going to change. It's not the other side of the planet!' Eva tried to lighten the mood as she spoke aloud the one thought that was keeping her going – it was only Cork. They weren't moving country, they were just going to be a bit further away. It didn't have to be that big a deal. As long as people stopped making such a fuss about it, she could convince herself that everything would stay the same, and she would do everything she could to make sure of it.

'But not having you in school will be so weird. And with sixth year next year, it's going to be so much harder to stay in touch,' Cathy spat. Eva wished she wouldn't be so negative.

'Cathy, please stop making it sound like I'm just abandoning you. I don't want to go, don't you get that? But I don't have a choice. Mum needs us.' Eva was as firm as she could be.

'But surely she has to realise that you guys are sad too. Even if not moving might push her over the edge, what if moving pushes you and Sarah over? She could go and you guys could stay with friends. I'll ask my mum – she won't mind.' Cathy was beginning to panic and Eva wished she could run over and hug her and tell her she wasn't going to go any more. But she *was* going, and a line was suddenly drawn between the two of them, a shadow of what was to come when they were no longer together. And it hurt.

The bell sounded and lunch was over. No one except Cathy had said a word since Eva broke the news, and even she had now gone quiet. Eva wished one of them would say something and tell her what they thought. But each one of them looked as if they'd been kicked in the stomach. They simply couldn't talk to her as they left the room to go to class. They filtered out until only Eva and Zac remained. She broke down in his arms.

'Why didn't they say anything? Don't they care?' Eva sobbed.

'Of course they care, that's *why* they didn't speak. It's too hard,' Zac assured her.

'I'm right, though, aren't I? It's going to be okay, isn't it?' Eva was desperate as she begged him for some trickle of hope.

'You'll be fine. We'll be fine,' Zac soothed.

'I don't want to lose you,' Eva sobbed.

'You won't. Love conquers all, remember? Come on, look at everything we've been through already together. Have a bit of faith in us, would you?' Zac tried to laugh, but Eva wasn't listening. She was in her own little world. He held her for a few minutes before she ran off to the bathroom to clean herself up and head to class.

*

Her final month in school flew by in a broken heartbeat, and all too soon it was the start of June, and the last day of term. As Eva heard the school bell ring for the very last time, the summer had officially arrived. As she walked through the corridor, towards her locker which she had emptied of all books, she willed herself to always remember her school. The bright light of the sun filtered in through the windows, grubby with handprints, but clear enough to frame the blue sky. The old posters that lined the walls told of cake sales and trips and raffles, all over by now, but their advertising campaigns still adding colour to the pale corridors. The sea of faces and casual clothes blurred her vision and she was sure she felt tears beginning to prick her eyes. She was sad, yet the warm light flooding around her and the comfort of memories that now filled her made her strangely happy. She hated the saying 'don't cry because it's over, smile because it happened', she'd always found it clichéd, but suddenly she knew that however upset she was to be leaving, she would always be grateful for the times she'd had there.

Lines and lines of lockers stood strong, as if to salute the students farewell for another year. Eva passed a group of sixth years and realised that they too were facing a similar departure to hers. But they'd had their time. Everyone had always known that six years was the time limit for their stay and the end for them had always been near. But Eva had had to come to terms with so much, so quickly. Throngs moved towards the door and rushed out to embrace their freedom for the next three months, but Eva wanted to put off walking out the door for as long as possible. She wanted to bask in familiarity and take in every inch of her surroundings before they were snatched from under her and moved from the part of her mind labelled 'present' to the part bearing the sign 'past'. There was only so long she could put it off.

She knew that everyone was waiting for her outside to hug her and kiss her and tell her they were going to miss her. She didn't want to hear it, it was all so final. But the sunshine lured her away from the interior of her familiar world and drew her out the door. Stepping into the clear air, Eva closed her eyes, just for a moment, and prayed that she would never forget.

33

Zac

Zac sat at his kitchen table, nursing a cup of tea and smiling at his mum opposite him. She'd blossomed so much of late. Zac was glad that the whole incident with his father seemed to have made her a stronger person. Her voice was smooth and even as she broached a subject that she expected an emotional response to. But Zac wasn't emotional. He completely agreed with every word she said and the only thing that surprised him was her fear that he would somehow be angry.

'Mum, relax, okay? I'm not upset or anything. I obviously saw this coming, and to be honest, I'm really glad,' he assured her.

'But Zac, a divorce is a big deal,' she insisted.

'I know, but after what he did—' he shrugged.

'I just don't want you to think I'm weak because I'm not asking your father to make another go of it. I mean, I know a lot of women ask their husbands to go to anger management or something, but I just don't think I have the energy to do all that,' she continued.

'I don't expect you to. In fact, *that's* what would make me upset, if you even considered for one second giving him another chance. So I'm really glad you're not going down that road,' Zac said fervently.

Zac's mother hesitated and then confessed something Zac knew was hard for her to do. 'I nearly did, Zac. I wanted to. I know what he did was horrible and terrible and unforgivable. But the thought of ending a marriage as long as ours and being all on my own again is scary. I've known your father for so long and he's the only man I've ever loved. It is hard to realise it is over.'

'But surely what he did made it easier to see what a prick he is. And it's not even like it was the only bad thing he's ever done. He treated you and I like shit, Mum. Surely that made you realise you don't love him,' he protested.

'But love is strange, Zac. Even when you hate someone it's hard to forget about years and years of love. I really did love him before he started getting his moods. He made me happy and then when we had you I had a life that was perfect and it felt nothing would ever spoil it. Little did I know,' she said ruefully.

'I know, Mum.' And Zac did know – he knew what love felt like. He knew how much it hurt to think of losing it. He felt for his mum, and knew that she'd had to be strong to have made the final decision and file for divorce. But she'd done it and he was proud of her.

'Mum, I respect you so much for how you've dealt with all this. I mean, I know it was probably really hard to realise, but divorce is the only option here really, after all he's put you through,' he said, trying to comfort her.

'I know, Zac. But after everything he's been saying to me since – that he's sorry for what he did and all his promises that it will never happen again…' she trailed off.

'What?' Zac was shocked. Had his mother been in contact with his father? Now that he thought about it, he probably should have guessed. He wouldn't just disappear because Zac wanted him to, but the thought that his father was playing the innocent and begging for forgiveness sickened him.

'Has he asked about me?' he asked.

'Of course he has, love. He wants you to phone him. I was going to tell you. It's just with Eva leaving, I figured you've got enough on your plate. I'm sorry, I should have told you. But he doesn't want to lose touch with you, that's for sure. How do you feel about that?' she asked anxiously.

Zac thought long and hard and realised he didn't feel anything at all. He never wanted to see, hear or meet his father again. And for the first time he realised that this whole thing was more than a family splitting up – it was going to mean the loss of a parent for him. But then he thought of Eva. For so long now he'd listened to Eva talk and cry and long for her own father to be back, wishing she could have both parents like everyone else. It was the one thing she wanted more than anything, and yet here he was throwing away a parent just because he was angry. Zac didn't know what to do. He hated his father, but to think that he would throw away something which Eva longed for with all her heart was hard.

But it wasn't the time to think about it. Maybe in a few months, or even years, he'd get in touch with his dad, but until then it was an issue Zac wouldn't think about for now. Too much already filled his head and he had to prioritise. Eva had only a month left in Dublin and Zac knew that between that and making sure his mother was all right, he was going to have his hands full.

*

A week later, Zac's mother was out for the evening with her friend Sue. Zac asked his mum if it was all right if he had Eva over for the evening and, as usual, his mum was cool and said that his girlfriend was always more than welcome to come over whenever she wanted. His mother was very fond of Eva. She was also being particularly sound about her departure, knowing it was very hard for Zac.

Eva arrived just after eight and she was looking very well. She wore tight, low-cut jeans and a tight blue T-shirt, but something was different that made her appear ten times more attractive than she usually did. Maybe it was just his heart playing tricks on him, knowing what they had planned for that evening. The butterflies inside him were having spasms and Zac was afraid he was going to explode if they didn't calm down. Eva must have sensed his nerves and gave him an extra long kiss, which in fact just gave the butterflies more ammunition.

They headed into the sitting room, where the low lights and television gave a reassuring atmosphere, as Eva told him all about her day shopping with Cathy. She explained how Cathy had spent a lot of time texting Johnny, as it looked like their relationship was ending, much to Cathy's dismay.

Zac nodded, knowing Johnny had already said he wanted to be single for the summer but then, out of nowhere, Eva kissed him. The kiss sent Zac's mind swimming again, and although he'd been momentarily distracted, he suddenly realised why they were there, and his heart raced again.

They'd talked about it for ages now and both Eva and Zac had agreed that they were both ready, and it would be perfect to do it before Eva left so that she would always remember it. They'd waited and waited, though, until the perfect night arose and finally here it was. Zac had had to make sure that Eva was in fact totally ready. He obviously was, but he didn't want her to be doing it for him, by any means.

'Eva, we can wait. Just because you're leaving doesn't mean we have to rush into something you don't want,' he murmured.

'Zac, shut up. I want to. More than anything,' she said firmly.

'As long as you're positive?' he asked.

'Of course I am. Zac, I love you. I want to have sex with you.' As soon as those words had left her lips, Zac knew that there was nothing more he wanted too. As they sat in his living room, both talking and laughing and kissing, Zac felt a childish apprehension that was exciting. He'd always been different from his friends – he'd wanted to lose his virginity to the right person. Although the lads had always slagged him and told him there was no such thing as the perfect 'first ride', Zac was adamant – and tonight he was sure was going to be it.

Eva told Zac to put on a CD. He clicked play on his stereo and hoped that whatever he'd been listening to earlier would be good enough. What he hadn't counted on was it being the most perfect song possible. They both paused to listen to the lyrics, and were brought closer than ever in that moment.

And this is our heyday, baby,
And we're not gonna be afraid to shine,
Cause we can make our heyday last forever,
And ain't that what it's all about,
Oh living in our own terrible way.

Eva said nothing, but looked at Zac and he knew that she wanted him to know that their heyday wasn't going to end just because she was moving away. Zac understood and showed her by leaning into her and kissing her. She responded instantly and as her lips caressed his, and as her hands pulled him ever closer to her, Zac's butterflies were awoken once more. They kissed and kissed and he ran his hands all over her wonderful body. She was pressed so tightly against him that their hips moved in time with one another. Zac's mind was ablaze with pleasure. All he could think about was how much he loved Eva and how she was the most incredible person in the world. Slowly, she drew herself from him and looked him straight in the eye. Neither said anything, but enjoyed the safety of each other's gaze. Finally Eva's soft voice broke the silence, though it was almost a whisper. 'Do you want to go upstairs?'

Zac paused, knowing he did, and with a kiss of confirmation, took her hand in his and headed up. His heart was pounding, but although he had expected his mind to be racing with anxiety and nerves, it was in fact perfectly calm. For he knew exactly what he wanted and who he wanted, and as she followed him, her fingers intertwined in his, everything was wonderful.

Forget the past – darkness lost to me,
For this moment will never leave.
And everything is how it ought to be.

34

Eva

Eva stared at her reflection in the mirror. She looked different! There was something new in her appearance that she couldn't put her finger on, yet to her it was glaringly obvious. She was scared to go downstairs because she was convinced her mother would take one look at her and exclaim, 'You had sex with Zac, didn't you?'

What was it, though? Eva suddenly realised the phrase 'losing your virginity' had a whole new dimension to it. She did feel like she'd lost something, but not in a negative way. If she was going to lose it, she wanted Zac to find it. She laughed at her weird analogy, but it was the only way she could explain to herself what she was feeling.

She'd felt so emotionally connected with Zac. But now that she did, she felt slightly more vulnerable too, like she'd opened another part of herself with a whole other range of emotions. It was all about trust, though. She hadn't been scared at the time because she trusted Zac – it would have been terrifying otherwise. But it had been good. She felt as if she'd crossed a bridge, another stepping stone in life.

That was what made it so unbelievable. When they were younger, she always imagined Cathy and Lisa losing their virginity *long* before she did. But now that it had happened as it did, it felt like the most right thing in the world. Thinking back to Zac's house, she felt giddy inside. It wasn't exactly romantic – neither had really known what to do, which made it a bit awkward. Obviously, they'd seen it all before and thought they knew, but then it didn't really work like that. It was confusing! Eva laughed. Thinking about it like that, it sounded far from special, but that was the thing – it had been so special. It had been the most special moment of her life. And despite the fumbling and confusion, once he was inside her, it had felt amazing. It was a moment she would never forget. Giggling to herself, she went downstairs.

'You're looking very pleased with yourself!' her mother commented as she skipped into the kitchen. Eva smiled inwardly. If only she knew!

*

For the following weeks, as if to give Eva the best send-off possible, Dublin was having one of the best summers in years. The sun was so fiery one day that they had to make the most of it. The gang met up in Dún Laoghaire, and Eva felt content as she, Lisa, Cathy, Zac, Graham, Cian and Frank strolled towards the cool, inviting water.

Zac and the girls walked on ahead, while the other three lagged back, deep in conversation over Graham's latest suggestion.

'How would you guys feel about going on a holiday or something, just before sixth year? Just the three of us and Zac?' he asked excitedly.

'I'd definitely be up for that! Puerto Banus or something? It'd be good for Zac too, take his mind off Eva leaving and all,' Cian enthused.

'Exactly! Or Amsterdam maybe? What do you reckon, Frank?' Graham turned to his other friend.

'To be honest, man, I don't think I have the funds. Plus I'll hopefully be working for all of August,' Frank explained.

'Working?' exclaimed the two others in unison.

'Yeah,' he replied flatly. 'Haven't got a job yet, but I've sent out a load of CVs, so fingers crossed.'

Cian couldn't hide his shock. 'What do you need a job for?'

'What do you think? Money, dumbass.'

'Frank,' Graham said, 'your dad's an architect and your mum's a senior counsel. Somehow I don't think money's a problem.'

Frank began to get uneasy. 'Yeah, but I can't just sponge off my rents anymore, especially not for beer money and stuff. It just doesn't feel right.'

'Feels fine to me,' Cian interjected loudly, high-fiving Graham before launching into his opinions on where would be the best location for their holiday, and just how drunk he planned on getting.

Frank just strolled along in silence, wondering why his friends didn't understand. He didn't like that they didn't, and for such good guys he couldn't see *why* they didn't. But he saw no point in dwelling on it and rejoined the conversation, which had now moved on to the idea of a trip completely based on the strip clubs of Spain.

The group passed Dún Laoghaire pier, and Eva stared at the volume of walkers who ambled along the stretch of boardwalk. The sound of chatting and laughter, fused with the gentle clink of boats and sea water, produced the perfect summer soundtrack. The boats bobbed softly, like ducks on a lake, and seemed to talk to one another like the babble of friends that surrounded Eva. The walkers were a sea themselves, all flesh and shades and tanning faces.

Sandycove Beach was completely covered in bodies, and children laughed and screamed and flitted from place to place. Sand castles and brightly coloured buckets created a city of life that looked like something one of the children themselves would have drawn. Towels of rainbow designs, with melting bodies lazing on them, turned the beach into a patchwork quilt, so only the odd area of golden grains were exposed to the roasting heat. Eva stood rooted to the spot, taking in all the sights, and as the smell of the salty water filled her, combining with the vague aroma of suntan lotion, she smiled. One of the groups had brought a radio to the shore with them, so that everyone around was exposed to thumping summer tunes.

People filled the water, and many gathered on the small pier so that they could throw themselves into the waves below. One particular boy took a giant run-up to the edge before forming a near-perfect dive, which was rewarded by loud claps and cheers by all his spectators. His body plunged into the swell before reappearing once more, with a smile on his rugged face. It was Zac. Eva felt herself beam with pride as she watched everyone discuss his dive. He was followed into the sea by two other boys, though neither even tried to match their friend's perfect display. Cian and Frank merely bombed downwards, sending splashes all around them, while they bobbed to the top, laughing and pushing as they treaded water.

Eva realised just how long she'd been standing there, trying to store every inch of the image in her memory. The others had moved on and as she scanned the sand, eventually she located Cathy, Lisa and Graham, who had set up a little patch of colour of their own. She joined them and looked forward to a whole day of pure relaxation, truly believing that just for a while, the sun's rays could empty her head of all thoughts and leave her feeling lighter than ever.

*

Eva's final Friday in Dublin arrived in the blink of an eye. With the party the following night, the Coonan household was a whirlwind of preparation. However, Eva had been given permission to slip off to Zac's house for the night. His mum was at a party in Sue's house and they wanted to make the most of having the house to themselves. Eva conceded this was probably the last time it would be just the two of them. Even the thought of Sunday and her departure made a lump form in her throat. This week had been so good; the thought of leaving was awful.

Eva strolled over to Zac's house in the early evening air and rang the doorbell. She lit up when he answered it and kissed him. Though it had never been officially stated, Eva knew that this last night alone was going to be taken advantage of, and she couldn't wait.

'You all packed then?' Zac asked lightly.

'Think so. There are still a few bits and pieces I'm too scared to do yet, though,' Eva admitted.

'It's just so weird. It still hasn't hit me you're actually going.' Zac looked into Eva's eyes and, in an instant, her lips were on his, kissing him tenderly. For the rest of the evening they continued like this and, every minute that went by, Eva fell just a little further in love with Zac. Each time he touched her, she was ablaze with pleasure, and as her clothes were slowly removed, she prayed the night would never end. They moved upstairs and lying in Zac's bed, Eva's body groaned with ecstasy. She savoured every second.

*

By the time Saturday evening arrived, the Coonan house was spotless. There was food cooking in the kitchen as well as a buffet spread in the dining room. Loud music filled the living room and candles burned throughout the house. The amount of alcohol in the utility room was criminal, but Eva knew that it would barely be enough. She decided she'd done all the organising she could and headed upstairs to get ready. The previous week when she'd been in town with Cathy, she'd bought an outfit for the night, announcing that she wanted to look brilliant, because it was her night and she wanted to go out with a bang. She finished off her outfit with smoky eyes and some pink lip gloss and was quite satisfied with the image the bathroom mirror offered her. She applied a final mist of perfume and, before she headed downstairs, Eva took one final look around her, breathed deeply and whispered, 'This is it.' And it was.

But it wasn't over just yet, and she was going to make sure she had the night of her life.

Her mother's and sister's guests arrived first and the house slowly filled up. Then her posse came. Lisa and Cathy both looked great and the latter enquired as to whether Johnny and Kev would be along. Eva smiled at Cathy and knew that her heart was bruised; Johnny and Cathy had decided to go 'on a break' for the summer, though the decision had definitely been very one-sided. Cathy hadn't been happy with the split and, since Johnny was just back from Spain, tonight would be the first time she'd see him since they'd put their relationship on hold. Eva had invited both Johnny and Kev as she'd become good friends with them through Zac. Though neither had arrived yet, it was clear that Cathy was very nervous about seeing her ex, and said she needed support. Eva offered it to her with open arms, but in an instant her friend had changed, her face aghast.

'Eva, I'm so unbelievably sorry. This is your last night, and here I am worrying about my love life. I'm so sorry, what am I like? Let's have a brilliant night, okay? I'm going to miss you so much,' she announced.

With that Eva was dragged to the centre of the living room and commanded to dance. Gradually more people began to follow suit and quickly Eva was surrounded by bodies, moving in time to the funky beat which boomed through her house. Then a hand met hers. Without even turning around she knew who it was. The fingers were so familiar to her and the soft yet firm grip they had on hers was one that pained her to leave behind. She spun to face Zac and the two of them moved to the couch where, for the night, Eva was in a cocoon of romance. She had to move very little from that spot to enjoy the party. Her friends simply joined her and Zac on the couch and chatted away to her, most of the time lightly, but the odd sentimental comment brought reality back to her.

Suddenly Cathy shouted that it was time to give the presents. Gathering in the kitchen, Eva was laden with cards and boxes, while flashing cameras lit up the scene. There was one present from her closest friends. The box was placed in front of her, while a crowd of expectant faces stared at her, wanting to know what she thought. She opened it tentatively to reveal a large, leather book. Looking inside, she was faced with over a hundred pages of solid writing. Puzzled, she looked at the first page, which declared:

Eva – this is your life. (So far!)

Cian jumped in and explained that each of them had written down their fondest memories of her and things they'd done together. Eva flicked through the pages and saw the different handwriting, each telling tales of the years gone by. Some had included photos, some just text, but each spoke of all the wonderful days they'd shared with her. She was speechless. The time and effort that must have gone into this was breathtaking. She'd never known the boys in her year to put effort into anything, yet here she was with a novel of memories which each of them had taken from the depths of their hearts and placed on the rich paper. Tears began to slide down her face and as she flicked to the last page of the book. Two words filled the page and Eva was moved more than she had ever been.

Never forget.

Beneath the words were the signatures of all those who had taken part in putting together the book. Cathy's name was there, in her rich, curly scrawl. Cian's messy scribble. They were all there. Kissing each one of them in turn, she thanked her friends from the bottom of her breaking heart for the best present she could have hoped for. Cathy and Lisa had both begun to cry and, even though the lads tried to remain cool, Eva saw that their eyes had glazed over too. But she wasn't going to let the mood dampen, and commanded everyone to return to the sitting room, turn up the music and dance till they dropped! Eva flitted from person to person, taking picture after picture, until she filled up three rolls of film, as if preserving the night in her camera, for she never wanted it to end.

But it did and, as she kissed and held each of her friends before they left, her heart slowly snapped in two. Zac was coming over again the following day to see them off, but for the rest of them, this was it. Each of them hugged and kissed her and promised they'd be in touch. The hardest goodbye was to Cathy. Eva held her, knowing it was their last hug for a long time. Zac could see the powerful friendship between the two girls, and he watched Eva's heart break as she let Cathy go.

Eva finally closed the door, and felt as if she had closed over a period of her life. As much as she ached inside, the party, and that summer, had been perfect.

She looked at her mother with glazed eyes, searching for some shred of hope that this had all been a joke, that they weren't going anywhere, but there was none to be found. Zac broke the silence.

'You guys *will* be okay.'

Eva was surprised at how much his words touched her, but she prayed inwardly that he was right. She loved him so much, but she also loved her mum and her sister, so maybe the future wouldn't be too bad. Her train of thought led her to ask, 'Where's Sarah?'

No one answered at first.

'Maybe she's upstairs,' Zac suggested, though now that he thought about it, he hadn't seen her in a while. The last hour had been a frenzy of departures as the remaining guests left and he couldn't remember seeing her since the start of the evening.

'Sarah?' Eva's mother shouted up the stairs. No reply. 'Sarah?' she tried again, louder this time. Nothing. 'I'll go check her room. Try her mobile, Eva.' There was a slight note of panic in her mother's voice, though Eva doubted anything was the matter.

She dialled Sarah's phone, but it just went straight to her voice mail. Her mother reappeared. 'She's not upstairs. Could you get her?'

Eva shook her head and wondered just how worried she should be. Surely Sarah had just gone to walk one of her friends' home, to say a final goodbye. But then why was her phone off? This wasn't like her sister at all, the most organised girl in the world. An unpleasant feeling began to grow inside Eva. Judging by her mother's face, she wasn't the only one beginning to fret.

'She's definitely not staying at someone's house?' Zac suggested.

'Of course not,' Eva replied, more curtly than she'd meant. But she didn't need stupid suggestions interrupting her as she racked her brain for ideas as to where her sister could be.

'Right. Zac, love, could you just go for a stroll, just around the block or something? Maybe she was finding all the goodbyes hard and needed some air.' Eva's mother tried to stay calm, but her voice wavered as she spoke. Zac headed out immediately.

'Eva, you start ringing around – her friends, people who were at the party. I'll do the same from my mobile. She can't have gone far. Can she?' Eva's mother's eyes pleaded with her daughter for reassurance and, despite her own worries, Eva had no choice but to offer it.

'Mum, relax. As you said, she probably just got upset and wanted to get out. She'll be home any minute now, wondering what the fuss was about, you know?'

'You're probably right, love. Thanks.' The two women began dialling.

*

It was half past three in the morning when Eva's mother finally called the police. She hadn't wanted a fuss and, more importantly, she had truly believed that any minute Sarah would walk through the door. But she never did. And now Eva was frightened and her mother was crying and the police were on their way. Eva was so relieved that Zac was there to help her, but it was hard too. She kept going to him, hugging him, holding him, not wanting to let go. But then she'd see her mother, standing there all alone, her face fraught with nerves, and she realised it wasn't right that she didn't have anyone hugging her. So she'd pull away from Zac and go to her mum, the two women united once more in hurt.

In that moment, Eva realised that ultimately she would have to make a choice. Going to Cork wasn't something she wanted. Leaving Zac here in Dublin would break her heart, but the love she had for him and the love she had for her mother were different, and at the end of the day Eva knew which was more important, which she couldn't let go of. It hurt, but her mother was so broken, and she vowed she would never leave her, even if it meant putting a strain on what she had with Zac. But they were strong too, and Cork shouldn't really affect their bond. But only time would tell, she conceded, and her heart ached for what was to come.

Two policemen arrived at the door and were ushered in by Eva's mother, who proceeded to talk very quickly, begging them to find her daughter. Eva realised just how tired she herself was, and the scene before her began to recede from sight as her emotions and exhaustion clouded her mind.

'Zac, would you take Eva into the sitting room while I talk to the sergeants, she looks as if she's going to pass out!' Eva's mum gave a nervous laugh, and Eva felt herself being led out of the room. She needed to stay awake, to help her mum, but her head was heavy with alcohol and frenzied thoughts. Where was Sarah? Would she and Zac be okay? Would her mum be all right? Why couldn't she keep her eyes open?

*

Eva woke with a start, staring around her in confusion. The room was bright, and a blue blanket lay cosily around her. Was it morning? A glance at the clock told her it was nearly eight o'clock. Sarah! She suddenly remembered. Jumping up, she ran to the kitchen, where her mother and sister sat deep in conversation. Where was Zac? Was it a dream? But as her mother spotted her in the doorway and invited her to sit down, her eyes wet with tears, Eva knew that this was a far cry from a dream.

'When did you show up?' she asked her sister.

'About an hour ago,' Sarah said quietly.

'Where the fuck were you? Mum and I were worried sick!' Rage suddenly surged from beneath Eva's exhaustion as she became hungry for answers.

'Oh, that's why you fell asleep, is it?' Sarah spat back.

'Girls!' Their mother wasn't in the mood for fighting. 'Please, it's been a long night. Eva, it doesn't matter where she was, the important thing is that we have her back in one piece. And Sarah, your sister was exhausted. Between the party and the panic you caused, you can hardly blame her,' she explained sternly.

'Sorry,' Sarah mumbled. Eva didn't follow suit. She hadn't seen her mother looking so weary since the night of her breakdown, and she wasn't about to let Sarah off for causing so much angst without a damn good explanation.

'What have you got to say for yourself? Any particular reason why you decided to spoil our final night, or was it just a bit of a whim?' Eva's tone showed just how unimpressed she was.

'I was just explaining to Mum before you decided to wake up!'

Eva opened her mouth to throw back some equally clever retort, but a look from their mother told both girls to settle down.

'I just needed to get out. Do something wild. It was our last bloody night in Dublin, I thought I deserved the chance to break a few rules,' Sarah declared.

'But it's just so unlike you, love. That's why we were so worried,' her mum said gently, trying to diffuse the tension.

'But that's the thing. How would you know? You honestly think

I'm the first fifteen-year-old who's stayed out all night? Of course not. But you guys forget I'm *only* fifteen. I do too, for God's sake. I'm too busy playing the fucking adult of the house. Oh Mum, don't look at me like that. I'm sorry. I just needed to remember what it was like to be a teenager. I haven't felt like that in so long.'

'What do you mean?' her mother asked.

'I can't… I feel so bad saying this… but you see, I'm supposed to be the strong one. Ever since Dad died, it was like this unwritten rule that I took care of us all, and I was okay, and I'd make sure things were all okay. I just never got the chance to show my feelings properly because if I broke down, the whole family would fall apart. I was the rock. It just got hard, you know? I needed to break free, just this once. I'm sorry.' Sarah began to cry and Eva realised she hadn't seen her sister do so in a long time, as if proving what she'd just said.

'Honey, I'd no idea…' Eva's mum was shocked more than anything, as was Eva. She'd never doubted the truth of Sarah's strength. She'd envied it, but she always believed it was genuine. But had she bothered to put herself in her sister's shoes? To suddenly be promoted from the baby of the house to the head? Sarah had no Zac, no brother Don. Of course it was hard. Eva cursed herself for never thinking about it before now.

'Sarah, I'm so sorry. I never… you should have said… this is awful. All this time…' Eva tried, but the words wouldn't come. Their mother cried beside her, and she knew that she, too, was struggling with what Sarah had said.

They talked for another hour before finally heading to bed. They had planned to leave for Cork later that day, but all agreed that another night in their house would be a good idea. Eva was welcomed by her bed and, as she lay there, wondered just what lay in store for them all. She and her mother had promised that they would start fulfilling their roles now, allowing Sarah to be a teenager again, both ashamed that it had taken such a fiasco to make them realise how out of line they'd both been. But at least now the three of them were reunited. Things were going to be different now, better, and Cork was the perfect chance for them to start fresh; a real family. Eva began to think of Zac, but she was too weary – sleep took over and, secretly, she was glad.

35

Zac

The moment he woke, Zac was hit with a stone-cold thought that smacked him hard between his ribs so that he was unable to breathe: today was the day, the hardest day of his life. The clock seemed to tick louder and quicker than usual and Zac felt paralysed as he lay in bed. Even though Eva and her family had postponed their departure by a day, this had done little to distract Zac from what was to come.

He dressed quickly, threw his jacket on and embraced his mother before heading to Eva's. As he walked through the silent streets, he realised that, more than anything, he was scared – scared to endure the ordeal that was about to come and scared that he wouldn't be able to handle what was thrown at him. He stood at Eva's door, trying to bring himself to press the bell. Was this actually happening? He knew the minute the door was opened, it would only be a matter of hours before she left him.

Eva opened the door and hugged him tighter than ever before leading him into the house. They went upstairs, where she was throwing the last of her things into a bag. She worked quickly, saying little. All the time he stared at her, watching as she appeared to take it all in her stride, while he knew that inside she was quivering with despair.

As their final hours passed by, it seemed that time was slipping through his fingers like melting ice. Finally, she was finished packing and sat beside him on the bed. Keeping her hand in his all the time, he looked at her, wanting to remember every inch of her. They spoke, but realised nothing they said mattered any more, only that they loved each other.

She handed him a note but told him not to read it for a while, until things had settled down and he'd got used to the idea of her being gone. He promised and kissed her once more before pulling away to give her one last thing, a small box.

'Open it.' Zac found his voice shaking slightly.

Eva opened the box to reveal a small silver ring. It was completely smooth and very simple, save for the raised square on which was engraved 'E&Z'. As Eva ran her finger over it, a glint caught her eye as she realised there was another inscription inside the ring: 'Always'. Eva instantly burst into tears. Zac held her, but it seemed as if she would never stop. As she tried to talk, it was as if her heart was truly breaking.

'Zac, it's perfect… I love it… I love you… but I'm leaving. I don't want to go, Zac. I'll miss you too much… I love you,' she sobbed.

Zac tried not to listen, because her desperate pleas cut him even deeper as he realised that the horrible feeling inside him was also penetrating the girl he cared for more than anything. As they sat there, encased in each other's arms, united in the purest love and the purest hurt, time ran out.

He carried her case down the stairs and into the car, which was loaded and ready to go. Every step he took seemed to be in slow motion and Zac could hear nothing, only his heart pounding and Eva's sniffles as she tried to hold back even more tears.

Sarah and her mother appeared and announced that they were going to lock the door for the last time. The three women gazed up at the house which held so many memories, but which would now become part of their past. The door was closed and the gate was shut. One at a time, Sarah and her mum hugged Zac and planted soft kisses on his cheek. Mrs Coonan in particular seemed to be finding this harder than she expected, her eyes were glazed with reluctance as she said goodbye.

'Zac, I'm going to miss you. You've been an absolute joy to have around and it's really felt nice having a man around the place. And not just any man – you've made Eva so happy and I know she loves you. I only wish her father could have met you. You took great care of her.'

Zac listened to the broken whisper of a very lonely woman and was touched by what she said. As he watched her and Sarah walk to the car, he prayed that life would be better to them than it had been in the past.

When he could deny reality no longer, he turned to Eva. Neither knew what to say or how to say it or just how to make the moment seem in some way better. It was impossible. Zac kissed her and she kissed him back, their tongues tasting every inch of the other's, neither wanting time to catch up with them.

'I love you, Eva.'

'I love you too, Zac.'

'Always?'

'Always.'

They pulled away and were separate, as they would be for a long time. Zac contemplated watching the car pull away until he could see it no more, but couldn't bear to stand there for a moment longer. He gazed at Eva for the last time as tears ran down his face before turning and running out of the estate as fast as he could.

He couldn't go home, so instead he sprinted to the main road, where he caught a bus that was just leaving and sat on the top deck, staring at the world that whizzed by. Out there, they didn't know. They didn't understand the pain he was feeling in that moment, and they didn't care. He wanted to stand up and scream at them and tell them what he was feeling. Buildings and trees and masses and masses of people blurred into a river of unfamiliar, unwanted mess, which made the hollow in his chest dry up even more so that he found it hard to breathe. She was gone. But he knew a place where there was still some of her left, and he wanted to be nowhere else.

Taking another bus, he reached the place, and as he searched through the trees, he located theirs. Their inscription was still in the bark and he remembered the day they'd spent there. The sun had been shining and life had been sweet and as he stared at the jagged lettering 'EVA & ZAC. ALWAYS' he knew that nothing would ever be the same again.

He sat beneath the tree, not knowing what to be and, even more, not wanting to be anything at all. His mind was so jumbled and yet so clear, as he felt only the stabbing pain in his heart. And then he remembered the note. She had told him to wait until he was less upset to read it, but now that he'd remembered it, the paper burned in his pocket.

Dear Zac

Right now I'm feeling so much but I'm afraid I may not be able to write it down. You know I love you and I want you to always remember that. They may just be words, but the feeling inside me means so much more than that. You make me someone I want to be and every inch of you amazes me.

You were my first love and I gave you all I could – my heart, my virginity and most of all my soul. You helped me through some of the hardest times of my life and knowing we have to be apart is killing me. But know that we always have our memories and our love to keep us.

Yesterday, when we all finally awoke after the party, I had another talk with Mum. A big one. And I don't know whether it was Sarah running away, or the fact that our departure was looming, but Mum gave me a choice. She said I could stay. She said she had watched me all night at the going away party with my friends, and with you, and realised just how happy I've finally come to be. So she asked if I wanted to stay. She said she had to go, there was no doubt of that, but that she was sure I could stay with friends up in Dublin, and just visit her at weekends.

Of course, the first thing I felt was pure delight. I wouldn't have to leave! I could stay with you guys, stay in school, be in the place I love so much. Best of all, be with you. But then I looked into her eyes, and Zac, I couldn't do it. She is just so pathetic. I don't mean that in a harsh way but, my God, she's in bits. She has so little, and to ask her and Sarah to live in a house on their own, to split up our family more than it already is, to ask Sarah to take care of Mum on her own having just told me how much she just wants to be young again... I couldn't do it. And it made me realise that I owe them so much, and that this move is something I have to do. It really is a small price to pay to see Mum smile again.

But we'll be okay, won't we? I can't lose you – that would ruin me. I hate admitting just how dependent I am on you, but I can't really deny the fact that you are my all. I love you, Zac, and it hurts so badly to say goodbye, but I know it's not the end. I'll visit as much as I can, and you're to come down every weekend.

We'll be perfect, just promise me that.

Never forget
Eva xx

Zac read and reread the words until he could no longer see them, for his eyes were blurry with hot tears. She'd had a choice? She could have stayed? And yet knowing how much he loved her, she *chose* to go. As if the pain of her leaving wasn't enough, Zac now realised that part of her had wanted to go. These words erased the one thing that had been keeping him going – the knowledge that she hadn't had a choice, that it ruined her to leave him and that she hated the fact that she had to. But she obviously didn't care, didn't fight for love. She expected him to do all the work now, visit her every weekend and promise her things were still perfect, when she'd had a choice? It was pathetic. He was broken in every way. As his huddled figure shook with sobbing, just for a moment, he hated Eva.

What's the point? It's been in vain,
My eyes never saw the same,
Forget them all, the lies I've lived before.

36

Eva

Cork was prettier than Eva remembered. The summer's rays caressed the busy streets and she breathed the air, smelling every colour. It was hard to imagine what their house would be like eventually, at the moment the piles and rows of cardboard boxes made it an obstacle course. There was a lot of space, though, and as light poured from room to room, Eva followed its trail, inspecting every corner of her new home. She decided to text Zac. In the car all the way down, the only thing she could think about was him. She missed him already and had wanted to turn the car around and be with him again. She ached for his touch.

HEY BABY SO WEV ARRIVD. D HOUS IS NICE ENUF, BT UR NOT ROUND D CORNER. DAT HURTS. MISS U ALREADY. LOVE U XX.

The message was delivered and she hoped she'd hear from him soon. Evening was beginning to set in and the dusty sunshine seemed different to Dublin. Sarah was upstairs, beginning to unpack, while her mother was in the kitchen with Don, who'd arrived to help them settle in. Eva didn't quite know what to do with herself. She was tired, yet spending such a long time in the car had made her restless. Her cousins would be arriving soon to welcome them too, and Eva couldn't shake the feeling that Dublin really was far away. She kept checking her phone, waiting for Zac's response, but nothing came. Eventually she gave up and decided to ring him, eager to hear his voice, as it felt like days since she'd done so.

'Hello?' he answered in the deep tone she loved.

'Hey, it's me. We arrived!' she announced, almost giddy knowing he was on the other end of the line.

'Yeah, I know, I got your text. How is it?' he asked, though his voice seemed to lack interest.

'Are you okay?' Eva was confused.

'Yeah, I'm grand. Just tired, you know?'

'Yeah, it's been a long day. Saying goodbye was so hard,' Eva conceded quietly.

'I read your note,' Zac interrupted.

'Oh?' Eva was slightly surprised, thinking he would have waited longer. 'And?'

'Honestly…' Zac paused. 'I was kind of pissed off.'

'Oh.' Eva was worried. What had she done? 'How come?'

'I don't know,' he lied.

'Obviously you know if you said it. Just tell me,' she coaxed playfully, unaware of what was to come.

'Okay. Well, honestly, I was pissed off because I hadn't realised your mum gave you a choice that you could have stayed. You kept telling me all along that all you wanted was to have a way of getting out of going, and then I just find out that was a lie.' Zac's voice was harsh and Eva began to panic.

'Zac, it wasn't like that. Please, I miss you, don't be like this,' she tried.

'I miss you too, Eva. It just hurts, that's all.'

'Zac, you know I didn't have a choice. Not really. She may have said I did, but there's no way I could have actually let Mum and Sarah go alone.' Eva was desperate for him to believe her. Did he honestly think she didn't wish more than anything that she was with him? 'Zac, I love you, but I had to do this for Mum. I love you, we're still together, isn't that what matters?'

'I suppose,' Zac sighed.

'Please don't be like this, it's my first night here, I'm already going to be crying myself to sleep as it is. I wish you were here,' Eva said, close to tears already.

'I wish you were here too,' Zac replied, though his words lacked emotion in comparison to hers. 'Text me later.'

'Okay, I will. Please don't hate me,' Eva pleaded, hoping things were okay.

'Of course I don't hate you, Eva. How could I? Text me later.'

'I love you,' she promised.

'Love you too,' he echoed, before hanging up.

Eva didn't know what to make of the conversation. Had he actually been pissed off with her? She hated the way this move had seemed like a decision about whether or not she loved him. Of course she did, more than anything. But why couldn't he see that things had to be this way? He did say he loved her and, after all, that was what mattered. But there was no denying the feeling of unease in Eva's stomach as she was called into the kitchen by her mother. Her cousins had arrived.

*

The days that followed were a blur of unpacking and meeting with relations. Eva was caught between remaining completely withdrawn from the whole thing, longing for Dublin, and being lured into the warmth of her reunited family.

Her cousin Ger was delighted to have her around, and took her into town one afternoon. They wandered the shops through throngs of August crowds. He met up with a group of his friends, some of whom Eva had met last Hallowe'en, and one specifically who was particularly happy to see her. She laughed to herself as she remembered turning down the very same boy so many months ago because she'd felt an attachment to Killian. How things had changed!

For the millionth time that week, her mind was filled with thoughts of Zac. They'd only been texting since that first phone call, as it seemed the gang back home were busy doing some hard-core partying before summer slipped through their fingers. She still replayed their chat in her head and wondered what it had all meant. Maybe it had just been a once-off. Maybe, like her, he'd had little sleep the night before she left, and his angry mood was just a result of tiredness. Emotions had been running high, after all.

It was only a fortnight until she began her new school, which left plenty of time for Eva to pop back up to Dublin for a few days. She watched her mother unpack each cardboard box, mindlessly unwrap each treasured ornament and give it a new home on some shelf or another and it was as if Eva was watching her put together her new world. Her new life. Although everyone knew Eva missed Dublin, Eva wanted her mother to know that, most of all, she was there for her, and that she was really going to make a go of things in Cork. Life *was* too short, and Eva had faith that love would keep her going. Far away or not.

37

Zac

August was warmer than it had been in years. Brown seemed to kiss random leaves, while the rest of the lush foliage remained green and dazzling in the late summer sunlight. It was three weeks since Eva had left and, although she'd been in touch, Zac had been secretly hoping she'd visit. It would have been the perfect end to the summer, but nothing was perfect, he remembered.

He was having good times, though. The group had been united in sadness at Eva's departure and they seemed to have become even closer. It was as if they realised that there was no way of predicting how long they all had together, so every day was important. It was as if a new wisdom had descended on them all, and if they could make it through losing one of their best friends, they could face anything.

His mother was in good form too and Zac believed that the sunny months had done her a lot of good. It was as if for all these years, Zac's father had made her a completely different person from the one she truly was, and at long last the real her had been exposed. She wore more casual clothes and let her hair hang loosely rather than scraping it back off her face. She spoke with more confidence and walked with her head high. Zac had learned a lot from her in that short time. He had realised that life isn't always easy, and that sometimes things happen that break your heart. But that doesn't mean they have to beat you. And just as his mum was overcoming her heartache, so too did he realise that no matter how hard it was not having Eva around, they were still a couple, they were still in love, and that was what mattered. He couldn't believe he was in a long-distance relationship. He'd always thought they were a silly idea, especially when it came to people their age. He'd always thought life was too short. But now that he was in one, he realised life was too short to let go of the best thing that had ever happened to him. Difficult or not, he'd have to work at it, and he knew that sixth year would definitely make things more difficult as both he and Eva would be studying non-stop, but it was worth it. She was worth it.

The air was fresh and the sun was warm and Dublin seemed happy to bask in the remaining warmth of summer. The buildings gleamed and the sea twinkled in the sunshine like chandeliers. The sky was a traffic jam of white, fluffy clouds in a pale blue lagoon of light, and they cast an air of happiness on the busy world below.

*

'Guess who?' Zac teased.

'Do you think I'm stupid? How're you?' Eva was delighted he'd called.

'I'm good. Tired though,' Zac admitted.

'Yeah, actually I meant to ask you, how was last night?'

'Good. Wild! We hit this new place in town and there was such a good crowd there. Bumped into loads of people I know,' Zac explained.

'Like who?'

'A few lads from my old school, Frank's mates from his area, a couple of girls. The usual, like.'

'Which girls?' Eva asked, surprising herself at the sharpness of her tone, but conceding she did want to know the answer nonetheless.

'Eh, I don't know.'

'Of course you do,' Eva insisted. 'Which girls?'

'Whoa, is this the Spanish Inquisition? Just girls in general. Megan, Rachel, Sue—' Zac listed.

'I hate that girl. She was always a bit of a tool!' Eva said.

'Really? I think she's cool enough. She was looking really well, just back from France. Savage tan.'

'Okay, relax there,' Eva said, unimpressed.

'What?'

'Go easy, don't get too excited,' Eva said sarcastically.

'What? I was just saying. You're the one who asked,' Zac defended himself.

'Yeah, but I don't need to know if you thought they were hot or not,' she said.

'Jeez, I was just saying. Relax, would you? I won't bother telling you who was there in future if you're just going to get pissed off.' Zac wasn't in the mood for fighting. He'd been looking forward to this chat all day, so he didn't want her ruining it because she was jealous of some girl he barely knew.

'What? So you're just going to hide it from me in future? I was just asking because believe it or not, I get jealous at the thought of you guys all going out together when I'm stuck down here,' Eva said, playing the sympathy card. But Zac found it hard to feel sorry for her when there was a very simple way to alleviate her pain.

'So come visit. We're not back at school yet, you could have easily got the train up for a few nights. I keep telling you this.' Zac was frustrated.

'You know I can't,' Eva cried. It felt like they were going around in circles. She fell silent. Zac didn't know what to say. He hadn't been planning on this.

'Look, Eva, I've been looking forward to this chat all day. You know I miss you so much. Please, let's not fight, it's stupid,' he soothed, wondering how they'd ended up here in the first place.

'Okay. You're right. Just remember it's hard, yeah? I miss being out with you. I hate the thought of other girls getting to chat to you in nightclubs and stuff,' Eva admitted.

'But you trust me, don't you?' The last thing Zac needed was for mistrust to start creeping it. It was always one of the fears when couples were apart, but he'd believed from the start that he and Eva were too strong for that.

'Of course I trust you. You love me, don't you?' she asked sheepishly.

'You know I do. Always,' Zac reassured, wondering why she'd ask such a question.

'Good. So, how're Cian and Graham?' Eva changed the subject.

Their chat continued, both easing back into things. Zac couldn't help thinking, though, that this was the first time since Eva had left that she'd seemed so unsure of things. Were doubts starting to creep in? Surely not. Of course he'd thought those girls were attractive, but never once did he consider acting on it. What he had was all he wanted. He just hoped she understood that.

He didn't want to say goodbye on the phone. Every time they'd talked since she'd moved, the end of the conversation was always so difficult. It felt like he was standing at her house all over again, unable to let go. They were doing well, though, and he was still as in love with her as ever – but the phone calls only reminded him of just how well they got on, just how much they clicked, and it pained him to not be able to know when he'd next have her in his arms or see her eyes. It was cheesy, but he couldn't help it. He longed for her and wished that she'd just come home.

Renewal of familiar light,
The photographs will break the night,
The warmth of reminiscing knows I'll
Never forget.

38

Eva

The high ceiling seemed too far from where she lay, and as she stared up at it she almost believed that it was in fact the sky, whiter than usual but equally unreachable. Eva was growing to love her new house and, although it was strange, she was slowly finding that it suited her and each room possessed a magic she knew she'd grow to love.

Her new bedroom was far bigger than the one in her house in Blackrock. A large iron double bed sat in the centre of the wooden floor, and Eva felt like a princess. White curtains hung around the huge bay window, which allowed a river of brightness to filter in and illuminate the room every morning. Eva loved Sundays and, since the weather was still warm, it felt safe to lie in a cocoon of duvets and watch the sun try to lure her outdoors. Her mother had been in just ten minutes earlier to open the curtains and encourage her daughter to rise but, if anything, the light that filled every corner of the bedroom was even more reason to stay in her nest, and smile.

She thought back on her week and was happy. She'd been petrified by the thought of starting a new school, but now that the first week had passed, she realised it wasn't all that bad. It did feel weird putting on a different uniform and hearing strange accents ask who she was and what she was doing there, but apparently the novelty of a Dublin girl was a very welcome one and everyone had taken her under their wing. Thankfully, she'd told her mum as soon as they'd been told about the move that her new school would have to be a mixed one so she would be able to make male and female friends. A tall girl called Mandy who was in her class had instantly warmed to Eva and was glad to show her around and help her get the run of the place.

'It must be daunting, coming into a new school in sixth year?' Mandy had asked kindly.

'Yeah, it's weird all right. Things just seem so different here from Dublin.'

'Better, obviously?' Mandy joked.

'Ha, we'll see! I just feel so out of place,' Eva admitted.

'Well, that stupid accent hardly helps you blend you in, but I've a feeling the lads in particular will be able to get over that pretty quickly, if you know what I mean,' Mandy teased, giving Eva a wink. Eva laughed, wondering whether to take her new friend's words as a compliment, but glad she'd at least found someone to cling to for the first while. She was going to need all the help she could get.

All week Eva was inundated with questions – what music she liked, where she used to go out at weekends, if she had a boyfriend. The latter made Eva's heart stop momentarily as she thought of Zac, and by the end of the week Mandy had commented on just how much she talked about him.

Checking her e-mail, Eva couldn't deny just how much she missed him. The rush of butterflies she felt on seeing she had a message from Zac was so strong.

Hey hows it goin
Just though I'd say hey. Sorry I didn't ring last night as promised – got a pile of maths homework which I didn't finish til like 11. I'll try calling later though. All's well here. Cathy and Johnny are still back 2gether but Lisa and Graham are still on a break.

Did you hear actually Cian's got some new bird on the go, but how long it will last nobody knows.

So, how're things? School going ok? School here just isn't the same without U. Sorry – I promised myself I wouldn't go all mushy in this email but U know I really miss U, Eva. I keep trying not 2 think about it, but when someone mentions your name, or I hear 1 of our songs on the radio, I can't help it.

And I don't want U 2 take this the wrong way, but this is harder than I expected. We're 1 week in2 6th year and already it's hard 2 find time 2 call each other. It's a month since I've seen U. And yeah, love is mostly about what you feel for someone, but not having U physically is killing me.

I'm sorry, I know how things have 2 be now, but I can't pretend I don't still wish U were here Eva, because I do. I never thought It would be easy, but I didn't think it would be this hard.

Visit soon. Please.

Listen 2 my CD – it won't let U 4get.

Later

Zac

Eva went very still as she finished reading what he'd written. The e-mail had been so Zac, so painfully honest and warm. But the last couple of lines hadn't been what she was expecting. Doubt lingered, becoming more and more obvious each time Eva reread it. Why was he so scared? She was missing him too, but it was as if he was so unhappy he wanted to reconsider the whole thing. And then a thought crossed her mind which made her want to get sick. Was there someone else? Every time they talked on the phone, if he made reference to this girl or that girl or an old friend or a new friend, Eva tensed up, wondering if there was something going on. She hated thinking it, but she couldn't help it. Zac was a good-looking guy, no doubt there were always going to be admirers. But when she wasn't there to shoo them away or make sure he didn't overstep the line, it was hard. Of course she trusted him, but the doubt in his words made her question her faith just the tiniest bit. But it was enough.

She decided to text Cathy.

HEY CATH WOTS UP. LUK, I NO DIS MYT SOUND LYK A WEIRD REQUEST, BT IM JUST FEELING KINDA WORRIED BOUT ZAC. WIL U KEEP AN EYE ON HIM? MAKE SURE HES NOT DOIN ANYTIN I WUDN APPROVE OF? I JUS GET SCARED U NO. TANX BABE, XX

Eva sent the text and felt relieved. She knew that Zac would never cheat on her but, still, if it would ease her mind to know Cathy was keeping an eye on him, then so be it. She read the e-mail once more, relishing the good bits and trying to puzzle out the not so good parts. He kept asking her to visit, but like he said, they were only a week into sixth year, so it was important for her to fit into her new school, to try and build up some sort of routine.

She was also wary of the bit about 'physically having her'. Did he mean sex? She hoped not, because she never thought Zac would have worried about something like that. What they had was beyond that. He was the love of her life, and she of his. Of course it was hard, but surely this e-mail had just caught a glimpse of Zac in a bad mood.

She logged off and decided to take a bath to relax and stop her thinking any more bad thoughts about the boy she loved. The steam rose up and Eva locked the door, shutting out the world, leaving just her, the candles and the bubbles. She stripped away her clothes and her worries and the smell of lavender soap surrounded her body as she stepped timidly into the warm suds and sank into the cocoon of heat. Closing her eyes, Eva let her mind float away so that for the first time in so long, nothing mattered. At first it was a strange sensation, and one her body was definitely not used to, but she was appreciative of the long-overdue break, and she lay for almost an hour in her little world.

*

A couple of weeks later, it was Eva's eighteenth birthday. Originally, she had thought this would be the perfect excuse to take a trip back to Dublin to celebrate but, now that it had arrived, Eva realised that she just wanted to keep it small. All her old friends had texted her to wish her a happy birthday and Cathy had phoned, but Eva couldn't deny that she was surprised Zac hadn't rung too. A simple text had sufficed, which made Eva's heart sink. But then she did concede that Friday nights meant grinds, so maybe he really hadn't had time to call.

Her new friends, however, had got wind of the occasion and announced that something had to be done to mark the day. Eva agreed to head out with a big group of them to get some food that evening. She wondered why she was finding the day so weird, but soon realised that the thought of officially heading into adulthood was scary – especially without her father. It felt as if she was declaring that she didn't need or miss him as much as before. But she really did, more than ever.

She decided to try and relax and enjoy herself and, as she ordered a bacon and cheese burger, she sat back to watch the rest of the group chat loudly in their twangy accents, laughing and teasing one another and reminding Eva of her friends back home. A good-looking boy called Ian was seated across the table from her and made sure that she was always involved in what they were talking about. He filled her in on who everyone was, who'd gone out with whom, who hated each other and generally all the underlying politics of the gang.

'So was there this much history in your group back in Dublin?' he asked jokingly.

'You have no idea, Ian. I think it's just part of going to a mixed school. Obviously when you all grow up a bit the novelty of being surrounded by the opposite sex all day wears off, but thinking back through the years, there was some serious scandal,' Eva laughed.

'I love it,' Ian announced. 'I seriously would die in a lads' school. Imagine!'

'I think *I'd* manage,' Eva joked.

'You little slut! Only messing! Mind you, I still haven't asked you the all-important question – Cork men or Dublin men?' There was a twinkle in his eye.

Eva paused. 'I'll give you my verdict when you tell me which you prefer, Dublin girls or Cork girls?' she declared, suddenly realising that she was flirting. Still, it was only harmless, and she was dying to hear his response. But Ian was playing it very cool.

'Your get your mates down here and then I'll judge properly.' He, too, was reluctant to answer the question at hand – it was far more fun beating around the bush!

Eva promised she'd try to get the gang down to visit her over midterm so that both groups could get to know each other. She was reminded of when Zac moved into her school, and how successfully he'd managed both sets of friends. That was what she wanted, and she had no doubt that that's what would happen. Although she still hadn't been up to Dublin, and none of them had visited her yet, she knew that things would settle down soon and they would all be reunited.

*

The next morning as she lay in bed, Eva's phone buzzed beside her, and her heart leapt – an early morning text from Zac? But instead it was from another boy.

HEY EVA. HOPE UD FUN LAS NYT. WOZ TINKN DUBLIN GIRLS R STARTN 2 HAV D EDGE OVER CORK GIRLS BT IL HAV 2 GET 2 NO U A BIT MORE B4 I MAKE THAT CALL! CYA MONDAY, IAN.

Eva didn't quite know what to make of the message as she reread it. She hoped she hadn't given him the wrong vibe the night before. But it was only a bit of fun. She knew that, and he'd known that, so instead she decided to be content in the fact she'd made a new friend. And a nice one at that!

It was times like this that Eva gladly admitted that life wasn't all bad these days as hints of joy crept slowly in. But she felt as if she needed to get rid of some of her thoughts before coming to terms properly with life. Then she remembered where she'd heard words like this before – Zac had always said something similar when he wrote songs. Could she do that? She hadn't played the piano in a while, but it was here in the front room of the house. She loved music, she knew a good song, she had so much in her head at that time – maybe a song was the best thing.

She got up and, sitting at her desk, Eva took out pen and paper and began to try and channel some of the thoughts, images and feelings onto the page.

She thought of Zac and her friends and her father, and the one thing which struck her was how much she wanted to see them all again and be as if nothing had changed. It was a wonderful thought and already Eva was scribbling down words as images began to form themselves before her eyes.

The next day she made for the piano and, placing her fingers on the cold keys, she allowed her hands to refamiliarise themselves with the instrument. They started slowly, warming to the touch of the ivory. Soon, certain chords began to come to mind and, matched with others, produced a tune which seemed to fit Eva's mood. Timidly, she wrote it down and slowly began to match it with the lyrics, changing both slightly so that the fit was perfect. In that moment, a song was formed, a song that Eva knew she could always play to help her think of the past and look to the future and hear and see things which made her happy. Was it about visiting Zac? Was it about dying and seeing her father again? Eva didn't know, but either way, it fitted. And she loved it. The future was scary, but it held a light which both comforted and excited her. As she played her song and sang loudly, a glow returned to her heart which let her know that eventually, she was going to be okay.

Through the mist, I can see your face,
Calling me home.
And I will be there, ASAP
Now that I'm sure I'm not alone.
It's getting darker, spirits come to dance,

But I tell them I only dance with you,
I hum our melody, memories they lurk,
But I know soon it'll all be true.

'Cause I know you're waiting for me on the other side
With a placard in your hand, reading my name.
And I know as sure as night becomes the morning,
Everything will be the same
Once more.

*

'Oh hey, Zac, I was just thinking of you, I've got the best news ever. I just wrote—' Eva began excitedly, delighted to hear her boyfriend's voice at the other end of the phone.

'Eva, I need to talk to you about something,' Zac interrupted, his voice holding a note of urgency.

'Okay, go on, but remind me to come back to this, I've been dying to tell you.' Eva couldn't wait to tell him about her song; he'd be so proud of her. But he was intent on telling her something. Quickly he got down to business.

'So we were out last night, usual spot in town. And we were all having a great time, getting pretty drunk, messing about,' Zac began.

'Yeah, okay.' Eva didn't quite get where this was all leading, but she listened on, unable to deny the jealousy which stirred inside her as she was once again reminded of the world she'd left behind.

'Well, I was talking to this girl Christine, a friend of Johnny's, really sound girl,' Zac continued. Again Eva felt that familiar knot in her stomach tighten, unable to bear hearing him talk of another girl in such a way.

'Go on,' she encouraged, despite herself.

'Okay. So then Cathy stumbles up to us, drunk as a skunk, tells Christine to fuck off and then starts giving out shit to me.' Zac's voice was beginning to get louder. 'So I'm just standing there, not having a clue what's going on, and she's going on all "How could you do that to Eva?" and "You don't know how lucky you are to have her!" and all that. So obviously I'm so confused, I mean, of course I know how lucky I am to have you. For fuck's sake, she knows I miss you enough! And anyway, I was only bloody talking to Christine,' he said.

Eva listened, unsure what to say. Secretly she was pleased Cathy had intervened, but she would have preferred something a bit more subtle. Zac wasn't finished.

'So then I basically asked Cathy where all of this was coming from. And she starts to tell me how you've asked her to keep an eye on me so that I don't cheat, and that you've been texting her and told her to keep you informed on everything because you're having doubts. I mean, for God's sake, Eva!'

Eva was silent. When it was put like that it sounded so ugly, but she couldn't deny it. Nevertheless, surely she could just make him see it was only because she missed him and loved him that she needed to know he was just as committed to them staying together as she was. She went to explain this, but Zac was off again.

'I just can't believe this, Eva. I mean, we've always said our relationship is built on trust and respect and love, but then you have your friends spying on me, telling every girl I chat to to fuck off. What the hell is your problem?' Zac demanded.

'It's just hard. I mean, anything could be going on, and I wouldn't know. Of course I trust you, I just get scared…' Eva tried, her voice beginning to crack.

'So why wouldn't you just talk to me about it? I get scared too, but I've no one down in Cork who would tell me if you did anything. No one. Do you know how that feels?' he asked pointedly.

'But Zac, I would never—'

'Neither would I, Eva. Why can't you see that? After all this time, do you honestly not know that?'

'Of course, Zac, of course. I just get so worried… not seeing you, not being around you – you've been kind of distant recently,' Eva explained, her mind thinking back to his most recent e-mail.

'Distant? What are you talking about? As for not seeing me, not being around me, ever heard of a bus? A train even? You promised you'd be up before now. It's nearly two months, Eva. You promised…' Zac's voice faded away before he heaved a huge sigh. Eva didn't know what to say. What was going on? Why couldn't he see that it was hard for her too? She was trying to get used to things, get set up, get used to having to study again. Time was precious for the moment. But that didn't have to change anything – that didn't have to affect them at all.

'Look,' Zac said, finally filling the silence, sounding calmer than before, 'why don't I come down next weekend? We can finally sort things out, talk about all the stuff that's making this so hard. Make it all okay?' Zac suggested. Eva racked her brains, wondering why next weekend rang bells, then felt her heart sink as she remembered – Don had surprised them all by announcing that he had proposed to his girl-friend. Everyone was a little shocked since they hadn't been together that long, but Don seemed on top of the world and was bringing them all out for dinner to celebrate. She told Zac as much.

'So get out of it,' Zac proposed. 'We can have the place to ourselves, put things right. Eva, we really need to,' Zac admitted sullenly.

'Zac, I can't. It's such a big deal to Don. This whole move is supposed to be about family, it's too soon to be getting out of things already. Mum's still very fragile. She's started to have nightmares about Dad's death again…'

'But you'll be with her all week, and all next week and the week after that. Eva, why can't you see? I get that she's fragile, I'm not trying to be insensitive, but don't you realise – we're fragile too. More than you know. We've got to start making an effort if this is going to work,' Zac finished, sounding heartbroken.

But there was nothing Eva could say. She couldn't leave her mum, and even if it was hard to see now, Zac would get it. She knew he would. And then he'd realise how foolish he'd been to try and make her choose between her family and him, and things would be okay again.

'Zac, you can't come down. Not yet. But half-term's not that far away, and we'll all have more time then,' she explained calmly, knowing he'd see sense.

But there was only silence at the other end. She could hear his breathing, but nothing else. She wanted to hold him and have him kiss her and tell her they'd be okay. But still he said nothing. And the more seconds that ticked by, the more Eva began to panic. Why wasn't he agreeing with her? Why wasn't he seeing how right she was? He wasn't doing anything. She had to break the silence; it was unbearable.

'I love you, Zac,' she said, hoping that that would awaken him. It was what mattered, after all – they'd always said that. But still he said nothing.

'Zac? Please say something,' Eva begged, her heart beginning to beat quicker and tears beginning to well inside her. What was going on? Didn't he love her too? She willed him to return her words. She prayed, called on her father to make Zac say the thing that would make it all okay again. But it never came.

'Eva,' he began, taking a deep breath, bracing them both for what was about to be said. 'I just don't know any more. We were so naive going into this. We didn't plan anything or talk about stuff; we just assumed that love would carry us through.'

Eva agreed, knowing what he said was completely true, but unsure as to what the problem with it was.

'But I'm starting to wonder if that's enough,' he announced. Eva's heart stopped. The tears began.

'It's just so hard, Eva. I need you so much. But we don't have time to talk any more, you still won't come visit, you won't let me come down, so when is it going to work? And that's the worst bit of all. I get why you moved to Cork. Hard as it was, I came to terms with that. I tried to put myself in your shoes and I realised that if my mum asked the same of me, I'd have gone. But every time you tell me you need to be there for you mum, or that you can't come up because of her, I get angry. And I can't forgive myself for that. Your mum's been through so much. I can't even begin to imagine how much your dad's death hurt her, hurt you all. So I hate myself for being angry with her. I can't do it any more, Eva.' Zac too began to cry. Eva was in shock. Each sentence was so honest and true and typically Zac. No matter how much what he was saying hurt, each word made her fall in love with him even more. She couldn't lose him. Not now. Not ever.

'Zac, please. As soon as things are better here, I'll be on the first train up. Don't you think I want to? I miss you so much, I miss Dublin so much. I still cry every night. I lost my dad, and then I lost you and it's hard. But I have to be strong, for her. And once she has some strength of her own back, I'm all yours, I promise,' Eva sobbed through the tears. Again Zac was silent, but not for as long this time.

'So let's wait. Let's wait till midterm. Because I can't face any more of this. Each day breaks my heart, and I pray that this will be the day she's okay, and you can be back to how you used to be. And I know that's selfish, but I'm not trying to be mean. I just mean, you need to focus on what's important right now, and that's your mum. So maybe we should put us on hold. For the moment. So that you can really concentrate on what's happening in Cork. And then, when things are better, we can see where we're at, if we're ready to make this work again,' Zac explained calmly, though his voice broke occasionally with the difficulty of it all.

Eva didn't know what to say. Had he actually just said those words? She couldn't lose him; she didn't want to put him 'on hold'. She needed him now more than ever. But she couldn't deny that deep down in her heart, she knew he was right. It broke her in every way possible, and she refused to admit aloud that she agreed. But no, surely she didn't – he'd just said it so nicely, her heart had obviously been tricked into thinking he was right. But he wasn't really. How could them not being together be right? They were meant to be. Their first love and their last. She couldn't do this.

The tears kept streaming and her heart was thumping hard against her chest. She hung up the phone and collapsed on her bed, unable to believe what had just happened. She stayed like that until night arrived and the shadows licked her into a hazy sleep, where she dreamed of nothing but him, and how things were supposed to be.

39

Eva hun it's Cathy,

I tried ringing earlier but there was no1 in so thought I'd send this and U can call me back whenever. Zac told me in school 2day what happened. Why didn't U call me? The poor boy is in bits. I really don't know what to say honey. Like, I never saw this coming. U guys were the perfect couple, nothing could shake U. But seriously, don't think 4 a second that its permanent – theres no way U guys will remain apart – its just how things are suppposed 2 b for now. Maybe a bit of space will show U just how much U need each other, and b4 U know it, you guys will be back on track. I guarentee it.

But look baby, Im here 4 U, U know that? When are you coming 2 visit? The months are creeping by and still no sign. I know you've stuff 2 deal with but it might do U good 2 come up, even just overnight. Just give me a ring to sort it out though because a lot of us are doing extra grinds in the institute on Friday nights, so timing's even harder these days than ever.

Again, don't worry about Zac. Im here 4 U. And he loves U more than anything in the world. I guess he just felt he was getting in the way, 4 the moment. But soon, it will all be sorted.

Love U loads darling.

Cathy

XOX XOX

*

Dear Diary

October has arrived and the leaves are turning browner and the warmth is fading away, and in so many ways the world is getting darker. It's over a week since Zac's phone call where he wanted to go on a break. For the first few days, we didn't talk – it would've been too hard. But then he texted me to see how I was, and no matter how much it all hurts, I can't be angry with him. Because I know it's tough for him too. He thinks he's doing the right thing and, honestly, he could well be. But who knew my world would come crashing down like this? We're supposed to be taking some time apart from each other so I can focus more on Mum, but all night at the celebration dinner, all I could think about was him, and how much I need things to sort out soon, because I love him now more than ever.

Everyone in school is being cool to me but I've been in a total daze all week – I can't concentrate on anything else. Ian's having a party on Saturday night which I'm invited to. They all said they can't wait for me to be there, which is sound of them. I don't know if I'll go though – I'm not in the mood for partying at all. But maybe it'll be good to take my mind off things.

School is so tough and I've piles study to do, but as I said, concentration just didn't happen this week – Zac fills my mind from the moment I wake to the minute I fall asleep every day.

Mum is in better form, though, which is good. She's made some new friends here and last night she was out for drinks with them, which she said she enjoyed. I hope she goes out again soon – I've haven't seen her as relaxed in a while. It's kind of hard to admit, but I can see why she wanted to move. I mean, she loves just making new friends and being in a whole new place in her life where she can start afresh. It enables her to have the chance to change how she lives from now on.

Sarah is still finding it hard – her friends back in Dublin haven't been that good about keeping in touch, which I think she's a bit upset about. She rings her best friend Megan a lot, but her gang aren't that good with the internet or whatever so she doesn't hear much from them. My friends are all being really great – I've an e-mail from one of them every couple of days, which is lovely. They all got in touch when they heard about me and Zac.

I think I'm going to call him this weekend. Just to talk. So much was left unsaid last time because I was just in bits. But I've thought about it more, and there are so many things I need to say. I need him to know that maybe he's right, I'm not sure, but we simply cannot be apart for much longer because it's killing me. I may not have been the best girlfriend since I moved here, but I can't be without him. Maybe this was what I needed to realise how much I have to have him in my life, no matter what else is going on.

I'm scared, though. What if this week has made him see that he's actually grand without me, that the whole long-distance thing just won't work so we should properly call it a day? Every night I run all these thoughts over in my head and I'm so weary from all the worrying. I can't let go of him. I just can't. So I need to phone him. Scary as it is, I don't really have a choice.

Life's too short. Love's too perfect to lose.

*

Well hello there gorgeous,

Your amazingly good-looking friend Cian here reporting for business! Can't talk long because I have homework coming out of my arse and hockey training 2 attend, but a quick break 2 talk 2 my favourite girl is always permitted.

Hope the boggers are being nice. Any hotties? U should send some photos up. I'm sure the lads are all fighting over U! I've a lady friend on the go at the moment but not sure if I'm all that Roy Keane if you know what I mean.

Well that's the craic. Giz a bit of a reply when U get the chance and keep on trucking baby.

Cian ;)

*

Dear Diary

Zac wasn't able to talk last night; he was out for dinner with his mum. He said he'd try to call me, but somehow I wasn't convinced. So I just sent him an e-mail and suggested maybe he come down next weekend. Mum said it was okay, and I was thinking that the best way to finally put stuff right is to do it face to face.

I hope so much that he can come. Ever since the idea entered my head all I could think about was seeing him again and how amazing it would be. But then I started thinking, what if it's weird? What if he looks me in the eye and says that he just doesn't love me any more? I got really freaked out and I couldn't stop crying.

Saturday night arrived and I had to get out to try distract myself. I went to that party in Ian's house – there were only about thirty of us. But the music was blaring and everyone was drunk and he was being so nice to me. Anyway, we were just talking out in his garden and suddenly we looked around and everyone was gone. And we were just looking at the stars and out of nowhere he goes, 'What a perfect sky.' And it sounded just like something Zac would say. I completely froze, not knowing whether I was going to burst into tears or what. But then Ian turned to me, and looked me in the eyes and tried to kiss me.

I have to admit, part of me almost wanted to. I actually nearly did. Somewhere in my mind, I started thinking that it would just be so much easier to start again with someone else, someone who didn't live so far away and who wouldn't break my heart by pausing our relationship when I needed them most. And his lips were almost on mine and I could smell his aftershave. I even closed my eyes, shutting out reality, pretending I wasn't vulnerable, pretending I wanted this. But I didn't. Thank God I realised in time! I had to push Ian off, I felt so bad. He wasn't too impressed, obviously. But

I didn't care. Because all I could think about was how much I was never going to be able to get over Zac, or think about anyone else in the same way. He's the one.

I know I'm young, but I officially dismiss all those who say love is impossible to feel or see when you're young. Because I know that I've seen it, and it's pure. Clear. Like dew. No, not like dew. More like a spider's web. Hard to see, but when it catches the light it glistens in all its perfection. Fragile. And easy to destroy. But skilled, all the same. Beautiful and skilled.

I fear I may have just written my first piece of literature. Only it'll never sell. No one wants to read about love. Not the perfect kind. Book love is passion and secrecy and sex and excitement. Not like the real thing. Not like the love I know.

Why do I do this to myself? Think so much that eventually I am worn to tears. Knowing life is hard on me now, I still seem to feel the need to break myself even further. Make it stop.

I must sleep – it's the only way I'll grasp any peace.

*

Song Title: Slowly
Lyrics & Music: Zac O'Dwyer
Inspiration: Mum & Dad

I watch him, he breaks you down (slowly)
I watch you, you think no one is around (slowly)
I tell you things are going to be okay
But suddenly it's yesterday

Chorus
And I wonder, how many times you will fall
And I wonder how many times is no more?

Slowly, slowly, slowly, slowly
Till he wipes you clean
I know you listen to my words
But love it tells you what you've heard
And I know there's things I don't understand
But there's only so many ways I can take your hand (slowly)

Chorus

*

Hey baby!!!

Cathy's weekly report as usual!

So, it's midterm at last – about bloody time! Still, you know Amy in our year? She's having an 18th in some swanky nightclub in town on Saturday night so we're all looking forward to that. Except there's one person who's excited about something else!

Poor Zac – he's been talking non-stop all week about how he's visiting you this weekend. Seriously, he's obsessed! And rightly so – clearly he's going to go down and everything's just going to fall back into place between you guys! I'm so happy for you – it's so stupid you guys being on a break – both of you are so blue without the other.

Oh by the way, we've started looking into booking our sixth year holiday – yes, that's right, as soon as we get the results, two weeks of pure alcohol and pure sun – sounds like heaven doesn't it? I presume you want to be included in that yeah? Cool beans!!

Anyway, as I said – enjoy your weekend with Zac. Behave, but not too much! I kind of have to admit – I'm a bit jealous. Wish I was seening you too. But still, promise you'll visit soon?!

Love U so much baby
Friends forever
Cathy

*

Hi Eva

Zac here, just thinking of U.

My bag's all packed – can't believe I'm actually going 2 see U 2morro. It's mad though because it's nearly Halloween and I moved 2 your school just after Halloween last year so it's like 1 year anniversary of knowing each other. It feels like more though – I could swear that for all that I know about U and feel 4 U, I've known U 4ever.

I'm so excited, but then again, a little nervous. Will it be weird? Please God don't let it be – if you're feeling something or want 2 say something 2 me, say it. Because there's no way I'm letting this get awkward after so long now.

But it could be wonderful. I don't want 2 think about it 2 much though – we'll just kind of see how things go when I arrive and take it from there.

It still aches 2 know that even though the few days in Cork will be perfect, not matter what happens, I'll still have 2 come home and know that I can't be with U again. But if we decide we're gonna make it work, we're gonna make it work this time yeah?

We're gonna do it right or not at all, coz what we have, or had, can be perfect, so why settle for less?

Listen I'd better head.

C U 2morro!

Always

Zac

XXX

PS I thought I'd feel much better after I sent this email, but I'm not sure that I do. I still don't have U Eva, and yet I still need U. Love's persistant isn't it? But it always wins. Never forget that.

40

Standing on the platform, listening for the screech of the train, Eva waited. The station was full of bustle and bodies, all coming and going and waving off and welcoming home. But to her, it was silence. Like an irrelevant vision that served only to distract her from the imminent arrival of Zac. Even the thought of his name made her stomach twist even more, she couldn't believe he was actually coming. Couldn't believe that for the first time in what seemed like an eternity, his eyes would melt her heart again, and this time either break it in two, once and for all, or restore it back to its former glory. She willed the latter to happen.

A distant rumble made her hairs stand upright, and sure enough, lights began to come into focus. He was here. She checked the clock – perfectly on time, not even spoiling her with an extra few minutes so she could compose herself. No; her ears were filled with the clickety-clack of powerful wheels and, in that instant, her future began. The hissing halt surrounded Eva and, almost in slow motion, the doors of the train opened. The passengers flooded out, eager to stretch their stiff legs after their long journey south. Like animals blinking into the light, they carefully took that first, timid step. Eva's eyes scanned the crowd, darting this way and that, searching for that ray of familiarity. Throngs surged onto the platform, but still she couldn't see him. What if he wasn't coming? What if there had been a mix-up, or he'd missed the train or, worst of all, decided the whole trip was a bad idea and left her standing there?

But suddenly something clicked. She knew that boy; that dark, handsome face in the crowd. But it wasn't who she'd been expecting. Not who she'd expecting at all – it was Graham! And then it was Cian. And then Johnny and Cathy and Lisa and, at last, that face she'd been expecting all along. Her heart pulse raced. There he was. Just as always, but there was something different about him. The end of the summer had given an extra glow to his face and made him look even more handsome. They all rushed towards her at once, smothering her with kisses and hugs and screeches of delight. Eva couldn't believe it. Her mind was hazy and their voices seemed so far away. Was this happening? Was it only her imagination? She couldn't quite work out where reality ended and delirium began. She was pulled this way and that, and all the time she struggled to find sense amidst the rush of happiness that had filled her. Zac, in turn, would have paid all the money in the world just for the look on her face in that instant – the mixture of utter disbelief and pure joy touched his heart, and he knew that the surprise had definitely been a good idea.

'But… how… all of you…' Eva tried, but couldn't quite string together a sentence, her shock was too much.

'Surprise!' Zac announced and, being the last to get to hug her, wrapped his arms around her and held her tighter than ever. Eva's heart danced as she buried her face into his chest, slowly realising that he had done all this for her; brought her the people she missed more than anything, just to make her smile. Well it had certainly worked! She pulled away from him, grinning from ear to ear.

'Thank you so much,' she managed through the overwhelming delight which had consumed her. And Zac stared into those familiar eyes, at that familiar soul and, in that split second, fell head over heels in love with Eva Coonan all over again.

The bus journey back to Eva's new house was a flurry of excitement, as each of them tried to recount everything she had missed, whilst she in turn tried to figure out where such an elaborate plan had come from and how she'd been so unaware of it all.

'Cathy, you even told me you guys were going out this weekend…' she started.

'That was your mum's idea actually. The sly thing! You should have seen the look on your face, baby! You didn't actually think I'd let Zac beat me to coming down here first did you? Hell no!' Cathy giggled.

Zac looked at Eva, cocking an eyebrow cheekily at Cathy's comment, before returning his gaze to the window once more – the streets of Cork zooming by – the city that had stolen her from him. But he wasn't going to be bitter anymore, or sad, because he was there now and, although they still had things to sort, seeing her had reminded him just how much he cared for Eva. He hoped she felt the same and didn't hate him for calling a halt to their relationship, even if it was only temporary. He still didn't know whether that had been the right decision or not but, once they got a chance to talk about things this weekend, he'd know exactly what she thought of him, and the call he'd made. He couldn't deny his nervousness.

*

No reunion would be complete without a good drinking session! Although Eva's house was more than cosy with all their guests, Eva's mum had made all the necessary preparations, unbeknownst to her daughter, and had them all well fed and watered before a night out on the town. Eva frantically rang around her new friends, trying to see where they were all headed and arranged to meet them all at the same nightclub in the city centre. A flinch of apprehension told her she was nervous at the two groups meeting but, since her body was still coming to terms with the whole situation, there was little room for anxiety.

Eva, Cathy and Lisa got ready in her new bedroom and, as they applied their make-up and dithered over outfits, it felt just like old times. Eva was so relieved that things weren't weird in the slightest and everything had felt exactly as before with each one of her friends. Though there was one exception. But although she longed to talk to Zac, to have that all-important talk that would determine everything from then on, for now she was completely content in basking in the bizarre but reassuring feeling that her two worlds were mixing together to make her feel truly at home.

They got the bus into town, again full of energy and chat and high spirits – since this was the first Saturday night of their midterm, all concerned were well set on having a wild one, not to mind the fact that the entire group had been finally reunited. In the club, Eva felt the alcohol go straight to her head, but didn't care, as she found herself in the middle of the dance floor being spun this way and that by Cian, as they tried to show Cork people exactly how it was done.

'I've missed you, Eva – neither of the other girls ever want to dance with me! Apparently I'm an acquired taste on the dance floor,' he feigned hurt, as he dipped her low once more.

'Well Lisa and Cathy never could quite match the connection we always had when it came to boogying!' Eva giggled in return. She was having so much fun! Then suddenly over Cian's shoulder, another body moved and swayed in time with the rhythm – it was Ian.

'Eva, how's it going? I've been keeping an eye out for you – it's bloody jammers tonight isn't it?' He gave her a hello hug and threw a strange look at Cian who continued to try to whirl her around.

Eva laughed, before introducing the two boys. They exchanged handshakes and Cian suddenly looked a little embarrassed at his previous antics – he'd forgotten he'd be meeting Eva's new friends! Ian and he began to chat and then the rest of her new friends appeared, each greeting her with big kisses and demanding to meet her Dublin convoy that had arrived.

Eventually, the two groups were brought together and began to chat and, with each vodka and lime, Eva enjoyed the night more and more. So this was what things were going to be like? This was what the coming months would be, and then she'd be back to Dublin for college, and it would be the Cork gang coming up to visit her. Why had she been worried? This was easy, this felt good and the future wasn't so scary after all. Ian bought her another drink, reassuring her that he thought her friends were all lovely, especially her two lady friends! Eva realised how tipsy she was as she gazed up at him, feeling her balance sway slightly, but was glad he liked them. Glad that he approved. He was a nice guy. They were all nice guys. In fact, she didn't know whether it was the alcohol or not, but in that moment she was pretty sure she loved each and every single one of them!

Zac watched her all the while. He'd noticed some sort of a connection between her and Ian and, unable to put his finger on it, wondered if it was anything to be worried about. Her new friends all seemed lovely – one girl in particular, Mandy, insisted that she'd heard absolutely everything about Zac and, despite being slightly embarrassed, Zac couldn't deny the little glow which surged within him – he liked the thought of Eva talking about him! He liked the thought of Eva full stop. Unfortunately, he hadn't got the chance to get her alone tonight, but it was probably for the best – neither of them was quite sober enough to discuss things properly and, anyway, it was important for her to enjoy the evening and see the two groups mix. He knew more that anything how good it felt to have your old friends and new friends break down barriers, and the certain sense of pride that comes with it too, knowing you're the reason they're all together.

There was no denying, as he sat beside Eva in the taxi home, her head resting on his shoulder as she drifted in and out of sleep, how much he still felt for her. That one night had shown him everything he'd needed to be shown and, as soon as he got the chance the following day, he was going to tell her as much. He prayed it wasn't too late, that he could still put things right. But suddenly he realised that he also wished she'd wake up because they had absolutely no idea where they were going.

'Eva…Eva wake up – we don't know where to tell the taxi to go…' he nudged her gently as she began to stir.

'What?' she grumbled from her pillow of his shoulder.

'Eva – your address. We don't know it. You're in Cork now remember?' he tried once more, noting the taxi driver's impatience. The rest of the gang were bursting with laughter from all corners of the people carrier. It was just like old times!

*

The following morning, a houseful of thumping heads woke, slowly but surely piecing together the night, but utterly convinced that it had been a good one. Eva cringed as Cathy recounted their taxi confusion, further embarrassed by the fact that she had absolutely no recollection of it whatsoever. Still, what she could recall of the night had been amazing. The dancing, the drinking, the catching up and the constant laughing; though she did begin to realise just how little of it she'd spent with Zac, and hoped that she hadn't said anything she'd regret. Cathy reassured her that she hadn't.

'Actually you spent quite a lot of your evening with that guy Ian – not bad Eva…' Lisa teased.

'Oh shut up!' Eva retorted playfully, only to realise that raising her voice in any shape or form was not a pleasant sensation, as the banging in her head refused to cease. She needed breakfast!

As they made their way through piles of bacon and sausages, marvelling at the spread Eva's mum had produced, they discussed their plan for the day. All agreed that nothing too strenuous would be appreciated, and a bus journey to the beach and a lazy stroll seemed perfect. They dressed slowly, but the food had begun to wake them up, and Eva once again was hit by the brilliance of it all – her gang in her new house, filling every quiet inch of it. The sunlight called them outside; a bright day in every sense. And as the rays danced through her bedroom, illuminating her tired but happy frame, Eva thought of her father, hoping he too was there in that moment.

The weather was surprisingly warm for October, and Eva and her friends weren't the only ones who'd decided that a seaside amble would be a good way to pass the Sunday afternoon. Dogs fetched sticks from the calm water, twitching with excitement as they awaited their masters' next command. Their tails wagged so furiously they looked like they were going to have a nervous breakdown, but their frenzied happiness was contagious, and Zac found himself watching them and laughing at every throw and fetch of the stick. He watched Cian and Graham paddle in the sea and splash each other like children – their delight was hilarious to see on such fully grown men. The girls were being chased by Johnny who was bellowing threats of throwing them, fully clothed, into the water. Eventually, he caught hold of Cathy, who wriggled to get free, but rather than punishing her as promised, he merely spun her around and kissed her so passionately and so deeply, that Zac's mind was cast back once more to Eva. He watched her play, shoes and socks off, the damp sand pressing up between her toes. Every so often she'd join Graham and Cian, paddling in the gentle waves which strolled in and out like lazy ballerinas, their white skirts flowing over Eva's feet. Zac went to the edge, reached down and scanned the drenched sand for a smooth voyager who would be gracefully launched into the welcoming sea. Finding just the right stone, he picked it up and with the flick of his wrist, sent it out to sea. One hop, two hops, three hops; it bounced along the calm water until it disappeared down to the seabed below.

The sun was gazed at its twinkling reflection in the water below, caressing the world with its weak but warming light. As Zac stared at Eva, she turned and caught his gaze. He cocked his head up the beach, indicating that maybe they should go for a walk. She nodded, and made her way over to him. He could feel the lump in his throat begin to rise, knowing what had to be done, but hoping he'd be able to do it. They set off down the strand, together, both nervous but excited about what was to come.

'I don't know where to start,' Zac admitted. He kept his head down, noticing how big his footprints were compared to her tiny steps in the sandy ground.

'Me neither,' Eva echoed, wishing she could just say all the things that were pounding in her head and in her heart – she'd been waiting all weekend for this and now the time had come, why couldn't she do it? Was she scared? Scared he wanted different things? He was the one who'd decided to go on a break, not her – what if his opinion hadn't changed? She realised how frightened she was, and looked out to sea, not wanting him to notice the fear in her eyes. If he was going to dump her, there was no way she'd let him see her cry. She'd done enough of that already.

But then she felt something she hadn't in so long – a hand on hers. It moved gingerly, unsure of what the reaction would be, but as she welcomed those fingers she knew so well, they intertwined and, as always, fit perfectly. Eva stopped walking and finally stared straight at Zac. She couldn't lose him. She had to tell him. She'd kill herself if she let the opportunity go. Fear was not a good enough reason to let the best thing in her life slip through her fingers. Taking a deep breath, she began.

'Zac, I know we haven't had a chance to talk that much since you arrived – it was all such a blur. An amazing blur – like, I still can't thank you enough for bringing them all down here. I needed it so much. But I need something else too…,' she was beginning to feel the fear creep in again – the fear of rejection. But once more she wasn't going to let it win.

'I need you Zac. So much. Like, just having you around these past couple of days, I keep looking at you and just realising how much I love you. I know things were hard when I moved. But I think we can do it. Like properly. Honestly, I don't think the alternative bears thinking about. We have the Leaving Cert. and then it's the summer and then we'll go to college together. But even just thinking about right now, you and me here on this beach – I can't lose this. And I don't…' she tried to continue, but was stopped by Zac's lips. He leaned in and kissed her, knowing that it was the thing he wanted to do more than anything in the world. Their lips met and tingled at being brought back together again. Their tongues softly caressed the other, remembering their taste perfectly. Zac pulled Eva to him, tighter and tighter, not wanting to let go. Her hands were wrapped around his neck and his whole being shivered with the ecstasy of it all. They kissed and kissed, making up for lost time, letting love stretch its wings once more and soar upwards. Until Zac pulled away, knowing what had to be done.

'Eva I love you. Being on a break was horrible. I know it was my idea, but the only good that came out of it is knowing that I still adore you.' He stopped, trying to gauge her reaction. This was hard.

'I know this time we'll make more of an effort and, even if it gets hard, I realise now that the alternative is harder. So let's do this. Let's be together,' he was beginning to pick up speed, as all the thoughts he'd clogged up came spilling out, desperate to be heard.

'Think of last year – everything we went through. Your dad, my dad, our mothers rebuilding their lives. So much changed but the one thing that I never doubted was that I had you. And you've no idea how much that kept me going. Even in the worst times, I never stopped loving you,' Zac admitted. He turned his gaze out to the infinite line where sea met sky, hoping in his heart of hearts this girl knew just how special she was to him.

'You're amazing – you know that? Everyone knows it. Sometimes I still don't know why you chose me – do I deserve you? But that doesn't matter; what matters is that I can't do this, I can't not have you,' he paused, embarrassed but not caring. He needed her. 'So let's do this. Let's be in love… I can't let go.' He held his breath as he awaited her response.

'Always?' she suggested with a wry smile.

'Always.' He affirmed.

As they walked hand in hand back up the beach to join the others, they didn't speak. Everything was how it was supposed to be again. Letting go was too hard, but in some ways too easy – they'd have to work at this. But that was what they wanted. It was all they wanted.

The sound of the sea was everywhere, broken only by the laugher of their friends. The clouds were greying the sky and seagulls chatted to one another, sharing gossip as their wings glided through the salty air. The tangy smell of the sea filled Eva and Zac. So this was what happiness smelled like? A final kiss and a look that said it all – love had won.

~And I know all of this, and yet I still long to be somewhere else. Life is discontent and the future doesn't seem to be bright enough to hold out her hand and pull me through this horrible cloud. Love is so heartbreaking and at the same time the most wonderful feeling life has to offer. I haven't even felt it to its fullest but even the shred of it that has touched me has been amazing. And even though from time to time we go out of tune, the melody is clear and even, and the trickle of happiness that fills me is nearly enough, even though I know I should be doing something else.~

Acknowledgements

There shouldn't be just one name on the front of this book, but hundreds; so many people helped me to write *Forget* and I can't go without mentioning at least some of them.

* Mum, for the never-ending support, late night chats and countless cups of tea, without which there wouldn't be a book.

* Dad, my hero, who taught me the most important thing in life; 'take your time, no rush'!

* Dave – even across the water he manages to make me smile and want to achieve everything that I can.

* All the rest of my family for generally just being the coolest bunch of relations a girl could hope for.

* Mrs Quin, for never letting the creative sparks inside me die, and whogave so much of her time towards this, and all my English endeavours!

* Alil – the world's most generous man! The one responsible for making the dream a reality.

* Patricia Scanlan – a true inspiration; constantly there for me, lighting candles and making it all happen.

* Breda, Claire, Ciara and all at Hodder for helping me along the daunting but exciting path.

And lastly

* My friends – the inspiration of the story. The girlies for always being there to talk to and cause havoc with. The lads, who never fail to put a smile on my face. And to certain people, for making the story come true. Class 2006!

Ruth Gilligan
June 2006

Permission Acknowledgements

'Star Star'
Written by Glen Hansard. Published by Perfect Song Ltd. Reproduced with permission.

Despite our best efforts, the publisher and author were unable to contact all copyright holders prior to the publication of Forget. Tje publisher will make the usual arrangements with any copyright holders who make contact after publication.